MY BIGGEST LIE

Luke Brown was born and grew up in Lancashire and now lives in London. *My Biggest Lie* is his first novel.

'Partly an extended love letter, *My Biggest Lie* is an attempt at sincere self-expression, and an examination of contemporary culture and the difficulties of communication in our technologically fraught era ... Rewarding and ambitious' *TIMES LITERARY SUPPLEMENT*

'Awesome new writing talent!' *COMPANY*

'A zinging and thoroughly LOL-inducing tramp around the London we know and love. It's got heartbreak, grown-up wisdom, gleefully vicious satire and a dreamy chunk of action that takes place in Buenos Aires' *THE QUIETUS*

'An unashamedly "literary" novel that nonetheless wears its learning lightly and is totally unpretentious. *My Biggest Lie* is a book within a book; a ludic, drunk, dizzying jaunt' *D.*

MY BIGGEST LIE

LUKE BROWN

CANONGATE
Edinburgh · London

This paperback edition published by Canongate Books in 2015

First published in Great Britain in 2014 by
Canongate Books Ltd
14 High Street
Edinburgh EH1 1TE

www.canongate.tv

1

British Library Cataloguing-in-Publication Data
A catalogue record for this book is available on
request from the British Library

ISBN 978 1 78211 040 8

Typeset in Sabon LT Std by Palimpsest Book Production Ltd,
Falkirk, Stirlingshire

Printed and bound in Great Britain by Clays Ltd, St Ives plc

This book is printed on FSC certified paper

MIX
Paper from
responsible sources
FSC® C018072
FSC
www.fsc.org

In memory of
Matthew Brown

Writing long books is a laborious and impoverishing act of foolishness . . . A better procedure is to pretend that those books already exist

Jorge Luis Borges

I've tried to be as honest as possible about everything

Diego Maradona

There was a time not long ago when I thought that lying was the most natural thing in the world. I was young and I had a good haircut and a girlfriend I loved. I had a best friend who was also my boss and he was friends with the most interesting people in London. I assume they were interesting. Looking back, I can't remember much of what anyone said. But I remember laughing. I remember everything being the funniest thing that had ever happened. I worked hard and stayed out late. We drew a high line between fuel and poison. I wore suits I couldn't afford in the hope that this was the way that one day I would be able to afford them. I always got the round in, and I always asked the barmaid her name. I never spoke to anyone about Sarah because if I did I'd have to tell everyone how much I adored her. I didn't want to overcomplicate the portrait. I'd made an experiment with my character, and it seemed to be working. It was fun. It was addictive. And I forgot, temporarily, what was true and what was false. Or it was simply that I preferred the false.

It was then that I was found out.

PART ONE: MY LOVE

Chapter 1

On the last day of what I kept telling myself was a happy month, I woke up alone.

I could hear children laughing outside on the estate. The block of flats Sarah and I lived in was built around a grass square and from our bedroom window I watched a boy with an Afro kick a football to a dog who was as big to him as a horse was to me. The dog scrambled over the ball and executed a perfect Cruyff turn, accelerating away to leap up at a young girl on a pink scooter.

Ben, you big tit, you've knocked Tasha over. Eric, next door, leaning out of his kitchen window. I had lived here for eighteen months with Sarah and I loved the place. Sarah was giving the keys back to the landlord tomorrow and I was flying to Buenos Aires in the afternoon. The flights we'd booked were non-refundable and still valid. Even now, eight hours before take-off, I hoped I could persuade Sarah to relent and come with me.

Sarah. I found her downstairs at the kitchen table, her head in her hands, looking from a slant at the same view I'd seen from our bedroom. It was Saturday, a spring morning, a day obscene with promise. Sarah turned from the window and looked at me.

I can see her face now, project it onto the white piece of paper I'm staring at. The wisdom is that I screw that face up in a ball and throw it in the bin. The wisdom is that I accept I made such a mess of things that she will never let me make things right. The wisdom is to draw a moustache on her and persuade myself it was all her fault, that I was mistaken about my love for her. Oh, the wisdom. The blunt realism. How do people live that way?

I took a deep breath and once again tried to make my case to her.

There is something you may have heard about me, the reason why some of my old colleagues won't speak to me any more. That wasn't why Sarah was leaving me – indeed, she left me on the morning before the night the other catastrophe happened, and she came back two days later because of it. That was the best bit about falling apart: it persuaded her to come back to hold me together. There wasn't anyone else who could have, and Sarah still cared enough to want me in one piece. The only other person I wanted to speak to was my former boss and closest male friend, James Cockburn, but he was in hospital with two broken legs and a dead mobile number. Under the terms of the settlement I had signed I was not supposed to contact him or any of my former colleagues. That was mostly fine. I had surrendered my own phone to the police as evidence and I used this as another excuse not to confront my shame through other people's eyes.

Sarah came back and, to begin with, something incredible happened: we fell completely in love again. Now our time was finite, we decided to make it last for ever. We saw in each other's faces what we used to talk about when we talked about love, we pinned down the word to describe this purity of feeling and intent. It was not a lie invented by poets, and if it was, who cared, it was the best lie they ever told. Love: at this late hour, you could still fall in.

For the rest of the month we drank and went to galleries, we took ecstasy and danced, we went to bed after ambitious dinners and expensive wines and lay on the sofa under a duvet with hangovers and high-quality HBO drama on DVD. But it was a paradise only made possible by its expiry date. This last month with Sarah had begun with us giving a month's notice on the flat and with Sarah deciding she was not coming to Argentina on the holiday we had booked to visit her oldest friend Lizzie. I didn't want to go without her but she made clear that was irrelevant. My boarding the plane was the condition of her staying with me until I did. We talked about Buenos Aires as the ideal place to write the novel I had always talked about: cheap, literary, atmospheric (we presumed). And haunted too, by a man I had watched die. You know of course who I am talking about. I had known the famous novelist for only ten hours but I would not let myself forget him or pretend it was not my fault he was dead. Ten hours, whatever others might say, is long enough to come to love a man. In Buenos Aires, where he had written his first novel, I hoped I could wrap myself in his experience and write mine. It was the only plot I could come up with, an escape and a penance rolled into one, and Sarah called my bluff and decided it was the answer to her problems too. My going alone would give her time to think things through without me. She might join me later; we would 'have to see'. We closed our eyes because we did not want to see what scared us, though it could still see us.

Four weeks we had, twenty-eight mornings when I woke with her next to me again. It was like plunging into water from a great height and swimming to the surface to gasp for air. To be alive and know how nearly we weren't.

I wanted to remember this feeling when I was gone from her, so I would never be complacent again – but I didn't kid myself there weren't equal and more alluring devotions in store for me. Good intentions? I'd had those before.

'Liam, please,' Sarah said, forcing a smile and cutting me off. 'It's our last morning together for a while. Let's just have some breakfast.'

I wasn't hungry but at least the ritual of making breakfast was something I could do for her. I moved towards the fridge. On the top of it was a delicately curved pot painted with intricate patterns by an ex-boyfriend of Sarah's from Brazil. Sarah worked in the art world, curating small shows and finishing a PhD, and our flat doubled as a gallery displaying the works of Sarah's previous boyfriends and current suitors. She referred to the current suitors, with less suspicion than me, as 'friends'.

'Why don't I make breakfast for once?' Sarah said, jumping up.

'It's all right,' I said, picking up a box of eggs.

'I want to do it. I'd been planning to. It will be nice. A farewell breakfast.'

'Farewell?'

'I mean, bon voyage.'

'I think you mean fuck off.'

Her eyes narrowed at me.

'Sorry, I'm joking.' I put my hands up in surrender and sat down at the table. 'One fuck-off breakfast and a cup of tea, please.'

Behind her on the wall was a colourful mural. There was a lot going on: helicopters, skeletons, marijuana leaves, bare breasts, men with moustaches, manacles, rifles, horses, stars-and-stripes on fire. I would be in a different continent tomorrow, one where my dead friend had written his first novel and fallen in love.

'How much space do you think you have to joke right now?' Sarah asked me. 'Because it's not as much as you think.'

The famous novelist I watched die has a name, one which to this day deters me from entering bookshops. It will be obvious that I am talking about Craig Bennett, though when I tell my story for the first time he is always the famous novelist. It adds ironic distance to the story that was not there, is not there, but is essential to the way I semi-survive these days. He haunts me you see, that lovely, corrupt man. In newspaper articles; in marketing emails from Amazon; A0-sized, six feet high on train platforms. I do well making light of it. He survives in his words, say the idiot fans, the ones you hear on Radio 4 saying, of course, Buenos Aires was the biggest *character* in his debut. Don't get me started on that type of idiocy. He survives in his words. For me he continues to die. I made sure of that.

The end of my night with Craig was horror, pure and simple. And it was my fault.

*   *   *

9

While Sarah made an omelette and I kept quiet I saw there was an opened envelope on the table, stamped Universidade de Sao Paulo. Sarah had been interviewed two weeks earlier on Skype for a job teaching a course there over the summer (their winter, hotter than our summer).

She put down our plates of food and saw what I was looking at. 'I got the job,' she said.

'Congratulations. That's really great. I really mean that. When do you start?'

'I haven't worked out yet if I'll take it.'

'That's really really great – what, really? You won't take it?'

'My deadline for my PhD's this year and . . .'

'Really?'

'Stop saying *really*. You don't know what *really* means. Anyway, I probably should take it. It's only for six weeks and I could use their library for some stuff it's hard to get over here.'

'When does it start?'

'Oh, er, not for a couple of months.'

'We wouldn't be that far away then, would we?' I suggested.

'Quite a distance.'

'Same continent, though.'

'Sort of from here to Moscow.'

'Just round the corner. I could pop over for a weekend.'

'Flights would be expensive. I don't think we should get ahead of ourselves.'

She was wearing pyjama bottoms and a vest top and I leaned down and put my head against her neck, smelling her hair, cheap shampoo and carpet static, feeling the warmth of her skin, the shape of the line from her cheek to her shoulder. She was unique in a way I could never truthfully express. The idea of chemistry we rationalise in conversation is chaotic in sensation. I was infatuated. It was the sound of her voice on the telephone, the absence of her body in the clothes hanging up in the wardrobe, spread out upon the floor. The way she walked down the street when she didn't know I was looking at her. It was true. She made me want to skip. I had made her believe that my love for her was perfect and never contradicted by other impulses. Isn't this the lie that is expected of us? Isn't this the lie we believe in ourselves? And for me, it could never for any other woman have been closer to the truth.

'Sarah,' I said, 'please, you have to believe me.'

It took two weeks from Craig Bennett's death for the funeral to be rearranged, but in the meeting in which I had agreed to resign in exchange for six months' salary, my CEO Belinda Wardour made it a condition of the deal that I would not come to the funeral.

The distraction of Bennett's editor having mysteriously fallen from a window the night before delayed journalists from seizing on my involvement. James Cockburn, the flamboyant publishing director for fiction at Eliot, Quinn, was a minor media celebrity in his own right, and the rumours suggested his broken legs were a result of Bennett having pushed him. The hypotheses were irresistible.

None of the few people who knew about my role in Bennett's death spoke out. I was to disappear. So, 'resigning to focus on my writing', I received my pay-off with a contract that prohibited me from speaking to the media or publishing anything about Craig Bennett. Belinda, in the

Bookseller's 'Moves' section, delivered the quote-de-grâce: 'It's disappointing to have Liam leave so soon after he arrived, but he's decided his career is not in publishing and we wish him all the best.'

It looked then like we had got away with it.

Cockburn was still in hospital. The man who gave me my job, my mentor, a role model. (He's a whole other chapter, a bloody novella.) He sent his own quote for the papers from his bed.

I deeply grieve the loss of our friend Craig Bennett. He was one of the most charming, generous men we will ever know, and the fact that hundreds of thousands if not millions of us feel like we did know him is a testimony to his extraordinary writing. I can't accept that I will never read a new book by him again, although many of his millions of readers who have not yet read his frank, acerbic and incredibly moving memoir Juice *will be able to when it is published in mass market paperback in June this year. A fearsomely honest, original writer, we may never see his like again.*

Rumours in the press make it important to clarify something: when I last saw him, the night before he died, before I drunkenly defenestrated myself at a party, we were the best of friends. It is rare in what has become sometimes a sterile publishing industry that writers' lives are as fascinating as Craig's, or their personalities as dramatic or exaggerated, and so we shouldn't be surprised that such a born storyteller should spawn some shaggy-dog tales about his final hours. If Craig can see us now – I won't say he's exactly laughing – he'd be too annoyed about not being alive, but I know –

* * *

I couldn't read any more of it, and avoided the papers for the rest of the month. It wasn't the only subject I was avoiding; it became much harder for Sarah and me to pretend we were happy as our last month together wore on. Our smiles stuck as we tried to think of something to say to each other that wasn't the thing we needed and refused to speak of. But as my flight approached, the panic overwhelmed me and I began to break the terms of our truce.

Sarah had finished eating and was staring out of the window again, watching the children play. Yes, we had imagined that too. She turned and looked at me.

'Please stop, Liam. I've listened. We did this at the time. We've done it since. There's nothing you can say to make things better. Perhaps being apart will work, I don't know. Just please, for now, stop talking.'

The worst thing about those words was how calm and placatory she was when she said them. Everything was not going to be all right, but she stood and came towards me and we kissed like love was simple, and then, for what I hope was not the last time, she led me upstairs back to bed.

If I never get Sarah back, if I ever stop trying to, I wonder how long it will take me before I am unable to recall the exact detail of her face, the sound of her voice, the way she moves. It would be romantic to say that she will never leave me, that I will see her looking back at me whenever I close my eyes. Oh, don't worry: I have said *this* to her.

Sarah is beautiful, though she's not so pretty you would fall in love with her from a photo. She's not the type of girl to practise how to come across best in 2D, and this was one of the things I liked least about her, her carelessness, her lack of artifice; it was not natural. Perhaps this is what love consists of: simultaneous repulsion and attraction to a feature of the beloved. I loved and hated that she was different to me, and because I didn't realise this I spent my time trying to correct the things I liked least about her that were in fact the things I liked the most.

There are physical similarities between us. Her eyes are brown, mine blue, though we have the same brown hair, hers falling in curls to her shoulders, her superb shoulders, two of the only things that can distract me from her legs. It is not that her legs are the type you see on the front of tights-packets or on teenage models in Sunday supplements, they're not as long as these, less exercised or less starved, no less the better for it, the legs I wrote poetry and cooked dinner for and lay between, the legs I watched to the detriment of road safety when we rode bikes together. They were *her* legs. I don't care if they make me objectify her: she was here! She was once here! So close I could touch her.

I had been best friends with Sarah for many years before we got together, though from the very first day I met her it had been an ambitious friendship. I had wanted her, and I had always wished she would split up with whichever boyfriend she had at the time. If it was not an innocent friendship I began with Sarah, when I sat next to her and listened to her voice rise and fall, when I laughed involuntarily at her stories and character assessments, when I plotted our adventures together, our happy ending, then there was nothing corrupt in it either. It was never the right time for us: I was not as forceful then as I have been since, and she either had an unsuitable boyfriend or I had an unsuitable girlfriend and we were never in the same place long enough to make the unsuitability incontestable. Sarah couldn't hold a job then (and perhaps now) for more than a year before she was bored and off somewhere – Korea, Brazil, India – to do another job and learn another language from another exotic boyfriend. These were years in which I could forget her except as a wistfulness, the warm promise of a distant reunion; make me happy, but not yet. I began to enjoy myself.

It was in the gap between one of Sarah's disappearances that I finally confessed how I felt to her. I had been single for a year, but she had a boyfriend back in Brazil, an artisan potter (they were always people with extraordinary occupations), and in her laidback way she assumed they'd stay together without being able to articulate how. In the meantime she had moved to Edinburgh for a job at the National Museum of Scotland, and invited me up to stay for a long weekend. It began on Thursday in a pub near her flat in Leith, one you reached by walking down a narrow street lined with prostitutes. We played a game – I can't remember who started it – categorising all our mutual friends by whether or not we wanted to sleep with them. I was delighted at how many people she didn't want to sleep with. Perhaps I lied a bit to suggest my tastes were less catholic than they are. And then we could no longer avoid it.

Yes, she admitted, with almost entirely disguised shyness, she would.

Yes, I admitted, rapturously, I would, I would, I would.

The next day we climbed to the top of Arthur's Seat and stood braced against each other as the wind tried to tear us off. On the way down her feet slipped and I caught her under the arms. She turned and looked at me incredulously, as if she hadn't noticed I had been with her until that moment. I had to say something but I couldn't.

She never had the right clothes for the country she was living in. That day she was wearing a summer dress with shiny black tights and flimsy canvas shoes – a thick blanket of a woollen overcoat on the top donated by one of her new colleagues after she had arrived to work two days in a row in a soggy denim jacket. The cold rain began to hammer down as we reached the bottom and she was soon sodden. We took refuge in a pub. She had stolen a lipstick that morning from Superdrug and came back with cherry-pink lips and soaking hair. Her lips were so bright they seemed to belong to another dimension. She was wonderfully disorganised in the way she assembled herself and I expect she will always be like this. I hope so.

I couldn't take my eyes from her. Something was going to happen, something was so obviously going to happen that I felt on the verge of being sick in case it didn't. In the end it was the word itself, unspoken for so long, that brought us together. That evening she had taken us to an ecstasy dealer's tenement flat and later, in a basement dive bar, dancing to house music, I had put my hands on her shoulders and said it: 'I love you.' It was the kind of thing you said on an E, but not in *that* tone. We knew what it meant. Its inevitability stunned her. She took a step backwards and smiled a smile that was without guilt, despite the boyfriend she would have to get rid of in the next month, and we kissed our first kiss.

We lay on her bed when we got home and she swam into a sharp new focus. She tied her hair back and I realised I had never seen her ears. They seemed enormous. She was suddenly a completely different person; her voice sounded more clipped than I remembered and I could imagine her playing hockey; she was a middle-class girl from the home counties, with a mother, a father, a brother and a sister; she owned and wore pyjamas; she thought her knees looked funny, her gorgeous knees pressed up against my jeans. It was fascinating to see her awkward, wondering if I should stay; she wanted me to, but she was a nice girl, a nice girl who shoplifted, and we decided we should take it slow.

I already had everything I thought I could ever need from her. She liked me, and I was lost.

Before I got up to go back to the sofa, I said something clichéd and untrue. 'From the start, it was always meant to be you and me.'

We lay there looking at each other, our bodies at right angles, our faces side-on, curious.

'I didn't know you felt like that,' she said.

'Really?'

'No, I knew!' She laughed and we looked at each other some more.

'You're not making any move to kiss me,' she said.

'I'm keeping still. I'm scared I might startle you.'

'Just approach slowly. No sudden movements.'

I stayed where I was and carried on looking.

Her prominent ears. Her funny knees. Her hungry smile.

My life together with Sarah finally ended with a long Tube ride to Heathrow that afternoon. We hugged each other through a pole in the packed carriage. We couldn't get the right angle to kiss. She still wouldn't meet my eyes. The day before I had borrowed a shopping trolley from a supermarket to haul boxes of my books to the nearest charity shop. I didn't even approve of giving books to charity – the publishing industry seemed in need of enough charity itself. But what was I supposed to do, bin them? I didn't have such a strong stomach. The ones I couldn't bear to give away I had placed, three boxes full, with my aunt. My friends had enough trouble finding space for their own books in their tiny London flats. Sarah's parents were coming round the next day to collect her stuff and she was going to live with them for a couple of weeks while she decided what to do.

We arrived at Heathrow and as we queued on the concourse to check in Sarah told me once again how much fun I was going to have. I put my hands on her shoulders and looked into her eyes. For once, she looked back at me. 'Please, Sarah, I don't want to go without you.'

'I'm moving home tomorrow,' she said, looking away. 'I'm twenty-nine and I'm moving home. I've got you to thank for that. If you don't get on this plane, what are you going to do? Where will you go? My parents certainly don't want to see you.'

We didn't talk about her confession to her mother that I had lied to her, or about her father's reluctant proposition then to beat me up. Her father and I had always enjoyed talking to each other. I wanted to ring him up and offer to help him kick the crap out of me.

'Sarah, I love you. We're supposed to be together.'

'It's just words, Liam. You're just words. And not even very original ones. I can't believe in them any more.'

'I'm not a liar, I told you the –'

'If you begin that again I promise that I will scream.'

'Oh, *please*. We're not simple people. We don't have to obey a soap-opera's sense of justice.'

'I will scream and I will walk away and any slender chance we have of staying together will be gone.'

I was crying by now. Unless I specifically tell you otherwise, assume I'm always crying.

'And stop *pronouncing* those tears.'

'Is it that slender?' I asked.

'Yes,' she said.

I turned back after I had my ticket and passport checked on my way to the departure gate. She was still there watching me. We reflected each other across five years. There aren't many looks in a lifetime like the one she gave me. You couldn't survive more than a few. She waved. I waved. She mouthed three words to me. 'I love you.' Or, 'Bye bye, Liam.' I could not be sure and mouthed three words back and she turned and walked away. She turned back once, she turned back twice and I waited for her to turn back again but that was all. Bye bye, Sarah.

Chapter 2

I had never been on a flight like the one I took to Buenos Aires. There was a stop-over in Madrid for eight hours and I used it to leave the airport, go to a bar in the city, drink ten small but powerful beers and compose a frantic letter to Sarah that during the time I was writing it convinced me I could make everything all right again. I posted the letter, got on the wrong Metro line back to the airport and nearly missed the plane. When I made it just in time I was drunk, but I was not alone. For the duration of the twelve-hour flight it seemed that nearly every passenger remained standing with a beer in their hand, wandering between other groups of upright and talkative Argentines. It was like a giant pub in the sky. I can't remember if we sat down even for take-off; it wouldn't surprise me if we hadn't, or if there had been barbecues sizzling in the aisles. The first half of the trip was a blur. I woke up, four hours in, sprawled across three seats, and immediately had to be sick. No one seemed surprised as I ran to the toilet with my hand over my mouth. Afterwards, I lay back down and hugged myself, crying freely but quietly, until an air hostess from the 1970s shook me and encouraged me into an upright position. We were about to land.

The taxi driver didn't understand my painstakingly prepared phrase-book instructions. I was asking for the Avenida de Mayo, which I pronounced like –ayonnaise.

'Que? Que?'

'De Mayo!'

'Que? Que?'

I pulled my piece of paper out and showed it to him. He read it and slapped me on the shoulder, spraying spit across the windscreen: 'Avenida de Mazcho!' And then he was off.

It was a bright sunny morning I did not belong in. The driver carried on a conversation with the radio as we sped through wide cracked roads lined with grand municipal buildings. It looked like Paris then Madrid then Milan; I couldn't keep track but I felt like I had been here before. I began to cheer up but when I arrived at my hostel at 7 a.m. they had no idea who I was and explained to me, thankfully in English, that they were full up. That was that, then. I had done my best. I asked them to order me a taxi to the airport because I was going back to England. On hearing this, they rang around and found me a place at a sister hostel and so, another taxi ride later, I arrived at the Tango backpackers hostel in Palermo. I'm not sure how the driver knew it was the right one because I learned later that every hostel in Buenos Aires is called the Tango backpackers hostel. In the foyer was a small young man behind a reception desk. He looked up eagerly as I came through the door then looked disappointed, a

21

look I thought was caused by my not being a woman. I felt sad for him too. Behind him was a wide bar, with fridges full of enormous bottles of lager labelled in the national blue and white. There was a music playing I had never heard before: chilled-out ambient beats and accordion solos. Electronic tango. At the time I found it quite beautiful, but I had been travelling for thirty hours and was delirious with strange emotions. I was to learn that no music but electronic tango played in the bar, for twenty-four hours, every single day of the week.

There was one private room left, a small white box just off the building's roof terrace. It had a single bed, a clothes rail and a window almost completely obscured by an air-conditioning unit which didn't work – a perfect monk's cell for me to begin my penance.

I had half of my redundancy money left and had applied for an Arts Council writing grant. If that came through, I could live like this for months. I would redeem myself through hard work, honesty and self-control. Honestly.

For the first few days I kept myself to myself and didn't explore far from the hostel. Without Sarah, I was in a state of shock, left to face head-on the reality of having lost my job and way of life. I suffered moments of vertiginous panic, but I can't claim I spent all my time realising hard truths. It was confusing. The hard truths seemed to have nothing to do with my being here in this airy hostel lounge, sitting at a table listening to endless accordion over crisp backbeats and earnest conversations between Americans. Not that all the voices were American, nor even the loudest. There were Scandinavians, Israelis, Aussies, English, Europeans, all sorts. There were even some Latins, though they were mostly staff. Over those first few days I divided all the guests into two categories:

the Kids and the Broken. Well, I had nothing in common with the Kids, with their tattoos and gym-muscles, their slender limbs and colourful clothes. They talked about mountains and beaches and marijuana. They were gap-year students, recently graduated and other idiots. I begrudged them their innocence, especially when they started to philosophise, which they did with a forthrightness that was difficult to ignore. But my greatest disdain was reserved for the inevitable moment when one of the Broken would take them seriously and offer his own opinion on the happy peasants of India. It was a point of faith for many of the Broken that there was nothing separating them from the Kids. The poor broken men (they were nearly all men). I refused to accept I was one of them in spite of the evidence. It helped that they were mostly slightly older than me, men in their mid to late thirties, fleeing lucrative careers in IT, accounting or management consultancy: lonely, dog-eyed men in checked shirts and baleful smiles looking all day for good news from Apple laptops, the very latest models, peering over the top for anyone to talk to. Looking at them, I realised that I had left a job and a life that I had loved. And so after two days of shock I could no longer bear to be around them.

I was staying in Palermo Viejo, an aggressively cool neighbourhood full of hipster boutiques, leafy streets and bar-lined squares where the late autumn sun dappled onto outside tables . . . all of that gloss. It would have been a wonderful place to be with Sarah. If she had been speaking to me. She had made me promise not to call her for the first two weeks and while there was still a chance she would forgive me I was determined to do whatever she told me. The nearest square to my hostel was Plaza Cortázar and I took this at first as a good omen, a perfect place to sit and read and write, to plant myself in the city's literary soil and try to grow something. Unfortunately the right books I'd packed were completely the wrong books: translations of the Argentine masterworks I had naively assumed would help me feel at home on arrival. Borges' gnomic, deeply un-reassuring stories made me want to weep every time I attempted them; there were times when I could not even get to the end of a story's title. Cortázar's supposedly read-in-any-order novel *Hopscotch* made me feel scared I did not know my way back to my bedroom, even when I was in my bedroom. I was too fragile and unplotted for either of them. I craved English realism to anchor me, but the books on the hostel's shelves had been left by children and hippies and the only readable novel I could find was *Bleak House* by Charles Dickens, an enormous over-corrective to the Argentine canon and the worst book in the world to read while watching the sensuality of Buenos Aires streetlife pass by. Fog, soot, grotesque characters and a saintly narrator. I recognised none of this around me. The guidebook mentioned an English-language bookshop, but when I went to find it one day it had moved. Borges loves this about Buenos Aires, his imaginary city, the image of which he says is always anachronistic. I gleefully hated him and resigned myself to *Bleak House*.

Though I had yet to start my novel, I was nevertheless writing something: daily emails to Sarah. I should have taken more care with these. I can't remember exactly what they said and I will never have the courage to look back at them in my sent items folder. But, hell, I know what they will have said, they will have said, don't leave me, don't leave me, don't leave me, and though I will have tried to be clever and present a compelling case for why it would have been better for her and not just me if she'd stayed, she would have seen straight through my manipulations to the real message: that I was selfish, that I was needy, that I was work. Whatever I was, I wasn't what I had suggested I was to begin with. And so it was that after a week I received a devastating response.

Before Sarah told me that it was over between us, for ever, completely, she told me how 'tired' she was of my 'silly romantic language' that didn't 'begin to redeem' my 'excuses and lies'. I was 'addicted' to trying to make people 'feel the way you want them to feel', 'like a politician rather than a boyfriend' who couldn't understand 'making someone happy is not pushing the right buttons in the right order' but being 'true and strong and open'. 'I don't know who you are.' It was over. 'I want you to have no hope.'

Amid the agony of accepting and refusing to accept what I had always known was going to happen, I suspect I quite liked the portrayal of me here, the compartmentalised, enigmatic multi-man. It is a sort of fun being a dickhead, that's why there are so many of us. It wasn't unique to me – did other people really reveal themselves truly to others? Were they better than me or did they just make a better job of pretending to be? I didn't believe it was only me who was so hungry, so weak.

What mattered actually was that Sarah thought there *were* truthful people around and that she was one of them, even if she was in a minority. There were better people than me for her to risk spending her life with.

I was desperate to go home, to make a dramatic gesture; I had to talk to her face to face, convince her she could believe in me.

I quickly saw how much worse this would make things. It was my constant presence in daily emails that had driven her to such a quick conclusion. She wouldn't want to see me; she would be disgusted at my additional cowardice, at my throwing away the chance to write the novel I had been talking about for so long. Perhaps if I gave her time to forget the vivid recent pain and remember the pleasure, my devotion . . . if I stayed here and learned something, wrote something to show her who I was. It was my only chance.

It was then that I decided to write the love letter, the love letter to end all love letters. I would take notes for months, write it all by hand – the pornography of the internet found its correlation in the email, instantaneous, generic, regretted. This time I would write slowly to Sarah, I would think and revise, I would find out how I felt about her and surprise us both with its truth.

This was my new faith.

But life was unbearable. I needed distraction, I needed a friend.

So I emailed Amy Casares. I had met Amy when I published her first novel, five years ago. She was half Argentine, half English, Argentine on her father's side, and had spent her late twenties in Buenos Aires producing a film at the same time as Bennett lived there (this was at the end of her brief first career working as the gorgeous daughter in the Oil of Ulay TV adverts). I had mentioned her to Bennett on the night I met him to see if he knew her, and he told me he had fallen in love with her and never forgotten her. I was not surprised about that, for I had been in love with her myself since we published her. She was ten years older than me and painfully beautiful. I didn't need to imagine her in her twenties or even thirties for I loved her as she was now, chastely, immaculately. The novel had done well, as these things go, but it had not made Amy a star, and Bennett had no idea it had been published until I told him.

It took some courage to email her. I knew that she would know some people out in Buenos Aires, but I did not know what she had been told about me, what she thought about Bennett's death. I didn't know whether she had gone to the funeral and, if she had, what stories people would have told her afterwards. Three days after I had sent the email, when I had had no reply from Amy, I decided she had made her decision about me. And so, despite my misgivings, I contacted Sarah's friend Lizzie on Facebook, the friend who had provided the initial reason for the trip. Lizzie sent me her number and I gave her a call that evening. She had a light, springy voice when she answered the phone, an accent that reminded me of Sarah's. 'So how is Sarah?' was almost the first thing she said. 'She's not here?'

'No, she's . . . she's got a lot of work on at the moment. I'm here for a while. She'll come later.'

'Are you missing her yet?'

'Lots,' I said truthfully, and we arranged to meet at her flat in Recoleta.

I walked to her apartment at nine that evening. The sky was a darkening regal blue at that time and the city felt poised, waiting to do something. Young men and women walked past me with groceries, old ladies walked dogs, couples sat on walls and benches tonguing each other unashamedly – it was still early, there was much to do.

I found Lizzie's apartment and rang the buzzer, and the

most beautiful man I have ever seen answered the door. He was clearly Argentine, and I can only describe him, as I apprehended him then, like something from a brochure: his long dark glossy hair, honey-coloured skin, perfect brown pools for eyes where one could drop one's soul and never hear a splash. He was smoking 'a fragrant joint'.

'You must be Liam,' he said, reaching out a hand and leaning forward when I took it to kiss me on the cheek. I'd read in the guidebook that this was how they did hellos and, though I liked it, it surprised me. I didn't know whether to return it, but he left his cheek there for me so I kissed him back. Behind him, the woman who must have been Lizzie was lying on her front, her feet raised up and casually wiggling behind her while she laughed on the phone and waved at me. His stubble scratched against mine as we separated and made me want to light a cigarette. Her legs made my initial. Behind her was an open balcony, with a view of many more balconies in the warm dark where the streetlights seemed to shine brighter than English streetlights, simply because they weren't English streetlights. Lizzie, folded up, looked like she'd be tall when she straightened.

He was introducing himself. 'My name is Arturo,' he said. 'You have just come to Buenos Aires?'

I nodded. It was calming to be in a real living room, without any calming electronic tango music playing. Arturo had a really good haircut. It shone. He shone. I asked him the question I already knew the answer to 'How do you know Lizzie?' and he just smiled and turned around to look at her. I remember the phone she was talking into was an old-fashioned one with a rotary dial. Her legs were tanned and the soles of her feet looked like they would always be dirty. Some men wouldn't have liked that.

But not me and Arturo. In fact, I just didn't know which of them to look at.

He offered me his spliff and, still stunned, though I hated dope, I took it and inhaled. Twice. Again. And then we were grinning at each other and embracing, as if enacting the second stage of the unusual hello we had begun before. 'You want a beer,' he told me.

While he was getting it, Lizzie hung up and tipped herself from the sofa like a slinky springing over a step. 'Liam!' In the same motion, she fell forward into me and hugged me doggily, pushing her chest into me, all coconut smelling, tall and limber, freckled brown skin still radiating the afternoon's sun. 'What fun.' It was a hug I was in no hurry to leave but we pulled apart as Arturo came back into the room with my beer.

He handed it to me and studied me more carefully. This alone should have been reason for him to relax if he was assessing me as a threat. He looked hard at Lizzie before turning back to me. 'But you are not here with your girl-friend, Liam.'

'She's had some work come up that was too good an opportunity to miss. She can't leave right now. Hopefully –'

'Oh, yes, let's talk about Sarah,' interrupted Lizzie. 'I want to hear all about what she's been up to – and how you met, what you do.'

And so, like the dutiful proud boyfriend I wanted to remain, I began to describe Sarah's blossoming career as a curator, her invitations to New York and Sao Paulo, how she had nearly finished her PhD, about the offers she had to teach short courses that summer at universities around the world. After years of having no money and having to admit at parties to being a student, she was suddenly in possession of a glamorous success story. I knew what that felt like, how useful it was, how heady the opportunities, how excited and self-absorbed it had made me. She would survive it better. It was perfect poetic symmetry that I had fallen just as she had reached her peak. She could do whatever she liked with her success now.

'And what do you do?' asked Arturo. 'Why are you here?'

'That's a good question,' I admitted.

I had tried to think of something plausible on the walk over. But if you are hiding some details of a story, it is always best to reveal others truthfully.

And so I started to tell them about my shame.

Chapter 3

I was sent to meet Craig Bennett on the opening Monday of the London Book Fair. I don't need to mention in which year. That morning Sarah had left me. After an entire night begging her not to I was almost grateful when she slammed the front door behind her, leaving me with one fewer of the bags of clothes she had thrown all over our bedroom.

In the shower I let myself collapse, sob and pray to my childhood God who only existed now during aeroplane take-offs and girlfriend emergencies. I turned all that off with the water and put on my best new suit. I had work to do.

Within minutes of leaving the house for Earls Court I became terrified of the conclusions Sarah would reach without my constant interruptions. I called her whenever I had a moment between meetings but she never answered. Each minute was madness. I started drinking at lunch, quickly working out which of my appointments wouldn't mind moving to the bar. I still have my tattered schedule for that day: apparently I met with fifteen different people.

I can't remember who most of them are, let alone the books they talked to me about. There were many tall, wonderful-looking women from the Netherlands and Germany, from France and Italy. There always are. I must have nodded in the right places and delivered my lines correctly; somewhere in the middle of that afternoon Belinda materialised in a cloud of exquisite perfume to tell me what a good job I was doing, and could I meet Craig Bennett in a restaurant in Notting Hill and look after him for a couple of hours before delivering him safely to our party?

James Cockburn would have normally been the one to look after Bennett but he was in hospital with the broken legs he'd acquired when falling from the first-floor window of a flat in Soho. I would have been at the party and witnessed this for myself if I hadn't been pleading with Sarah not to leave me.

Cockburn's fall was the talk of the Fair that day. People flocked to our stand to find out what had happened. I heard six or seven different versions, including the most lurid: that Craig Bennett, gripping Cockburn's shirt, had leaned him out of the window, demanding his advance be increased, and when Cockburn only laughed, Bennett had shoved him, perhaps half in jest, straight out the window onto the street below. It was a good story, but I heard another that was far more in character for my hedonistic mentor, that Cockburn decided to climb out the window and scale the narrow ledge around the edge of the building – why? – to surprise two actresses known for their roles in BBC costume drama who were sitting on an adjacent windowsill. This was just the kind of idea Cockburn would have found attractive, particularly as he had been drinking since the Sunday lunchtime kick-off of the QPR home game he'd taken some New York publishers and agents to.

There were other stories too.

Eighteen months earlier, when I had come to London to start my brilliant new job and move in with Sarah, I had done my best to correct my hedonism. I had been using my father's disappearance at sixteen for far too long to justify my excesses; I was no longer that damaged teenager. Sharing a flat with Sarah seemed to be the perfect point to give up the long boozy stimulant-filled weekends of the previous five years of our lives – and earlier too, when we had been best friends attached to the wrong people. Now we had our own living room in which to watch films and DVD box-sets on our own sofa. We could make love on a shaggy, purpose-bought shagging rug. The lies are so easy to believe in: I would read manuscripts and the canonical works of European literature; fresh coffee, jazz on the stereo, my drug dealers in Birmingham sending me promotional text messages I was too far away to take advantage of.

We moved into a flat in Hackney in an old council block. It didn't look much but I loved it. The sun came through our thin curtains and woke me up at five in the morning in the summer. I've never been much good at sleeping, never a member of what Nabokov calls 'the most moronic fraternity in the world'. (I had my own moronic fraternity united by the refusal of sleep, with Cockburn our founder and spiritual leader.) I would quietly watch Sarah sleeping until I got bored, and then sneak into the living room to read a manuscript for an hour or two before she woke up. I was good at my job then. Insomniacs make diligent readers as well as talented hedonists.

But Sarah liked the drugs too, and a couple of weeks into my well-intentioned abstinence, she began to wonder where they were. 'Have you not got – literally, not got *anything*? Oh. Oh . . . *good*.' It was my fault. I'd always had something squirrelled away; I'd created expectations. (That euphemism: we were *expected* to drugs.) There was a point in every party when we realised how easy it would be to have *more* fun. How boring it would be not to.

We decided the sometime in the non-urgent future when Sarah got pregnant would be the new deadline for renouncing our lifestyle (or we'll regret it then, said Sarah) and we went back to normal. It was not hard to find new drug dealers. I asked a literary agent over lunch, and she pitched her entire list to me, central, south, west, east, north . . . I bought them all. And suddenly drugs were almost legal as mephedrone appeared, combining the effects of cocaine and MDMA and speed, great pillows of which were available over the internet for almost nothing. Everyone was taking it. Everyone stupid was.

What I love (I am trying to say loved) about drugs is the way they engender the temporary suspension of disbelief, poetic faith, negative capability, whatever you want to call it. You can invent magical new characters for yourself when you're on them, and if you start to believe in them others will too. Perhaps an aspiring writer's instincts are riskier, more hospitable to the reader's desire for titillation, for secrets and extra-marital intrigue. Perhaps. This type of grand disingenuousness annoyed Sarah more than anything. So it should have. I just liked getting high. It isn't only writers who make themselves into characters: it's one of the commonest failings, one of the purest joys. And you don't have to be a liar to be a writer: that's a book festival cliché you hear from midlisters aspiring to midlife crises. Becoming a vainglorious prick has never been fundamental to creating literary art. No. I did that because it was fun, because I was morally exhausted and it was easy to pretend my behaviour was separate from my essence. But if the man careering around town in my clothes wasn't me, then why did I feel so bad, and so proud, about the way he talked to women?

It hadn't always been this bad or good. I'd arrived in London from a small press in Birmingham with a reputation for frugality, integrity and luck. Everyone loves a plucky indie. It made people at the conglomerates trying to poach our successful authors feel good about themselves to know we existed, that there was room for us. I was embraced at book parties. Have you met my mate Liam? People thought I was a nice guy. I *cared* about writers. Well, I always had a lot of compassion but outside of work it mostly overflowed in the wrong directions, to the people who least needed it. To the people who exhibited moral failings, by which I mean the people with the option to. The carnal people, the libertines, the charmers. The lookers, the liars, the reckless. The success went to my head. That's the *point* of success. I was drawn to the promiscuous and the criminal, like my mentor and the other JC, and who knew London publishing would be such a fine place to find these two qualities? It was with my reputation in mind, and with Cockburn lying in an expensive private hospital – not his first trip to an expensive private medical facility paid for by the company – that they sent the ingénue out to look after Booker-winning Craig Bennett. We had never met but by coincidence we shared the same literary agent, Suzy Carling – I had written one bad novel no one wanted to publish but she had managed to place a story of mine in *Granta*, and this had blown a gale into my inflating ego. I must have seemed just the man for the job. My task was to talk books, flatter, reassure him that in spite of the rumours, we knew he and Cockburn were the best of friends. I was to order the drinks as slowly as possible and *on no account allow him to take me with him to score drugs of any kind*. His publicist Amanda Jones briefed me. He was due at a party at ten; all I had to do was get him there, and then she and Suzy and the rest of the cavalry would take over. If there were any problems I was to call. Belinda hoped we would hit it off in a purely professional way, that I would be an option to take over the editing of his books if, despite our assurances, Cockburn's mysterious fall proved fatal to their working relationship. There was a lot riding on it: his last novel had sold nearly half a million copies.

I understood why they trusted me: I was polite, I was unpretentious (unpretentious for publishing, very pretentious for elsewhere) and I got on with people. They couldn't have known about the damage I successfully concealed. When Craig Bennett is written about in the press, his name is usually prefaced by phrases such as 'combustible', 'iconoclastic', 'self-destructive', even 'Bacchanalian', which tells you more about journalists than about Bennett. (I once heard a literary editor describe James Cockburn as a real-life 'Dionysius', by which they meant he wore his shirt unbuttoned and took cocaine at parties.) Such tags were relative. Most novelists don't make good copy for the news pages. If Bennett wanted to turn up on stage in the middle of a seventy-two-hour bender and abuse crowd members for their 'intellectual cowardice' then I was all for it. If he wanted to grip Julian Barnes in a tight bear-hug whenever he saw him in a green room and repeatedly lick his face until prised away, then what of it? (Bennett was 'not welcome again' at the Hay, Edinburgh and Cheltenham festivals.) He was a little old for such behaviour, but so are many people who behave this way. I am not in the first generation of men who refused to grow up. That evening I was expecting to meet someone completely normal. I wasn't at all worried about Bennett's reputation.

I arrived twenty minutes late at the glass-fronted French restaurant in Notting Hill. Or rather, I was on time, watching him through the window as he poured himself three consecutive glasses of wine. Sarah had finally answered her phone and was telling me it was over and to stop calling her so much. I pleaded with her to see sense and she objected to my definition of sense. Over the last twenty-four hours I had maintained a firm faith in the power of reason to defeat chaos. If I could just keep talking, if I could talk all day and all night, she would have to realise what I had done was not so bad, that it was not in fact *me* who had done it. I would have gone on for ever, listening to my voice grow more impassioned and articulate, wavering on the edge of real tears, if she had not begun to cry herself, something she hardly ever did, and in doing so remind me that she was something more than an obstacle to my will, an exercise in persuasion. She was Sarah and she was miserable. I would never have the right or the power to convince her otherwise.

I looked at my reflection in the restaurant window and listened to her cry. She was not a crier; I'd made her take on a role that wasn't hers. We criers are the moral infants of the world, the sensualists. We like the way it feels;

though we don't admit it, we're yearning to be miserable. We want a fix. Behind my reflection Craig Bennett was looking at me curiously. I waved at him and something in the friendly childishness of my gesture stabbed me: how far away I was from that pleasant boy I'd taken for granted and forgotten to stay in touch with. I wheeled around and after two minutes of desperate, abruptly terminated pleas to Sarah, I wiped my eyes on the sleeve of my shirt and entered the restaurant.

'You look fucking awful,' he said, after I introduced myself and sat down. Some people may have thought the same of him. You will have seen the photos: the rich craggy drinker's face; its pink tributaries crawling through reddish stubble, sunken blue eyes, bleached of emotion by hot weather and late nights. A surly face. Well, that was the photos, or the photos the papers took, or the photos the papers used. He might have been trying to look surly but it didn't convince me, and I was glad to take his comment as friendly. I have a lot of friends who, if they don't have faces like his already, are working on getting them.

'Yes, I do,' I said, nodding.

'And you're twenty minutes late,' he said.

'Yes,' I continued to nod gratefully, 'yes I am.' I reached out and poured myself the last glass of wine in the bottle, immediately raising it towards the waitress. 'Another of these, please.' I took a swig. 'This is nice,' I said. 'I'm sorry for being so late –'

And then I turned my face and just about swallowed another sob that threatened to spill over the table.

Craig Bennett continued to gaze at me curiously.

'I am sorry,' I said, pouring the rest of the glass down my throat. 'I'm not normally so incontinent.'

'What's happened?'

'Oh, I've just been dumped. Last night. She's not going to have me back.'

'I'm glad about that.'

'Pardon?'

'Don't get me wrong. We'll get into that. At least we *can* talk about that – if you're not too boring about it. You may even be wrong. I mean, I thought for an awful moment that they'd sent someone whose mother had just died or something.'

'We wouldn't put *that* on you,' I said, speaking as the company. 'That'd be awful manners.'

'A spurned boyfriend is far better than a grief-stricken son.'

'Yes? You're probably right. They wouldn't have sent me if they'd known how miserable I was.'

The waitress came over and showed me the bottle of wine. 'Just pour it please,' I said.

'You're doing all right,' said Bennett, like a command.

'Yes,' I beamed, as the waitress filled our glasses. 'A shaky start but I feel much better.'

'Good man.'

'My girlfriend would dispute that.'

'Your ex-girlfriend.'

'Oh, yes . . .' My irony wasn't robust enough to joke about that yet.

'How old are you anyway?'

'I'm thirty.'

'You lucky bastard. So then you better tell me what happened. Be warned: I don't have infinite sympathy for young lucky bastards.'

I didn't spend long telling him. It was mundane and predictable. I lied. I made out I was better than I was.

And when it was obvious that I was worse than I'd pretended – to myself as well as her, with the poems, surprise gifts, underwear and holidays – I lied harder and was caught out in increments until I was worse than what I had concealed. When I finally told the truth, it was unrealistic.

'What shall we eat?' I asked.

'I'm not really hungry. Why do you people always insist on meeting in restaurants? What's wrong with pubs?'

'We'd have to pay for our own meals then. But I'd have been very happy with a pub. I think I've given up food. I've thrown up everything I've tried to eat since Saturday.'

He looked at me steadily. 'Ah, mate,' he said, and he reached out and patted me on the arm. 'So it is serious? You love her? It's mundane but I know it fucking hurts. I've been there too.'

He was talking, I found out later, about Amy Casares, the half-Argentine novelist I had published. It was no coincidence that she would appeal to us both. Regardless of this chance connection a friendship was growing, or more precisely he was trying to rescue me, as I have been rescued by strangers before and since. The most cynical and duplicitous of us are often the kindest. There was no way, I knew, I could persuade Sarah of this. Because, probably, it isn't true. But that night Craig Bennett and I were convinced it was.

'Exactly,' he roared, pouring the last of the third bottle. (We had realised that we did like food, as long as it was food you could consume like drugs: we liked oysters – and had been necking them like tequila shots for the last half hour. We were elated.) 'Liars understand what people want, what they don't have. They have imagination! Empathy! They understand complication and contradiction!'

I was lapping it up. Instead of being a self-destructive liar I was now a self-destructive liar – in a good way. In the toilets, almost without thinking, I locked the cubicle door behind me and scraped out onto the cistern half of the remains of the coke that I had left in my wallet from the weekend.

As I walked back into the dining room I felt I had turned the corner into a happier life. I had meant to keep to myself what I had done, but he had been so kind that before I knew it I had passed the wrap across to him and told him to finish it. I'm terrible at doing drugs on my own. They make me so generous-spirited. A flash of concern crossed his face, before he broke into a grin. 'So,' he said, 'it's like this.' Then he was gone, leaving me to take in my surroundings properly for the first time: the inch of wine left in each of our glasses, the tall stems drawing the eye upwards, to the high ceiling, the glass chandeliers, and outwards, to the French waitresses and waiters, young people, in their early twenties, undaunted, poorly paid and incorrupt. My hands were shaking and I thought I could feel everyone looking at me.

Is it really possible to fall in love over the space of a few hours, the way I fell in love with Craig Bennett? Easy to want to, to think you have – isn't that what love is, the opposite of loss? The strength of the feeling is the proof against it having occurred too soon. What I felt that night was that I had found someone to reverse what I had lost. Someone who was pure gain.

My father is ten years older than Bennett, though he looks younger, smoother, like the past has sheared off him in a wet shave. A kind man, his new friends tell me. He wasn't always that man: there was another man who made decisions which neither he, my sisters nor I knew at the time would so blunt our memory of the father he had been before to us. We don't bring up the three years in which he disappeared, the years when we only knew he was alive because of phone calls he made every few months to our grandma. He wouldn't speak to his own father, divorced from grandma, or tell grandma where he was living, what country even – 'It doesn't sound like he's in England,' she'd say. (It's been years since he's sounded like he's on fucking earth, I would reply.) Something had snapped in him during his second, awful marriage, two years after he left us, and after 'an incident' with his new family, an incident we were never told or would ever willingly ask about, an incident that even he, in the height of his madness, recognised as madness, he had simply run, and when all his madness had burnt out he had returned to earth, complete again and a stranger to us. He may have been a stranger to himself too. He certainly wanted to be. In that first year back from the dead we saw him once or twice around the table with his new fiancée, Shelley, who ran a New Age shop in Milton Keynes and on each occasion gave us a gift of a scented candle. Shelley had departed, but we still met with Dad around a table once or twice a year. There was often another woman there. Each time we faced again the absolute impossibility of asking him a serious question. He looked startled when we did, like he was about to run for the hills. We didn't want to risk that. I was sixteen when he disappeared, my sisters thirteen and eleven. I was the lucky one; it's normal up on the Blackpool coast to be drinking heavily by that age; my sisters were jolted into a more precocious start. It didn't do us any superficial harm. All of us are (or have been) well-paid professionals. At the time I didn't feel the lack of a guide; I could work out how a man behaved from my friends and reading the books I liked about the Rolling Stones and other swaggering outlaws. There are advantages to adopting such role models: a certain charm or roguishness, the sad, warping half-truth that girls (and boys) like you more when you treat them badly; that some people get away with murders while others get broken. Most of all there was the glorious opportunity to blame someone else, someone absent, for my own self-indulgence. I met Craig Bennett on the night my dad, Mick Jagger and Keith Richards had all let me down. I came to believe that he had knowledge to impart to me, knowledge that could save me: and I decided to love him.

Chapter 4

Lizzie and Arturo had been letting me speak but now Arturo interrupted. 'How do you mean, you loved him? Like a woman or a brother?' It was not an aggressive question but slightly exasperated. I had been careful not to reveal all I had been thinking, particularly the details about Sarah, and perhaps he could tell I was hiding something. I had probably revealed more than I meant to.

'I've never had a brother,' I said to him. 'I loved him like a friend. Or like a father.'

Perhaps I looked sad then because Lizzie reached over and put her hand on my shoulder. 'What happened next?' she asked.

Craig and I were in a cab, heading to Soho, up some stairs to be greeted by a golden-haired actor. He looked shocked then surrendered to an open-mouthed grin. 'Craig – you came back! What a delight! What *chutzpah!*'

I hadn't seen Bennett abashed before. He was staring past the actor at the two windows on the other side of the room.

He hadn't explained where we were going in the taxi, just that he'd made a new friend who'd be able to sort us out before we went to the party where we were due. 'Now we've started, we'll need it or it will seem like a dreadful evening,' he'd insisted, though he didn't have too much insisting to do. 'And he's a good man: Fergus, an actor, a pleasant host.'

As Bennett fixated on the window I realised where we were. The cardboard crates full of empties confirmed it. We were all suddenly surprised at the situation. We probably needed more drugs. I had a sachet of mephedrone in my wallet, but it was a bit more engulfing and lasting than cocaine; not as socially acceptable. I bit my tongue and introduced myself to Fergus. 'As you can see,' he said, 'the last party feels like it finished about three minutes ago.' He pulled a mostly-full bottle of Prosecco from a cardboard box on the floor: 'Sorry it's not cold, fellas.' He rinsed out three mugs – 'God *knows* what became of all our glasses last night' – and Bennett discreetly recovered himself and drew Fergus aside.

As they conferred, I wandered over to the window and looked down to the pavement below. I don't know what I thought I might see: a cartoon James Cockburn-sized imprint, perhaps. On the other side of the road Eros Videos and Soho Video Club seemed wildly anachronistic, as if they were funded by the council as tourist attractions. A thin ledge ran under the window and around the side of the building. Fergus was speaking into the phone now and Bennett came over to stand with me at the window. We both peered down. 'Is this where . . . ?' I asked. He didn't answer. 'Fifteen minutes,' said Fergus, putting the phone down.

Some people, some writers, like to lyrically describe the reveries they've experienced on drugs. It's an even more boring and shameful habit than taking them. Cocaine was done and did what was expected of it. In the course of consumption we acquired two actresses and four missed calls from Bennett's publicist, two from our mutual agent and one, worryingly, from my CEO. We had moved to an upstairs members' club round the corner where the barmaid had greeted Bennett enthusiastically. I'd still made no contact with James Cockburn, suspecting, correctly, that I had been sent on a mission to betray him. It was midnight. We were two hours late to the party, but the party would go on late, and so I told myself that the situation wasn't irretrievable. Bennett was perfectly happy where he was and didn't share my CEO's sense of the importance of meeting export buyers, foreign editors and the producers of TV book clubs. The actresses' names were Lucy and Charlotte and they were the costume drama stars who had been at the party the night before. They were the kind of intelligent bohemian young women that a Cockburn would go to dangerous lengths to impress. My work credit card was behind the bar and we were drinking champagne. Bennett had stumped up the cash for an eighth of good coke and no one was being shy about taking it.

Eventually, I got all five of us into a taxi. We would arrive with an hour left of the party. I texted Amanda to say we were on our way. The response was immediate: that would be very fucking wise of you.

Leaving the taxi, we faced the usual gastro-enormo-bar in Kensal Green. In large part because of James Cockburn's copy-friendliness and connections with film directors,

46

conceptual artists and indie rock stars, our publisher's yearly party was officially *the* place to be at the book fair. Part of the fun was guessing which rock and rollers would turn up to be drunk under the table by the real hedonists. A voluble chunk of the international publishing industry would be in there.

A bouncer checked my name off and waved us all through. Inside, the cavernous first-room was decked out in what passes for classiness in posh pubs: wine-dark walls interspersed with flock wallpaper, oak tables and Chesterfield sofas. It was heaving; I immediately lost Bennett and the actors as I pinballed between double- and triple-kisses. The crowd was perhaps seventy per cent female and around a third of the remaining men were gay: to a man of imagination this was publishing's great perk and peril. I grabbed a drink and fought my way outside onto the teeming smoking terrace. Here I found myself next to Olivia Klein, a literary reviewer I would rather have avoided. I had been trapped in a disconcerting conversation with her at a Christmas party. She had said the rudest things to me about the books I published, all the time smiling winningly and moving me closer against the wall. She was young, in her mid-twenties, one of those eerily tall Oxbridge girls with skin so pale as to be translucent. She would have grown up in the country, miles from her friends, with only her horse, her mother's neuroses and her father the doctor's well-stocked library of Russian novels for company. As a result of which, she was far cleverer than me.

'Now when are you going to publish something a bit more *avant-garde*?' she was asking. 'Where's the new Calvino? Where's the new Borges?'

'I'm trying to publish books that large numbers of people will *buy*,' I explained. 'It's my job.'

'So you're happy to be complicit in the dumbing down of our culture?'

'Where is this new Borges, anyway? He wasn't in Birmingham.'

'You probably wouldn't recognise them if you saw them,' she said dismissively.

'You don't have any recommendations? Nothing you've read recently in the original Catalan?'

'Don't be facetious.'

I tried to change the subject. 'I hear you've written a novel, Olivia.'

(I had chatted to some literary scouts that day. Literary scouts are book spies employed by foreign editors: they always know everything that everyone is reading.)

'Who's your agent again? I could ask them to send it to me.'

Her body tensed, so much that I prepared to jump out of the way. She breathed deeply. 'Your broken-legged buddy has already anatomised what he perceives as its failures to my agent. Not enough tits, or something like that.'

'Well, James does have quite an instinct for that kind of thing. Have you considered putting some more tits in?'

'Oh, grow *up*. I'm looking forward to reviewing the next masterpiece you publish.'

She walked away then and I wondered if I might be able to damage her career before she did any damage to mine. I didn't know that I had only a few hours left of my career and at the time I quite relished the fight. An enemy can be more fun than a friend, more enlivening, more intimate. I didn't have as many as I would have liked. People liked me, or at least the people I liked liked me, or at least I thought they did. Then I thought of Sarah crying on the phone and realised things might be about to change.

'Liam Wilson!' My agent was walking towards me. Suzy Carling is only a few years older than me but seems at least two generations more advanced. She is striking in appearance and exhausting in conversation. She refuses to answer any questions or remarks that don't interest her, regardless of how useful they are to me. Tonight she was glamorous in a sleek black dress and blue suede boots with frightening long heels. Behind her, I caught a glimpse of Bennett through a window, striding somewhere with Jay McInerney in tow. Suzy pulled a Gauloise out of her handbag and leaned over to me. I lit it for her and she straightened up.

'How are you, Suzy?'

She blew smoke at me. 'Yes. So, what is the news with James? I can't get through to him. Have you spoken to him yet?'

'No, I haven't but I spoke to Belinda this afternoon and he's –'

'Yes, yes. I've spoken to Belinda. I saw you come in with Craig – and by the way, Belinda sounded very exasperated you were so late – so of course you have heard the rumours going around about . . .'

'Whether he was pushed?'

'Or *dangled*?' She laughed. 'I heard some girls earlier saying they were at the door when Craig nearly dropped James on their heads. They had to dive for cover, they said.'

'Who were they?'

'Oh, some publicity assistants. Of course it *wasn't* true – and if it was, it still wouldn't be. They looked rather scared when I butted in and asked for their full names and where it was they worked. So how's Craig holding up?'

'He's fine. I think. Actually, he took me to the flat where it happened earlier.'

'When you were *supposed* to be here.'

'Must you keep mentioning that?'

'And what did he say about it?'

'Nothing. He was staring down from the window where it happened, looking down at the ground.'

'Liam, you said he was staring down, that's where the ground's kept. Is that all you've got? What you need is an editor. Talking of which, aren't you nearly finished with that novel you've been promising me? I rather think you should meet Helen over here.'

And with her marvellous, instinctive gift for a change of subject I was led around for the next twenty minutes, pitching my entirely fictional novel (in the worst way, in being unstarted) to editors, many of whom were friends of mine. This was excruciating, for there are few things more undignified than an editor who writes.

I should explain that, in general, we hated writers. Awful people. Scavengers. Needy little vultures, picking around in creative writing classes, sending in expenses for dinners they had eaten on different dates and in different cities to the events they had not turned up for. Fine artists, the lot of them, experts in cover art. Parasites. Imperiously rude and/or sleazy to editorial assistants. Lazy readers of their own work. Hungry bastards. Reviewers of their friends. Reviewers of their rivals. Making young women cry. Making them sick. Making advances. Not earning advances. Making them pregnant. Making line graphs of Amazon rankings. Sending you these line graphs. Seeking plot and motive in them instead of their own flimsy storylines and characters. *Accidentally* ccing you into correspondence berating you to another needy little vulture. Being 'glad, in some way, that this mistake happened'. Never more than a metre away from the booze table at a book party. Obsequious chairs of literary events until the sixth drink in the follow-up dinner. Quoters of Goethe and Schiller. Owners of *The Mammoth Book of German Aphorisms*. Twitterers. Shitheads. Carrion-pickers. Slobs. Sociopaths. Laptop-dogs. Wolfes. Woolfs. Carvers. Lushes. Lishs. Gougers. Hacks. Mice. Lice. Writers, they were the worst, the most awful, we pitied them but loathed them more; because if it wasn't for them, the job really would be a pleasure.

My confrères listened to me with suppressed amusement. They had all seen me arrive with Craig Bennett and were polite enough to skip over my pitch completely and ask me the same set of questions when it was over.

'So, is it true Cockburn was screaming for mercy?'

'And the window wasn't even open, I heard!'

'Well, someone told me he was holding him by his shirt collars, just, y'know, to shake him up, and the fabric just ripped – he hadn't actually meant to drop him.'

'Yah. Apparently there's a whole chapter missing they didn't print and he'd only just noticed. A whole *chapter*. If that was me, someone would definitely have gone through the window. Who can blame him?'

'Someone said to me it was actually Nick Cave who pushed him.'

'Really, because I'd heard it was Bret Easton Ellis.'

'No, no, it was F. Scott Fitzgerald,' I said, and fled to

the bathroom, bumping straight into Bennett in the corridor heading the same way with his publicist in pursuit. Amanda glared hard at me as I pushed the door open and went in.

'Thank God, I thought she was going to follow us in for a minute,' he said.

'Shall we?' I asked.

'Oh, yes,' he said and we ducked in together to the free cubicle.

We had conspicuously avoided the subject so far (I had been advised not to bring it up) but I had been made giddy by the speculation outside, and I couldn't resist asking him any longer. 'So, go on then, what did happen with you and James?'

He paused and shot me a disappointed look. I'd said it gleefully.

'From the tone of your voice, I think you'd like to believe I pushed him out. Imagine if I had done that – what an appalling thing to do. Is that what you think of me, Liam? You sound like you wish I was that man, like you wish I was indecent. Is that how little you think of James?'

He delivered this soliloquy turning between the cistern and me, gazing into my face then back and with economical movements setting out two large lines.

'I'm sorry, I was being glib,' I said. 'I would much prefer you to be decent.'

He finished rolling up a note and pointed it towards the cistern. 'And this – is this compatible with decency?'

I searched for a truism to excuse our behaviour but came up short. 'No, it's really not.'

He leaned over and snapped up his line. 'Of course it isn't, and if you're going to behave in a certain manner it is important to name it correctly – or else how will you recognise and resist it one day?'

He passed me the note. He had still not told me what happened with him and Cockburn. 'To decency,' he said.

'To decency,' I repeated, and leaned over.

Chapter 5

'You like drugs?' interrupted Arturo.

'He *loves* drugs,' said Lizzie quickly, and I wondered how she knew before I realised she was talking about Arturo.

'I used to like drugs,' I said. 'But I don't take them any more.'

'Why no?' asked Arturo.

That was the easiest and hardest question in the world to answer. Because drugs made me so hungry and irresponsible. Because that was the best thing about them.

Bennett and I exited the toilets together to a welcoming party comprising Amanda, Belinda and Suzy. They scrutinised us and in the surge of enthusiasm the coke had inspired it felt like being caught doing something heroically wrong at school. Bennett roared with approval at the sight of them while I tried to keep a straight face. I'd examined myself in the mirror and given my face a good rub to eliminate any stray traces of powder, but under the test of those three meticulous and knowing gazes I felt transparent. When I looked over at Bennett I could see a smudge of white on the tip of his nose.

'*Craig*,' said Belinda. 'I'm so glad you're getting looked after so well by Liam. Now, could I impose on you for just a few more minutes? There's a very *attractive* and also quite *important* supermarket buyer whom I'm sure you'd love to meet.'

'I can't promise I'll fall in love with her,' said Bennett.

'I promise you won't want to marry her,' I said, and all three women turned to look at me as though I had made a racist joke: this despite Belinda having last described the woman in question to me as 'that half-price desperada *cunt*'.

I had been becoming someone else for quite a while, or someones, but that was the day when it became clear to me that I had chosen a role that did not become me, that was pushing the people around me into roles that did not become them. I liked these women. They were clever and sophisticated and knew far more than me about almost everything. I had wanted to be their colleague, learn from them, assist them. But as I lost my equilibrium we lost our common ground and could see each other only as cut-outs: the brash, know-nothing fool; the cold, unfeeling bitches from hell. By acting as one of these I had forced them to act as the other.

Bennett read their animosity correctly and tried to come to my rescue. 'Thanks for setting me up with Liam, by the way. He's been a good companion.'

But he was already being walked away by Belinda and Suzy, leaving me alone with Amanda. 'You realise, I presume, that we have not taken that as a ringing endorsement?' She made to walk away and then turned round again. 'What has gone on? All that earnest bullshit when you joined – commitment to editorial development, championing voices from outside the mainstream, blah, blah, blah. We all thought you were boring. We thought you were safe hands. He's got a huge rim of coke under his nose, and you're obviously fucked too. Jesus, you're not the only ones,' she said, looking around her. 'But earlier I told you quite clearly that he had a heart condition. Can I strongly suggest you do everything you can to try to remedy this situation?' She shook her head in disgust and walked away.

That was a shock. Had I been told about a heart condition? Not by her, I was sure. But then she had spoken a lot of words to me that afternoon when she arrived at my table to brief me; had they all contained meaning? If so, she should have said. My head had been full of Sarah and now I felt awful. Bennett still had the coke. I would have to get it off him and lose it. Or *say* I'd lost it. I'm very much my mother's boy; I may be susceptible to guilt but I abhor waste. I thought Amanda was probably exaggerating or lying to cover herself, but I decided I had best be safe. I stepped off the corridor into the room where the dance floor had got going. It was entirely made up of young women. I recognised a couple who'd started with us recently; I had no idea who the others were. The women looked so lovely there, dancing with each other, un-protective and slightly embarrassed, like they were at a children's birthday party. And then we began to arrive, the men. The DJ was the publisher of Sweden's most hip literary imprint: he had put on '1999' by Prince and was celebrating by jumping up and down behind the decks with his hands in the air. I looked around for Craig and got sadder about Sarah. And the older people arrived on the dance floor, the publishing legends, the members-club raconteurs, the eccentrics and the elegant, the sharks and the chic and the scouts and the Indians and the auctioneers and the earnest-faced editors-who-really-edit, the recently-fired and recently-promoted, the recently dry and the recently high, the rehabbed, reformed, retweeted. It didn't usually feel this febrile and poignant to me; perhaps it was the lyrics about ignoring the impending apocalypse. The way the book industry was about to change, we might all be out of a job in five years. But my friends were facing the prospect with courage and so I stopped feeling so sad for a second before I realised who I was missing from the centre of the floor: James Cockburn.

Cockburn and I had become friends at various ceremonies and private-members clubs during the two years when the books I published from Birmingham were winning prizes. A hedonist easily recognises another hedonist, often in the queue for a toilet cubicle, and as we were both from the North, lads in a feminine industry, we became friends quickly. At book fairs he'd introduce me to the funniest and drunkest of the foreign editors and agents. I don't believe European women are naturally more alluring than British, but at the time their accented English and the fact I hadn't met any before made them seem so. As men we were outnumbered and popular, despite the limitations of our looks and characters. I won't pretend I didn't enjoy it, that it didn't give me an impression of my attractiveness and charm I could never have believed in as a teenager; but I was in the first glorious wave of love with Sarah and never did more than flirt. James was more used to it than me, more adapted: he felt entitled to his luck and whatever else he wanted. He had made a myth and come to rely on it for his place in this world.

He had to keep creating stories for people to tell about him at book fairs; he was the notorious James Cockburn, outlaw publisher. I knew he loved this role, but I also saw how it trapped him. He was frequently in trouble with Belinda because of it, but it was also this persona that allowed him to do his job the way he did it. He was the ideal editor for a writer like Craig Bennett, and they were the very worst influences on each other.

What was certain was that there was no room for two James Cockburns in our office, and that Belinda wouldn't hesitate to sack me for similar behaviour. For both our sakes, I needed to separate that coke from Bennett – but now he was trapped between Belinda and the producer of a TV book club. As I moved closer he saw me and shouted over, 'Liam! Cocktails! Three mojitos!'

'Oh, I don't like rum,' said the TV producer.

'And, of course, whatever the ladies want.'

Belinda looked hard at me. I betrayed Bennett rather than her, coming back with only one mojito and some wine for the women. Belinda was gesticulating to the TV book producer as I handed them their bowls of white, and it gave me the chance to talk under my breath to Bennett. 'Do you mind if I do a line while you're engaged with these?' I asked. I wasn't going to mention what Amanda had told me, but I had to correct the mistake I'd made when I'd offered him a line at dinner. I'd have an accident and drop the lot in the toilet.

'Of course I do,' he said. 'I'll come with. Belinda! We're just going for a fag,' he called to her, ushering me away with a hand on the small of my back. He propelled me down the corridor towards the smoking balcony. I caught a glance of Belinda's face as I was pulled in a swift right angle into the toilet.

Again, I was bundled into a cubicle, and there, finally, I had to confront him. 'Look, I'm sorry, Craig, I can't allow you to do that. Amanda's told me about your heart condition.'

He looked over his shoulder at me from where he had placed his wallet on the top of the cistern.

'I feel awful for setting us off on this path tonight, but I can at least get us off it,' I went on.

He shook his head at me and went on doing what he was doing, opening the wrap and shaking coke out onto the surface.

'Seriously, please give it here,' I said. 'I can't be responsible for something else awful. And I really like you too.'

'I do not have a fucking heart condition,' he said, not looking my way. 'Unless maybe heartlessness.'

'Come on, that's not you. You've got too much heart. Let's look after it.'

'What do you fucking know about it?' he said, rounding on me. 'It's not what they say in articles about me, is it? I'm "wantonly cruel", "animated by spite and distrust".'

'Journalists, mate. I don't recognise that picture, and no one could from your books.'

'And I don't recognise whatever picture Amanda gave you. Look at me: I'm too young to have a heart attack.'

I *was* looking at him. He was red-faced and dry-lipped, licking around his teeth.

'They'd say anything!' he carried on. 'They do anything to make you do what they tell you to!'

'But let's not now, hey? We'll save it up for later.' I heard my voice as though it was someone else's. I had the forced tone of an HR assistant who'd just come back from a 'persuasiveness' 'workshop'. I knew I'd got it wrong.

Craig held me by the shoulders. 'I like you,' he said,

'because you were honest with me. You didn't flatter me. You told me about yourself and let me talk to you. Simple qualities, found in many places, but not always here. But I am free to do what I want to do, and you are not responsible for my actions. We hardly know each other. We don't know each other at all. I absolve you of any responsibility. I will not listen to you. There is nothing wrong with my heart and I intend to do a line of cocaine right now. You may join me if you like.'

Although his words were robust, they no longer sounded true. It was a performance without point, playing the version of himself he'd tried to disown to me earlier. I think I could have spoken to the man behind the face, if I had really wanted to. In fact, I'm sure I could. And it is this that makes it unforgivable that I accepted the line he offered and charged out of the toilets, past Belinda's stare and onto the dance floor, where I twirled around and poured my drink on the feet of a pretty editorial assistant, whose number I found later in my BlackBerry, 'girl with wet feet'. I would like to say I deleted it and that I haven't thought about calling it since. I would like to say much about myself that I cannot. There is something wrong with my heart too.

Chapter 6

Lizzie sniggered. I had been hamming it up a bit. Arturo looked at her with an appalled expression.

'Lizzie, there is something wrong with his *heart*!'

'I'm sorry, Liam,' Lizzie said. 'I'm sorry to hear about your heart.'

We looked at each other then, and I smiled back. I couldn't help myself. I really liked the woman. She had a forgiving smile: I know you are ridiculous, but I like the way in which you are ridiculous.

'I didn't mean that literally,' I said to Arturo. 'I was exaggerating too.' And in an instant his wide, innocent eyes narrowed and a sly grin cut through the concern he had affected. 'I know, Liam,' he said, and laughed, and I realised I had made two friends.

The party in Kensal Green came to a sudden end at two, far too early for my liking and the other guests with 'stamina'. As we queued for taxis, we gravitated towards each other, all asking the same thing: 'Where now?' There was a gang of about twelve of us, editors and agents, buyers for book chains. The assistants and the marketing and publicity people would have to go to work in the office tomorrow, and while it was possible to work at a book fair after only two hours' sleep and enough booze that you were still drunk at lunch – was in fact something to boast of in your half-hourly meetings – your wild eyes and slurred speech would be more noticable in the office. Fergus the actor was still here with his two friends. We waited for Bennett to appear. When he did, he was surrounded in a triangle by Amanda, Belinda and Suzy, as though he was being escorted back to prison after a day in the dock. Suzy caught my eye and immediately strode over to me. 'Liam: are you in the middle of arranging an after-party?'

'I think some people are –'

'Stop it right now, or pretend to Bennett it's not taking place.'

'But he's been to this party before. He's not really going to believe we're all going to bed now.'

'Well, Cockburn's not here this time, is he? And can't you just *help*, Liam? He's supposed to be speaking at the Fair at midday tomorrow, chairing an event on the Argentina programme. If he carries on he won't have gone to sleep by then. He should not be doing this any more.'

Nor should I. She was right; it was time for my empty bed and Sarah's strewn clothes on the floor, to start to tidy up the mess I had made of my life.

'Sorry. I'll go and tell everyone to pretend the after-party's off. Come and help though. They all love him, they won't want to let him go. I need you to help me threaten them.'

'With pleasure.'

But it was too late. Fergus and the actresses had found a cab and as Suzy and I made our pact, one of them opened the door and called out to Bennett: 'One space left, Craig, get in!' Before anyone could stop him Craig had darted towards it. 'Craig, come back!' we all shouted. The door closed behind him and the taxi accelerated away.

'Oh, fuck,' Suzy said.

Belinda and Amanda appeared either side of me.

'I blame you for this,' said Belinda.

'I was trying to help Suzy get him home,' I protested.

'He was,' said Suzy. 'You can still blame him, though.'

'Do you know where he's going?' said Amanda.

'I can find him,' I said.

'Find him,' said Belinda. 'Stay with him. Has your phone got power?'

'It has,' I said.

'If you fail to answer your phone to Amanda or me, your day will begin tomorrow with me taking a long look at your contract of employment – do you understand? I have never been so angry in my life. Just get him to his reading tomorrow, or get Amanda to him tomorrow morning in time to get him to the reading. Just take control of the situation, for fuck's sake. Sober up, stay awake and go and find him.'

I found him the first place we looked. I was in a cab with three of an endangered species, Irish booksellers, one of whom had been at the party the night before and knew exactly what had happened between Cockburn and Bennett. 'He was fucking Cockburn's wife,' he told me. 'It's sure. I heard them arguing over her just before it happened.'

'I know his wife,' I said. 'I'm pretty sure one maniac's enough for her. There's no way that was happening.'

'Ah, you say that, but humans, you know – they're always surprising you.'

We pulled up at the scene of the crime and looked up. A man was leaning out the window, contemplating the ground beneath him. As we got out of the car he finished his cigarette, waved and bounced the glowing tip on the concrete.

'Nice escape,' I called up.

'Is that what I've done?' Bennett called back. 'You better come in then.'

Three more cabs showed up: Fergus was a friendly host. Half of the guests had been at the party the night before and immediately began to whisper the story of Cockburn's fall to the half who had not, inclining their heads towards the famous window. I was busy talking to Bennett about our mutual friend Amy Casares, hoping he wouldn't notice, and he was animatedly telling me about the adventures they had had in Buenos Aires. All of a sudden, he seemed very sad. 'Can we get out of this room?' he asked. 'I know they're talking about me.'

We found a bedroom and Bennett shut the door behind him. We sat down on the bed. 'It's good to talk to a friend of Amy,' he said. 'Amy was always the one for me. When she moved to Madrid, I should have followed her. She would have let me, I'm convinced she would have. You can never know you were wrong if you never tried. That's what we want most sometimes, to know we were wrong. I'll never know. I had my set-up in Buenos Aires, I knew what I was doing there. I had attachments. But when she left, they were different, the attachments. They weren't fun any more. I can see you're being brave about your girlfriend. And you should be brave. But I wish I had been courageous earlier so I didn't have to pretend to be now. That's what being brave is: pretending to be brave. That's what it's for. What I'm trying to ask you is, do you love her?'

'Yes,' I said.

'And have you thought about what that means?'

'I've thought about it. I haven't reached an answer.'

'Do you want *me* to tell you what it means?'

'I think I had better work that out for myself.'

'There may still be some hope for you. Is there any chance you can win her back? Do you deserve her?'

'There's a chance. I hope so. I hope there's a chance.'

'Then my advice is – should you give advice if it hasn't worked out for you? Nevertheless, I will. I am a romantic, Liam, as I see you are. People will tell you there are many more fish in the sea. And yes, there are. There will be more women if you want them, or men, some of them younger and physically more attractive than the one you love. You will always desire them. Accept that. You will always have opportunities. It is the most popular deviancy among young women: their attraction to old men. I don't see the world changing in this way. It's the imbalance of the species. I've benefited from it myself. Benefited? I've been kept young by it. When what I've wanted is to grow old. You see, the only way to grow old is to grow old with someone. Because the people who've grown old don't recognise you unless you've grown old too, and you don't get old hanging around with young women. But you're not *really* young either. Tantamount though it may be to declaring my idiocy, I am a romantic and I believe in love. If there is something unique in you that recognises something unique in her, then that can never be repeated.

You can never love in the same way, only less or only more. And for me it's only ever been less. I made the mistake of fatalism. There is a finite amount of falling in love available to you. Don't spread it too thinly. You cannot love a hundred more girls. I understand: you're curious. You want to know all of them, all of their secrets and joys and sufferings, their unique qualities, but you will not have the energy. You will not even have the memory. Win her back if you can, and if you can't, don't fuck around for too long with too many. Or you'll end up alone, and what's worse, you won't really care. I thought I was more alive when I was lying, preying. But it kills you, Liam, it makes you dead inside. It kills you. You are most alive when you love.'

We were interrupted at the close of Bennett's speech by the Irish booksellers staggering through the door, looking for somewhere to take cocaine. 'You'll join us for a line, won't you, Craig?' they asked. He looked at me sadly. 'Do you see what I mean?' he said. 'Please don't,' I said. 'Don't what?' he said, shaping his face to inflame to an insult like a Glaswegian on holiday in Blackpool. I decided it would only provoke him into taking more if I made an issue of discouraging him. 'I'm going to look for a drink,' I told him. 'A rum and coke, please,' he said. 'With just a very tiny bit of coke?' I asked. 'Just a tiny bit,' he sighed, in a calmer voice.

More people had arrived in the lounge since I had left and I became caught up saying hello to friends and strangers. I found myself repeating the speech Craig had just delivered to me. After a while I began to feel guilty that I was making fun of him, that people thought I was being ironic. I was not laughing at him. I was laughing in delight because of him, because I'd come to know him. I went to find him. Bennett and the booksellers had been joined on the bed by the two actresses. A steady stream of people moved in and out to hear Bennett hold forth on various topics: the nature of love, the derangement of the senses, advances in vineyard machinery, the Australian literary scene, the importance of courage and its illusionary nature, where to buy cocaine in Palermo Viejo, house prices in the Gower Peninsula, etc., etc. I had lost him to the crowd. I couldn't get near him.

I told myself not to panic and rejoined the gathering in the living room. Time passed in a flurry of quick conversation. When I looked at my phone, it was *late*, 4.30 a.m. The party was thinning out. I went to use the toilet and bumped into Bennett at the door.

'Come in here with me,' he said. 'I need a sensible fucking conversation.' I went back in and sat on the bath. He pulled the toilet cover down and sat on that. 'I don't even need the toilet. I just wanted a fucking breather. Don't these people on cocaine talk?'

I couldn't help laughing at this.

'Hey, fuck *you*. There is less hypocrisy in that statement than you assume. At least I have given what I say some thought in advance. That's the way to take cocaine – you need to have prepared some interesting conversation earlier. They have not. And they keep trying to nudge me onto the subject of Cockburn without just asking me straight out what happened.'

There was an awkward silence. 'So, what did happen?' I asked.

'They're half right, some of them out there, you know? I was arguing with James about his wife. It was because we were arguing he ran off and tried to show off. But we weren't arguing about her for the reasons I've heard. I do love her but I'm not *in love* with her. I think she's wonderful. Do you know her?'

I had met Ella a few times. She's a quiet, satirical woman, a psychologist Cockburn has been with since they met at university, and I like her for the economy with which she ridicules James whenever he switches into his performance role. Just a word or a look to put his feet back on the ground. She's from Manchester and has kept her accent, and it has enormous power as a corrective to his bullshit. I've neutralised my Northern accent, softening it while keeping my flat vowel-sounds. James picks and chooses his depending on his mood. When he plays James, laddish, down-to-earth football fan, who happens to be able to recite lines of poetry by Ezra Pound, he comes on like a Renaissance Gallagher brother. But in his publishing speeches, he elongates his vowels, becoming almost mid-Atlantic (apart from the rare occasions when he introduces a Northern writer, when he comes over like the manager of a cocky indie band from Salford). The difference between James and Ella disappeared when they were together: they played up to it and acquiesced to each other, they were a holiday from themselves. Ella was pregnant with their first child.

'Yes, I love Ella too,' I said.

'And you know he was talking about leaving her?'

'He's not, is he? Who else would take him?'

'Talking about it anyway. Who knows how serious that man is about anything? But if he was prepared to talk about it, I was prepared to take him seriously.'

'But who for?'

'For a woman not nearly as interesting a human being, not nearly as good for him. Whose very appeal is only that she's not nearly as good for him. He wants to destroy

68

his life, his happiness, so he feels more alive. Ah, fuck it, why did I think I had the right to get involved? In the end, this is how we measure our happiness, by how much dramatic unhappiness we have to narrate, by how much interesting misery we have inflicted on others. This is how we make our mark. Not by love but through cruelty. Isn't that what tempted you to cheat on your girlfriend? To say, I inflicted pain. I abandoned conventional morality. People *noticed* me. Yes, people thought you were a vain tosser. Just like me. Like our awful role models. What more drugs do we have, Liam? We need more drugs. Let's lift our spirits. What's that stuff you were telling me about earlier that you had, the stuff the kids are buying off the internet these days? I'm so pleased about that, that someone's worked out a use for the internet that isn't wanking. Let me have a look at that stuff.'

'I don't think that's a good idea.'

'To look? Oh, *come* on, don't patronise me. I'm not your granddad. Don't you owe me some trust? There's nothing wrong with me. They're just trying to make you feel bad.'

I was tired of arguing. I pulled the packet out and handed it to him. He held it to his nose and took a cautious sniff. 'That's *quite* disgusting,' he said. It was. The powder smelled of gone-off eggs. 'Do some,' he said. I took a dab, hoping that would be enough for him. Someone was knocking on the door of the toilet. Another gang had arrived via a deviation to the Groucho. They'd brought two famous conceptual artists with them, friends of Cockburn's. They looked past me as I opened the door. 'Craig! How are you?' they called and pushed past, squeezing me out of the door.

*   *   *

The mephedrone whooshed up in me straight away and I found myself in a corner of the kitchen with Lucy, one of the actresses, talking quickly about something and inviting her out to dinner. I offered her some mephedrone but couldn't find my packet when she accepted. She had some coke anyway and we did a line of that. Her boyfriend meant she couldn't come out for dinner with me. That was fine: I felt deranged, entirely separate from myself. I was doing my best to break the connection altogether, because when I remembered . . . We talked and talked and time went by. I was searching through my pockets, looking for the mephedrone, when I saw Bennett walk in the room, clutching and kneading the top of his left arm. He walked over to the kitchen sink and pulled the cold tap on full, looking around for a glass.

I bounded over and hugged him. 'Here,' I said, handing him a pint glass from a cupboard. 'Are you all right?'

He filled the glass up and drank it down. He turned to me. His face was bright red, scared. 'No, I'm not. Quietly, please, will you ring me an ambulance?'

He was sucking for air, holding his shoulder and wincing. I knew immediately it wasn't a joke, could see how scared, and yes, embarrassed he was. He was trying to deceive himself that he was simply making a shameful exit from a party. The rest of the guests were looking over at us. I put my arm round him and rang 999 with the other.

Before they arrived he was on the kitchen floor, groaning. He had pulled my bag of mephedrone out of his pocket before collapsing. Fergus threw the rest of the guests out, even the actresses, and we could hear their voices rising up from the spot outside where James Cockburn had landed the night before. It was twenty past five. The paramedics would be getting used to this address, and the police too. Bennett could barely speak and neither the actor nor I knew what to do. I felt for his pulse: it was there, jumping. 'I'll stay with Craig, you just make sure you're covered if the police come round – clean any drugs up,' I told him and bent down over Bennett and held his hand. 'Don't speak,' I said, from concern, but also because I could not imagine what I would say to him. 'You're going to be all right. You're going to be fine.' I remembered aspirins were good for heart attacks in some way. 'Have you got any aspirin?' I shouted through. 'Shit, yes,' he called back through, and came back with a tub. 'Can you swallow?' I asked Bennett. He nodded. 'No, fuck that – will you crush it up?' I asked the actor. 'It'll work quicker. Do a couple.' It felt completely counter-intuitive, watching Fergus place a note over two aspirin and rake a credit card sharply over them, chopping the powder down finely as I had done so many times with ecstasy pills. I asked for some on the credit card and leaned over Bennett. 'Can you snort? It's aspirin – I think it will help, it thins the blood.' I held the card against his nostrils and he rasped a breath in, blowing the powder over his chest, perhaps inhaling very small quantities. I mixed the rest up with a small amount of water and fed it to him. Then I tried once more with the card to see if he could inhale some, and that's how the paramedics found us as they rushed in, a middle-aged writer, on his back, mid heart attack, being encouraged to snort powder from a credit card. It must have looked like attempted murder.

Bennett lived on his own and so, in the absence of family to call, I phoned Suzy. I had never in my life been so right-fully attacked. She ordered me to ring Belinda to explain, and in a daze I tried to, but she didn't answer. They would only let one of us go in the ambulance, and Fergus, who had known Craig for a couple of years, went instead of me. I stood on my own in a street in Soho. It was not light yet, but the sky was taking on a vibrant blue, something burning behind it. I had a day of meetings at the Fair beginning at ten. The police would have to be in touch, I realised, but no one had told me to wait for them here. The paramedics had taken my name and address, and we'd told them about the drugs Bennett had been taking. I'd given them the bag of mephedrone too. I wanted more than anything in the world to ring Sarah, who was staying at her friend's in Camden. But I flagged a cab down instead and headed to our empty bed. Here I picked up one of her jumpers and fell asleep hugging it. It smelled of the wax she rubbed on her hair when she got out of the shower to control her curls. It smelled of Sarah.

It must have only have been an hour or two later when I was woken by a knock on the door. Two police officers, a man and a woman, looked at me with distaste. On the other side of London, the Fair was about to resume. We were a long way away from there. I invited them in, but they didn't want to come in. My good manners had no currency here. I had to go to the station with them. 'How's Craig?' I asked. I knew the answer already from their presence, from the look on their faces, but I did not know I knew it then.

Chapter 7

When I finished the story, there was a silence.
Understandably, they were deciding whether I had made most of it up. I was not as truthful then as I am now and I had left a few unfavourable details out.

'I think I hear about him dying,' said Arturo.

'He's quite popular here in translation,' said Lizzie. 'He used to live here, didn't he? The ending of the story, that's not really what happened, is it? Is that a joke?'

'I wish.'

'God,' said Lizzie. 'No wonder you've decided to get away.'

'It is not good to die of drugs,' snapped Arturo. It was a comment of such obviousness it might have been uttered by a TV football pundit, if not for its brittle anger, as if Arturo had been personally inconvenienced by this dead man with the wrong idea.

'I'm sorry,' I said. 'I'll understand if you'd rather I left now. It's a bit much.'

'Oh, shut up and don't be silly,' said Lizzie. 'It sounds

like he was going to do what he did whether or not you gave him the drugs. You didn't make him take them.'

'Whether or not that's true . . . I've lost my job and I'm hiding here in disgrace. So, I'm here on holiday, basically. It might be a long holiday.'

'How long?' said Arturo.

'Oh, for ever, I guess. Until I run out of money or get bored. It could be as long as a year.'

'On holiday for a year?'

'I know, it sounds awful. I don't even like being on holiday.' I laughed, and Arturo blew a puff of smoke into the room and laughed with me.

'You can do my job for me if you like. You can drive a motorbike?'

'Ride a motorbike,' Lizzie corrected.

'I can't drive or ride one, or a car.'

'Sarah said you were a writer?' she asked, prompted, I presume, by this statement of uselessness. Many writers and editors do not know how to operate a car.

Arturo shrugged. 'I *ride* a motorbike, make deliveries.'

'I'm not a writer. I've had one story published, that's all.'

'You must have written it then,' said Lizzie.

'Or driven it,' suggested Arturo with a grin. 'It is not hard to *ride* a motorbike. I could teach you.'

I had never liked those writers who sonorously pronounced, 'I am a *writer*,' as if pretentiousness were qualification instead of side-effect, but in the end I confessed that I *was* writing a novel: it was slightly less embarrassing than continuing to admit that I had no idea of what I was doing there. Easier too than trying to explain the obscure penance I hoped to enact here for Bennett's death.

'It's so good that you and Sarah can trust each other to be apart,' said Lizzie enthusiastically, looking at Arturo.

Arturo shot me a wounded look as if I had conspired against him. It was a look familiar to me from watching international football. 'Do you not miss her?' he asked.

'I'm used to it. She goes away for months at a time for her research.'

'Arturo's sad that I'm going to visit a friend in Rio next week without him,' Lizzie chipped in. 'You'll have to keep each other company.'

'Does she not miss you?' Arturo persisted.

'I hope she does,' I said. 'I miss her lots.'

After his initial suspicion, Arturo seemed to have hopes I could become a comrade in the struggle against inattentive girlfriends.

'Lizze, look! This is what he looks like without his girlfriend!'

'Oh, Liam, that's sweet,' she said, coming forward and throwing her arms round me again. I could see Arturo's face over her shoulder. 'You look so sad. It's a sacrifice, isn't it, to allow each other freedom? It's so *generous*.'

Arturo shook his head in silent disgust and pulled out a packet of crayon-green marijuana from his pocket to roll a spliff.

'What is your novel about, Liam?' he asked viciously.

I'd planned for a while to write a novel set at the peripheries of the Rolling Stones and the art world in 1960s London. I'd spent years reading tall tales about these characters as a teenager and thought I could put them to good use. Suzy had already tried to sell a coming-of-age novel I had written in my early twenties set where I grew up in Blackpool. My alter ego's life was far more rebellious than mine. He took drugs as a teenager in the amounts that I had only graduated to in my late twenties. Suzy had liked the novel but no one else was interested.

I tried halfheartedly to explain my new idea to Arturo and Lizzie, but even just talking about it was an act of impoverishing foolishness. I should have known from my once-promising career that if you ever try to explain the plot of a novel without gusto it always sounds like a very boring novel. It's like making a tackle: you have to throw your whole weight into it.

'Why do you write about this?' asked Arturo. It had stopped being an aggressive question. He was curious. I started to tell him about what an interesting time it was historically – the end of empire, the breaking down of the class system, the last throes of the Establishment seeking to crush rebellion – but I was answering a different question to the one he asked: Why do *you* write about this?

'I don't really know,' I concluded. 'I think I've always had a weakness for bad role models.'

'The Rolling Stones are very popular here,' Lizzie said kindly.

Arturo – who, with his full, feminine lips, looked like a prettier evolution of Mick Jagger, like one of the fabulous Jagger daughters – asked, 'When will you find out why you are writing this?'

'Soon, I hope,' I said before finally managing to change the subject and ask them about themselves.

They had met each other six months ago. Arturo's band were playing in the bar next to Lizzie's college and they had stared at each other throughout the set with the unabashed confidence of the beautiful at the beautiful.

76

When they came offstage he had headed straight in her direction and asked her for her name, standing in front of her and letting his eyes do the work for him. His languid confidence annoyed her, suggesting he knew exactly how the evening would proceed from then on, and so instead of answering she had leaned forward, put a hand through the back of his glossy dark hair and yanked him in for a kiss. When she had finished his eyes had changed and his smile had grown from a playful smirk into a broad grin. He looked delighted, surprised, and she liked that, that he was happy to have lost his cool. She wasn't the type of girl to fall for poseurs, no matter how handsome they were.

I got a simpler, more proprietorial version of this story from Arturo while Lizzie started to cook. She had gone to see his band, she had stared at him, she had run towards him and kissed him. 'She surprised me,' he said laughing, 'she came out of nowhere!'

There was still something adversarial in the air when he spoke about Lizzie. 'Tell me about your band,' I said.

When he spoke I tried to avoid his eyes: as he relaxed they became so mouth-wateringly appealing I felt as guilty as if I was staring directly between a woman's legs on the Tube. Out of a sense of propriety I found myself looking away to notice the way his thighs filled his skinny jeans, the calve-like curve of his biceps as they appeared beneath his T-shirt's short sleeves, and then I gave up and surrendered to his gaze. When he finished I realised I had not listened to a word he said.

'We are playing on Tuesday,' he said.

'You should go! Keep him company while I'm away,' Lizzie said.

'We'll get wasted afterwards,' he said. 'I will have some cocaine and ecstasy.'

'I'm sorry, I really meant what I said. I don't do drugs any more.'

He studied me again and smiled. I realised that he was a perceptive man.

I spent that weekend thinking about Lizzie and Arturo on his mini motorbike, riding along the highway in the pampas, her tanned thighs squeezing his waist. To distract myself, I began to look for an apartment of my own. Lizzie had recommended starting on Craig's List and here I was immediately drawn to the section 'chica busca chico'. I thought it might teach me how to flirt in Spargentinean but all the adverts were in English, locals looking for foreigners, tourists, sugar daddies, a bit of fun, pampering, dinners. Less tentative posts offered the elite companionship of educated, discreet models. The 'chico busca chica' was far worse, American men offering to spend money on women who were sweet, didn't play games, were a surrogate mother, weren't materialistic or argumentative. The negotiations depressed the hell out of me. They were the opposite of love.

Lizzie had recommended a price region I should be paying for a flat but it took me hours of wading through tourist sites charging much more – feeling increasingly desperate as the electronic tango music in the lounge swelled like the theme from *Countdown* – before I found the places the locals used. After three or four excruciating phone calls with estate agents who couldn't understand my diffident Spanish, I began to understand they were all asking about a *garantia* and talking about two-year contracts rather than the six months I wanted. I decided I would be better off waiting for Lizzie and Arturo to get back and holding out for longer in the hostel.

I was, I admit, reluctantly beginning to see some appeal in living in the hostel. Something had changed in me since meeting Lizzie and Arturo: I had begun to lust again. The shock of leaving Sarah, of losing Sarah, had temporarily overridden desire for anyone else. And now I realised how much better this had been, for as I began to look at the women, the *girls*, in the hostel and imagine myself with them I began to imagine other men with Sarah. Thoughts of what she could be doing with the artists and curators and students who had always surrounded her, thoughts of what she *liked* to do, appalled and delighted me. But any delight I felt was not worth the horror. Any delight *was* the horror.

It had been years since I had been jealous like this. I had quickly forgotten how fraught the first months had been, the constant worry that she would go back to the boyfriend she had left in Brazil. She still spoke to him and he wrote her long emails about his plans to move to Europe. It took months before she told me she loved me, and during this time I developed further my persona, the man who didn't mind as much as I did, the man who looked at other girls and flirted and would spring into action if she ended things suddenly.

As months and years went past and I came to know she loved me, and, by extension, so did the world, I became a complacent, un-jealous boyfriend. I had even said to her, jokily, seductively, towards the end, that she could sleep with other men as long as she told me. This became one of our favourite fantasies. The idea of her fucking another never filled me with the terror it seems to imbue in most men. I think I really believed this. A fantasy is not very powerful unless it is also a real possibility. There were times I watched her kiss another man on the dance floor in a club or at a festival, times when she watched me kiss another woman. Delicious, shocking and unsustainable: we would spring straight back to each other, delighted at our daring, relieved at our restraint.

I had of course brought this up in the arguments in which I made everything worse. 'We had an understanding! I would have forgiven you! I wouldn't have cared!' This she chose to interpret as a sign I had never understood, had never cared for her, was incapable of caring for anyone. And, stupidly, unjustifiably, I exploded at this illogic. But it is *not* as simple as this, is it? This monogamous pact has not become the only definition of love, this selfish, fearful possession?

They make iPhone apps now for lovers so we can track each other's position as we go about our day. It's hard to imagine as a Christmas present but I bet they're given. We abolish infidelity by making cheating administratively awkward. The opposite of love. Or the true test. Cheating gets *hard*. Casanovas drop out in droves. The ones still going for it, now *that's* sexy.

And in my rage, because I thought we were better than this, I had oversimplified Sarah's point. You can't apply logic to fix betrayal. She had her own logic: I had lied, not just to cover my back but to mislead her in the extent of my devotion to her. It was not about my freely chosen moral system, it was about my refusal to admit to it, to wanting to have it both ways. I wanted to have my cake and have other cakes want me. She could have handled a revolutionary but not a petty criminal, not a con-artist, not an expenses cheat. It was just as bad as if I *had* fucked the girl I shared a bed with, the couple of girls I'd kissed on dance floors and never told her about. The only reason I didn't was to leave me a loophole with which to lie to myself and to her.

I hated that she was right, picturing her with the conceptual artists she hung around with in London. Oh, I hated them. Their idealistic politics, Chomsky paperbacks, lack of jobs. Their activism, their outrage. Where did it come from? Hadn't I once been like them?

Once, I had thought so. Now, I was in no state to judge anyone. I was becoming bitter. It had been years since I'd suffered the causes of bitterness. Lack of imagination, money, love: that's what soured people. I had had love and money but forgotten how to imagine; now that love had gone and money was on its way after it I had nothing left but to try and reawaken my imagination. I decided to start by thinking kinder thoughts about the sad-eyed men in the hostel bar, the awkward gatecrashers at an international conference of children's TV presenters.

And with my change of heart, I quickly found people to talk to. The TV never stopped showing football matches, wonderfully violent football matches, and I watched them with my notebook firmly shut besides a steady stream of litre bottles of Quilmes and harsher-than-normal Marlboro Lights.

'That's not normal, is it?' I asked the guy next to me, as a game erupted into a full-pitch brawl and a referee was knocked out by a flying kick from a Mexican right-back.

'From what I've seen over the last two days, it's not *ab*normal,' he said. He had the polite, efficient English of a North European.

'If you were prone to stereotyping you might make conclusions about the Latin temperament from watching this.'

He smiled and pinged my lager bottle. 'Or about the English temperament from watching you.'

This was Hans. He was German. We embarked on a conversation about Bayern Munich and their powerful midfielder, Bastian Schweinsteiger, which some Geordie lads began to take interest in too. I asked Hans if it was true that 'Schweinsteiger' translated literally into 'Pig Fucker'.

'Yes,' he said, 'you are absolutely right in this matter. It is a rural name.'

The tragedy of life was not only tragic, or it wasn't yet; to smoke and drink and discuss football in all its exhaustive, erudite pointlessness was a convincing simulacrum of content.

I got smashed and somehow ended the evening on the roof terrace with Hans, talking to gregarious tattooed Danish teenagers, three girls and two boys, who asked me where they might be able to score some cocaine. The thought of it made me woozy, disgusted that it was so exciting. 'Sorry, I don't do coke,' I said. Hans made the mistake of accepting large pulls on the joint they were passing round and wobbled away looking green. Then I made the same mistake. I stood up and tried to walk casually to the side of the building where I leaned over to look at the street below, thick with traffic and people on the pavement. It was not a place to be sick honourably, if such a thing is possible. My room was just across, so I let myself in, mumbling something at the Danes, and collapsed on the bed where, too late, I remembered there was no toilet or sink in my room. The girl I had been talking to, the single one, knocked on my door and called through to ask if I was all right. I lay on the floor next to the duty-free carrier bag I had vomited into and kept quiet until she went away. On Sunday morning, as I walked through the lounge with the same knotted carrier bag in my hand, I kept my head down. This kind of company was not good for me.

I spent the day in a corner of the roof terrace, dark glasses on, reading *Bleak House*. The digressions and never-ending parade of unlikely new characters were unsuited to my restless mind, but thank God the book was so long, nine hundred pages typeset in tiny print. I was dreading finishing it and having to resort to the least worst thing remaining on the hostel's bookshelves. It was genuinely possible that I was going to read a whole novel by Paulo Coelho. I might even have to read two. Of the same novel. There were eight. At one point the nice Danish girl I had been chatting up came up to sunbathe, waved at me, but sat at the other end of the terrace. I lay there looking at her, pretending to read, and when I had just about worked up the courage to go over and apologise for my sudden disappearance, two French boys appeared and bookended her. One of them was carrying a copy of *The Alchemist*, perhaps now making that nine copies in the building. I watched them all laugh for ten minutes and dreamed of Sarah before I decided to go for a walk.

The sun shone through the jacaranda trees and onto the fruit stands and café terraces, reflecting off the window displays of bespoke T-shirts. On nearly every street was an independent bookshop adjacent to a lingerie store. Whenever I saw a woman reading I felt a stab in my heart at the thought of the baroque quality of the underwear she must be wearing. It was Paradise, but I was locked out of it by language or, as it felt at the time, by sin. I stopped for a coffee and a cheese and ham toastie. I was beginning to get the hang of ordering my coffee at least. '*Café con leche, por favor*,' uttered in an English accent, would receive an incredulous, '*Que?*' The trick was to utter it with the cadence of Bob Dylan berating a journalist backstage in his amphetamine-fuelled mid-Sixties heyday. Either that, or in the accent of an enraged Mafioso extorting protection money at gunpoint. This was how everyone spoke out here. It was taking some getting used to.

After I had threatened to smash the waiter's skull in with my tone of voice, and he had called my mother a whore with his, I settled down to pretend to read *Bleak House* while the beautiful creatures from another world walked past.

When the loneliness became too great, I bought a phone card and called my mum, my sisters. It was lovely to hear their voices, but they weren't the people I needed to talk to. I was still too cowardly to tell them about Sarah, that I was a cheat, an idiot, that I was suffering. I still believed I might be able to sort things out without disturbing them. It was Sarah's voice I was missing. Even on her long trips away, I had spoken or written to her every day, kept a running account of all the interesting events and dialogue that became significant only in the telling of them to her. She was the shape in which sensation made sense. Now I was dispersing.

The last man I expected to need in a crisis was my father, but I was thinking about him more and more. He knew what it was to run away, to have done something shameful. I had not gone to him for advice since I was a teenager. I thought he might be grateful to be asked, might be grateful even to be listened to. But whenever I tried him, I got his answering machine.

'Dad, it's Liam. I've run away to Buenos Aires. Honestly. Send me an email. Tell me when I can call you. Answer the phone.'

I tried a few more times but had no answer. I was alone.

I was cheered up when I stopped at an internet café on the way back to the hostel and found that Amy Casares had replied to my email.

Dear Liam

How are you, my darling? But I know how you are: Craig's dead, poor Craig! And you blame yourself. Well, don't do too much of that, Liam, no more than's necessary. Craig was always perfectly capable of killing himself without assistance; but he did like to have people around to talk to when he was doing it.

You wrote about him beautifully to me, about the bit of him he showed people. His generosity, his childishness, his charm. He was a noble soul, a gentleman, but he was a mess too.

If it helps you for me to answer the questions about him and how he lived in Buenos Aires when I knew him there, then I'm happy to help.

But – and this is going to sound blunt and dismissive, but I'm risking it – you barely knew him and there's no reason why it shouldn't stay that way.

So I won't answer unless you ask me again.

Enjoy the city. It's a beautiful place.

Dangerous too. Don't get lost.

And don't let your guilt about Sarah get put onto Craig. It's Sarah you should think about. You were so happy when I last saw you both, just before you moved to London to be with her and start your new job. Don't you belong back there? Are you sure there's nothing left to fight for? Can't you go to her and sing your song?

I'm very angry at you for fucking things up with her. That is your fault. Craig is not.

Now, listen, you'll be just fine.

Love from Amy

So, that was me, off the hook and free to get on with my life. Good old Amy. If I could have believed her. But I couldn't. Bennett died because I was too weak to challenge him. Sarah dumped me because I was too vain to resist being tempted by a beautiful woman, because I was both too cowardly to go through with it and too cowardly to come clean about it.

I wrote back to ask Amy to tell me more about how she had lived here with Bennett. I was no use on my own. He had walked these same streets when he was my age. I would try to invoke him and carry him with me.

Chapter 8

I t was the day of Arturo's gig. Lizzy had flown to Brazil
that morning and Arturo had emailed a few days earlier:
Liam, Black Kittens play on Wednesday – will you come?
I didn't need reminding or persuading: it was to be my
first proper night out for weeks. I had a strong thirst, and
not only for liquids. I was lonely and every day became
worse at speaking Spanish and I was bored of pretending
there weren't pills and powders that might solve these
problems. That they'd created these problems didn't mean
they couldn't also alleviate them.

The Black Kittens were a three-piece. Arturo, the tallest
and most desirable member, was on bass and backing
vocals, sharing the front of the stage with Hernán, short,
stocky with a cropped haircut, playing a Les Paul copy
and singing lead in a high falsetto. Behind them, on the
drums, was Aleman, the German, who was very Argentine
and legendary, Arturo told me, for his habit of bribing
bouncers at swingers' clubs to let him in as a single man.
He ran a bar and sold a bit of weed and coke, a useful
man to know.

In a fit of restlessness, I had arrived at the venue two hours early, just in time to see Aleman's van pull up. I received three different man-kisses in welcome, and helped carry in the amps and equipment. We did a lot of smiling at each other, Aleman, Hernán and I, more articulate and less stressful than our attempts to use each other's languages. And Arturo translated when he could be bothered (and perhaps changed much to wind me up). He played the role of a pretty bimbo very much to his own advantage; I was beginning to see there was a sharp humour and cunning behind his ingenuousness.

Having to translate for me was ruining their dynamic so I told them to carry on with things while I tried to write my novel in the corner – but not before I'd placed an order with him for a hundred pesos' worth of cocaine, a small amount of sterling that made a shockingly large amount of cocaine five times the strength of what we had back home.

I found this out just before the gig started. It was ten, the venue was half full, and some very attractive women were embracing members of the band. Arturo had pulled me into the toilets and handed me a small white pebble wrapped in a snipped-off corner from a carrier bag. He swiftly unwrapped a separate pebble of his own and delivered two key scoops to each of his nostrils. That was how he always did it, without any of the careful ceremony and portioning favoured by the English. He loaded it up again and held it out to my own nose. I sniffed it up.

And then he was on stage, pogoing with a big grin as Las Gatitas Negres began their English-sounding indie-rock. Arturo hit thumping bass lines over Aleman's crashing symbals and Hernán sang Kurt Cobain-style vocals over them in a mixture of English and Spargentine.

The coke arrived and immediately made me bilingual. '¿Que tal?' I said to the girl next to me. She smiled and said lots of things very quickly. 'Lo siento, no hablo Castellano. ¿Hablas Inglés?' I said. 'Oh, yes, you speak lovely English,' I said. 'No, I can't hear you either,' I said, and then we stopped speaking, not before, I thought, a certain rapport had been established.

Between songs I shouted fluent Spanish at the girl next to me, which made her giggle and answer in English. Her name was Ana-Maria. She was a fashion student and worked in a clothes shop on the Avenida del Libertador. She spoke good English, enough to understand me when I spoke clearly and slowly, and so chatting her up proceeded with much less pace than it might in England when I had a package of cocaine in my wallet. But that was nice. I was too frantic at the best of times. At one point, I swear I am telling the truth, she said to me, 'I like your style.'

I wonder if I have sufficiently emphasised what a vain man I am, like any sensible man should be who isn't blessed with the good looks of a Brad Pitt or the absence of a libido. Women have eyes too, even if they're not as foolishly, sensually imbalanced as us. There's no sense in squandering our slight advantage by not being able to dress ourselves. Knowing how to dress themselves is one of the reasons why women are indubitably, objectively, more attractive than men, whatever one's sexual prefer-ence. It's easy for me to say this, I know: my taste being mostly for the straightforward. The guys I liked, like Arturo, I liked because they were as pretty as girls. I liked that they weren't girls too, but if they hadn't been girlish I wouldn't have noticed the opportunity for transgression, wouldn't have lusted for it. Pretty boys were the exception that proved the rule. And I would accept any kind of attention. I was susceptible to flattery. I tried hard for it. I was still slim and fit from cycling and playing football. I spent money on suits, shirts, shoes. I aspired to be a tart and I was pleased she had noticed. I liked women who cared about these things, who thought surfaces were deep. You could run your fingers over a surface.

'Thank you,' I said. I was having a great time. Later, I asked her if she knew Arturo.

'Oh, yes, I know Arturo,' she said, smiling as if she had suddenly remembered something pleasant.

'A man could get jealous seeing you pull that face for Arturo,' I said, and I don't think she quite understood or heard; but she looked past me to Arturo, who held his bass on stage in the position a discus-thrower holds himself before letting fly, frozen in the moment of taut energy before unravelling, staring at a point beyond his shoulder as though he had plans for someone waiting there.

'Arturo, he is fun,' she said. 'Only fun.'

Then what contrast could I offer her? I tried to imagine the opposite of fun. Pain? Work? Love?

'I'm only fun too,' I admitted. 'Just not as much fun.'

And then I leaned over and kissed her and she kissed back. Can you believe that women continue to do this? And it was an enjoyable kiss too, soft, nicely shaped, like a sip of the red wine she'd been drinking. When I looked back up at the stage Arturo was looking at me with an expression of theatrical surprise. It was only then I remembered I had a girlfriend.

He caught up with me at the bar and wrapped me in a damp hug. He was very happy. Now he stood back, raised

his eyebrows and laughed. 'You *are* enjoying your holiday.'
There was a new affection in his smile; he was less guarded.
Perhaps it was only the elation of being on stage.

'Oh, it's not like that,' I said.

'How is it like?'

Now would have been the time to confess the truth.
I'm good at spotting these moments in retrospect.

'We have a sort of . . . open relationship,' is what I
managed to say.

He looked at me doubtfully. 'You do not *mind* if other
men *fuck* your girlfriend?'

'Um . . .'

'You do not mind if Sarah is being fucked by another
man, by his big cock? It is hard for a *macho Argentino* to
understand. But, OK, I believe you, you *Englishmen*, you
like this, it is normal. Here we would not like that. Over
there, you do. Where you are, it is fun, *tradicional*?'

'Fuck off,' I said, laughing.

He patted me on the back and looked at Ana-Maria.
'Don't worry. I don't tell Lizzie.' Then he winked. 'And
you don't tell Lizzie.' With that he turned and walked in
the direction of a woman in a mini-skirt.

Events progressed quickly from then on. Ana-Maria and
I kissed some more, I talked a lot between kisses and at
some point she said, 'I think you are on cocaine.' I apologised and offered her some. She was polite enough to say
yes and then the conversation became less one-sided. I
learned she was from Cordoba, moved to Buenos Aires to
study, got work occasionally pattern-cutting, which was
well paid and good experience, but she had to work as an
assistant in a shop as it was sporadic. She had learned

English at school, and had worked as an intern for Stella McCartney for three months in New York, an experience that had nearly bankrupted her. She had split up with a boyfriend six months ago but was enjoying being single now. She said that with the fierce expression of people enjoying being single now. Me? I had that to look forward to. I hated being single and told her so. She thought I was funny, I apologised too much, I was nervous, I was sad, I was very English, I was sweet.

Soon we were in a taxi to a club. Arturo sat in the front and I was sandwiched between Ana-Maria and Arturo's new friend Lucila on the backseat. I learned almost nothing about Lucila; she was talking quickly across me to Ana-Maria while Arturo delivered a rapid pep talk to the driver. I was happy not to scratch the surface, to sit in the epicentre of two beautiful portenoritas, contained like a quote between feminine legs. "Lucky." "Amazed." "Very high." Since I had stepped from the plane, I had thought all these people belonged to a completely different world to mine. I kept quiet, hoping not to scare them off.

Hernán and others from the gig followed us in Aleman's van, and we met in the queue for the club. Inside it was booming, loud house music; the club just beginning to fill up at one in the morning.

I went to the bar with Ana-Maria. 'Who's the girl Arturo's with?' I asked, looking round to see him lean down and whisper something to her. She grabbed his arm and stood on her tiptoes to whisper back into his ears, pushing her high heels another two inches off the ground.

'Just one of those girls, you know, you bump into, in the clubs, in the bars.'

'She's a friend of Arturo's?'

She raised her eyebrows. 'They are friendly now.' Arturo was leaning on his forearm against the wall they were standing by, the back of her head brushing his arm. Their faces were only inches apart, kissing distance.

As the barman brought us our drinks I noticed something strange. Hernán, standing away from us, where he had been talking with Aleman, was now staring directly at Arturo and Lucila. He had a very intense look on his face, and I watched it change from incredulous disgust to a quiet, determined rage.

It could have been my imagination.

'Hernán, does he know Lucila?'

'I don't think so. Why are you so interested in Lucila?'

'It's Arturo I'm interested in.'

'I think I will find someone who is interested in talking to me.'

'Oh, God, not like that. Come here. Come *here*.'

It could have been a more excessive night. The cocaine was strong but we only mixed it with alcohol. At least I was in my own – *oh* . . .

At four in the morning, Ana-Maria announced I was leaving with her. We'd been dancing for the last hour with Arturo and Lucila. We were all really drunk and I knew the feel of everybody's body pressed against mine in an embrace. Lucila looked from Arturo to me with a grin of immense confidence. When she left us for a moment she would spin around with a flourish and stride away. Arturo, acting his part, would pretend not to notice, but

I caught him following her with his eyes on a couple of occasions.

Before we left I took Arturo to one side. 'Arturo. Remember Lizzie? Lovely Lizzie? Be careful.'

'I am careful. And Sarah's lovely too, right? I've seen photos on Facebook.'

'You don't understand – it's not the same situation.'

'Pah – why not? Don't you worry about me. Worry about yourself.'

He hugged me again then. I felt his heart going under his T-shirt. I didn't know him well enough to know if he was going to do something stupid with Lucila. It was arrogant of me to warn him against something he may have been too good a person to consider. That's what I decided. 'Before you go,' he said, 'take this,' and he pulled out a large green bud of skunk and pressed it into my hand. I tried to give it him back but he wouldn't take it. So I thanked him, kissed him goodbye and left with Ana-Maria.

The sex itself was great. Just the idea of an Argentine fashion student was mind-blowingly exotic to a man who had never stopped being amazed by underwear from Topshop. And we were high. Drugs don't only improve our linguistic skills. People who don't take drugs don't realise how good at sex they make us too. It's one thing us addicts can console ourselves with: we are genuinely better lovers. Fuckers, anyway. We go on for ages. We have *no* inhibitions. We'll say *anything*.

It's the aftersex and the afterdrugs that drugs don't help with, when the revisionist history writes itself. Waking up with not one but two strangers. The words you hastily sketched your identity with last night exhausted and without them you feel . . . nothing. There is no you.

Politeness remains, a diminished vocabulary, the lack of a subject, the urge to make a promise you won't keep. The transactional I won't tell if you won't tell. Last night you had said *everything* and now you have to find something extra before the small talk gets smaller and smaller and disappears altogether and you begin again or run away. And sooner or later, you *have to* run away. Or they do.

This all came afterwards. We were excited as we found our way to her room in a shared apartment. It was a wonderful room, like one of Palermo's boutiques: a desk with a turntable on it next to a two-metre slant of records on the floor. One wardrobe, one chest of drawers. A saucer used for an ashtray. Two dressmaker's dummies, covered with cascading fabric, dresses in progress. Nothing on the walls but white paint. I was just part of the installation.

She was naked in seconds, completely unembarrassed. When I went down on her she held my head in a firm grip against her with her hands, rubbing against my face with wonderful selfishness until she came. Well, that was fun. Was that an Argentine thing? An English woman might think it bad manners. Not that I had any recent experience of English women besides Sarah. I thought sex was anyway too varied and personal a deviance to ascribe national characteristics; that was for TV sexperts and that awful American who wrote *Sex and the City* and had a grudge against English penises.

We fucked and I fell asleep and if someone had picked me up and carried me still sleeping back to my room, it would have been OK. But when I woke, she woke too and there we were, staring at each other with naked surprise. *You.* There hadn't been much sleep, three or four hours, but the sun was pouring in through the windows and there wouldn't be any more now, not for me. She pressed her face into the pillow so I didn't have to. I hope she was thinking what I was thinking: *get out of here*. It's not to say we didn't like each other. But I think we both agreed that we didn't have to demonstrate we liked each other *now*, unprepared, defenceless and surprised as children. 'Are you all right?' I asked. I had had to bite my tongue not to ask Sarah this every ten minutes in our last month together. It was always less a question than a statement to the reverse.

'Mmph,' she said, turning over onto her side, facing away from me.

'I'll let you sleep,' I said. Then I leaned over and kissed her on the cheek, the casual, natural gesture of the long-term boyfriend I still was. I froze the second after my lips brushed the softness of her skin. She was the wrong woman. *Sarah*.

I'm sorry.

I fell out of bed, pulled my clothes on, most of them – there was a missing sock not worth the seconds – and I ran away.

I got lost trying to find my way out of the apartment block. It was like the Library of Babel. At one point I had to lean against the wall and force myself to breathe slowly, my hand holding my heart as it tried to escape my chest. A spiral staircase sunk abysmally below me and soared upwards to great distances. After I'd calmed myself, I found my way out into the sunlight and flagged down a taxi. When we pulled up at the hostel, the driver tried to charge me a *cinquenta* for what couldn't have been more than a ten-peso trip. I gave him everything I had, twenty-three pesos, a stern look, and walked out the door followed by a stream of gleeful abuse, *la concha de tu madre!* He had to act outraged, even though he had in effect received more than a 100% tip. The fucking drama of the place.

England. Sarah. Home.

I let myself go to pieces for a few days then. I felt a swoon of exhilaration, of swooping hard and fast. After that, the monotony of being miserable took over. I cried with the regularity that I smoked cigarettes. My heart was blackened, blasphemous; I thought in the language of a Cormac McCarthy novel. One of the dreams I'd been clinging to was that when I returned, chaste, to the UK, Sarah would have forgiven me and we would go on as normal. But now I would have to tell her about Ana-Maria, a month after we split up. I'd lost the ability to lie to her; she knew what I looked like now when I did.

After a week I began to pick up. I stopped trying to write magic spells to make Sarah go back out with me and started again with the novel. I had known all along that I was a comic rather than tragic character. I had wept for a week because I had slept with an *Argentine fashion student.* I imagined my friends' reactions if I told them this, the incomprehension, the merciless piss-taking. Being cruel is one of the kindest things men are to each other. I normally preferred the company of women but I could never understand how they could bear so much sympathy from each other in the face of disaster. You had to keep thinking about the disaster then. The best thing, in my experience, if you had been dumped, was for a mate to make a joke about the woman in question being ecstatic-ally fucked by a jazz musician. Because the thing is she *might* be, was what you were thinking: much better to make a cartoon rather than a documentary out of it.

I had decided one thing for certain: I was not going to risk sleeping with any more women if that's how it made me feel. I would just have to hope my libido took notice.

Though I was desperate to email Sarah, I forced myself not to. I continued to write to her by hand, in my notebook. I could not trust my feelings as they arrived. I would write her the best love letter I could, as true as Tolstoy, as romantic as Fitzgerald. The best love letter the world had ever seen, or I wouldn't send it. In the face of this awful hope, I pushed on.

Chapter 9

It took Amy Casares two weeks to respond to my request for more information about her life with Craig Bennett in Buenos Aires. Her email, when it arrived, ended with a warning, and a tone of suppressed annoyance – who was I, after all, to continue to claim anything other than fatal significance in the life of this man I knew so briefly?

Well, I could understand that, but she wasn't there. The man had tried to help me at a time when I had thrown away the happiest luck of my life. He made me feel briefly that I could survive the end of the world, or better still, that I might not have to. When he suggested I fight to keep hold of Sarah, with him by my side, to help me make my case, I believed I might be able to.

Perhaps it wasn't a coincidence my friends were mostly men much older than me. But was it paternal guidance or just a precedent for bad behaviour I wanted from them? James Cockburn seemed to have deserted me but would never anyway have enquired deeply into the wisdom of my behaviour, for fear that I would enquire into his own

– and I had always thought I was grateful for this unspoken
pact of ours. In the company of men who lunge to
unburden themselves, it is sensible to be on permanent
guard. What frustrates me. What I want. What isn't
working. When did it become acceptable to be so bald in
our demands? It was hard to see how the emotional life
could be discussed in these terms; how it would not be
deformed by precise language. Love, I had thought, should
be spoken of on the slant. Or not at all. But that night
Craig had given me permission to talk about it, to hope
and have faith. I didn't feel strong enough to have hope
without his permission, without him. I needed to make
him live.

Dear Liam

I met Craig in BA in the mid-90s – 95 I think. I'd been
working as a producer's assistant on a few films, just
eking a living with long months not working between
jobs. A nice time, when I wasn't worrying about money.
I'm not sure I ever worried that much. Something always
came up when I needed it desperately. It was my first
long period of time I'd spent there as an adult and it
was so exciting to feel the Argentine part of me come
alive again, although, with my accent, everyone still
thought of me as the *Inglesa*.

People began to ask me, 'Have you met the
Englishman?' I was intrigued at first: who was this
Gatsby? Then, when the stories invariably involved
three-day drinking and drugs sessions with his lawyer
Alejandro and whoever would join in, I was less interested.
I knew enough bloody drunks in London, enough
wannabe Bukowskis and Hunter S. Thompsons. But there
were rumours about the film he had written in Spanish
and was trying to get made, rumours he was talented in

spite of rather than because of the drinking. No one seemed to understand what his connection was to Argentina though he spoke perfect, dirty Spanish, knew all the *lunfardo*. And he wasn't really English either, though his family was originally from Yorkshire. His accent when speaking English could veer from Aussie to Leeds to aristocrat. He was an impersonator, and I don't think I ever discovered which of his roles was the main one, the real one I guess, and this is why I think I couldn't be with him any more. The film he was making: he had written it, but I never saw him do anything else apart from talk about it. Still, he talked about it well, and people liked to listen to him talk, you know this, and once we'd been introduced we saw each other a lot at parties.

In fact, he did have a development grant for the film, one he was recklessly enjoying with his 'colleague' 'lawyer' 'business partner' – it changed daily – Alejandro, his best friend who he'd met at boarding school near Sydney when he was a teenager. When they met Alejandro had just moved to Australia with his parents from Buenos Aires, and Bennett had just been sent to school for the first time in three years after being taught by his father on his remote vineyard – they lived together just the two of them there, with his mother and his sister in Melbourne. It was a last-ditch effort to get him a standard education, to socialise him.

So there were three of us hanging out in Buenos Aires, all displaced early on, and used to making a life wherever we turned up.

They had a game they'd play when they introduced themselves to someone. Alejandro would start, 'Let me introduce myself, I am Alejandro Miguel Marques Montenegro, and this is my dear friend and colleague Craig Bennett, the gifted film-maker.' 'No, that is too much,'

Craig would come in, 'I am merely the sidekick of this man here who of course you have heard tell of, Alejandro Miguel Marques Montenegro, the criminal rights lawyer, artist and Renaissance man currently assisting me, or rather directing me, in a small art movie I am about to begin to film.' There's something so sweet and charming about two men so clearly in love with each other. At first, anyway. It became a bit contentious between Alejandro and me. Sad really, particularly now I hear Alejandro and Craig never made up before Craig died. That relationship was really a lot more important to him than ours was. He wouldn't admit it, though.

You can probably find Alejandro if you're determined. Try their favourite bar, L'Espada. It's still around. But try to forget and get on with your own life. There's not much I can tell you about him that I feel will help you. I hope you find what you're looking for, but are you sure you're looking in the right place?

Love, Amy

If I was going to snoop around a bar asking for a mysterious fantasist called Alejandro Miguel Marques Montenegro, there was nothing for it: I'd better learn to speak Spanish. It would provide a diversion from repeating Sarah's name in my head.

There is a popular theory, unproven by rigorous analysis: that it takes half the length of a relationship to adjust to its demise. Sarah and I had been together for four years so I only had two years of misery left. I'd done a month already: a whole twenty-fourth of my time. Well, it wasn't that bad. But if I counted the year before we got together, a year in which I'd kissed her and been entirely obsessed with her, made promises and yearned across continents . . . I'd done somewhere between a twenty-fourth and a thirty-sixth of my time. They might let me out of my cell slightly earlier too, for good behaviour. Good behaviour? Unlikely. And this wasn't counting all the years I had loved her without telling her. So, if Sarah wasn't a special case, and I thought she probably was, I had somewhere between a hundred and a hundred and fifty weeks before I'd be able to have sex with a woman without crying. I certainly had time to learn Spanish.

I remembered Hans telling me he had been about to start a Spanish course and kept my eye out for him in the lounge. I was dangerously close to finishing *Bleak House* when he walked in and sat in front of the TV. As usual, there was a violent football match in progress.

'Hello, Hans,' I said, walking over and sitting next to him.

'Hello, Liam. How are you?' he asked.

'My girlfriend dumped me by email. So I slept with another woman last week. After that I went to my room and cried for five days.'

He looked at me askance. 'I had thought you had not been around,' he said casually. 'The other girl, the one you had sex with, was she very ugly or very right-wing? I have never cried for five days, only four. I thought they didn't make them *that* ugly, *that* right-wing.'

'She was pretty,' I said. 'Much more than me.'

'Poor girl.'

'Yes, poor girl.'

'I'm sorry you're sad, Liam. But it sounds like this girl would be better off with someone better-looking, more charismatic, no?'

He said this with what, to me, was heartbreaking tenderness. I could have hugged him.

*   *   *

103

We started Spanish on Monday and I was immediately grateful for the purpose. Coming to Buenos Aires to learn Spanish made a far more positive narrative than I had managed to cobble together so far. The classes were in Lizzie's language school and I looked around for her, wondering if she was back from her trip to see her friend in Brazil. I hadn't contacted Arturo since our night out together and I was worried about what he might have told Lizzie about my adventure with Ana-Maria. There were a lot of potential misunderstandings and, more to the point, understandings that could arise.

It's melodramatic to say you can taste lies. I'd lied frequently and joyfully throughout my life without feeling the awful anxiety I did now. It was danger I could taste, mechanic, chemical – but I'm not sure it was only this new sensitivity to exposure. It was acid, the taste of the slow digestion of the person I'd pretended to be while the other person grew inside me, eating me at the same time as I was emulating his voice, his turn of phrase, laughing at his jokes. The more lies I told, the more that man grew familiar. He was no longer eating me alive. I was eating him.

I ran into Lizzie in the corridor after my first lesson. Hans looked at me with increased respect as she embraced me. She didn't seem surprised to see me and she didn't appear angry either.

'You're back,' I said.

'Was I away? That seems like a long time ago. I heard you had fun with Arturo.'

'Um . . .'

'Um? An um is rather worrying where that man is

concerned. Really, um? I hope I don't need to be filing reports back to Sarah about you.'

'Ha ha!'

She looked at me curiously.

'I'm learning Spanish!' I said.

'I can see your textbook. Both of your textbooks.' She said something Spanish to me, I think it was Spanish . . .

Hans, a continental, said something Spanish in return. They both laughed and shook hands. 'Would you like to go for a coffee soon or something?' I asked.

Lizzie had the next afternoon off work and was keen to check out the newest exhibition at the MALBA. I agreed to meet up with her after my class the next day and go with her.

After I had answered Hans' questions about how it was I knew such an attractive resident of the city, I had nothing to do for the rest of the day. I had a brainwave and headed straight to the gallery.

It was a simple thing, but it reminded me I was actually here on a kind of holiday. Going to galleries is one of the few things I do on holidays. I'm not sure there's much else you *can* do on holiday in a city: read plot-driven novels on café terraces, visit famous nightclubs, try to locate and not to get ripped off by drug dealers, get drunk on wine over decadent lunches . . . the list soon runs out for a man of my imagination.

I hadn't been to a single gallery so far in my month in Buenos Aires, simply because they reminded me too much of Sarah. We had had a good system in art galleries: I'd go round quickly, looking at everything that struck me until I got moved by one thing. That's all I wanted, to be moved by one more thing. One beautiful or startling work to hold in my head and pass on to someone else.

I'd leave her to the meticulous analyses while I found the bar, bought a beer, wrote in my notebook and waited for her. I was never any happier than in those moments waiting to find out what I'd missed and what I had found.

If Sarah was gone for ever, I'd need more beautiful things, not fewer.

So I faced up to it, and instead of feeling sad, I felt the most at home since I'd arrived. The calming décor of the international contemporary art space. Every one of them done up like Brook's *Dream*, a blank canvas, an Ikea lounge, a photographer's studio. A place without background, a space to teleport into.

Art galleries are also the only places in the world where I like to get stoned; and I had been carrying Arturo's large bud of skunk around for the last week.

I shimmered into existence in front of the international doe-eyed brunette who sells the tickets on reception in every one of these institutions. Her fringe was perfect, as real as a photo in a magazine. She smiled the same smile she'd smiled at Sarah and me when we'd gone to the Hamburger Bahnhof on our holiday to Berlin a few months ago. It was a smile that recognised I was much reduced. *I know*, it said. *I saw. You idiot. But you are still welcome in here.*

'*Muchos gracias*,' I said when she handed me my change, and on a whim I asked, '*¿Como se llama?*' She smiled again but she didn't answer. No one knew her name. She was *Untitled. Sin Titulo.*

Moving on, I climbed the escalator to the first hall. Here I walked around some fluorescent sculptures and checked the cards, wrote names down in my notebook to Wikipedia later. 'Ah, León Ferrari!' I might say tomorrow. 'I really wanted to see his show in the New York MOMA

106

last year with Mira Schendel.' I was relieved to see I wasn't the only one doing this: I saw a couple of other young men and women reading the cards too. One of them was even making a sketch.

I was back the next day with Lizzie and smiled with complicity at the woman who sold me my ticket again.

'Oh, I love Antonio Berni!' I said as we were greeted by a multicoloured alligator, a girl's legs in over-the-knee black socks hanging out of his jaws.

Lizzie peered at the tag.

'I always think it's a shame he didn't do more sculptures.'

'Yes,' she said.

She turned and looked at a large painting on the wall opposite.

'Xul Solar. I think that's another of his over there. I like this one best, though.'

'My God, Sarah's got you well-trained.'

'Oh, it's not Sarah. I've always liked art. Actually, what really makes me like art is getting stoned. You don't fancy nipping out for a spliff, do you?'

'Have you got one?'

'Courtesy of your boyfriend.'

'I should have guessed. Well, why not?'

We walked down the stairs and round the back of the building and I lit the joint I'd prepared earlier.

'How is Arturo anyway?' I asked at exactly the same moment Lizzie said, 'How is Sarah anyway?'

She laughed. 'Aren't we boring? Surely we've got something more interesting to talk about than our other halves?'

'We are boring. And think about that expression, "our

other half". Does that mean we're half a person without them?'

'I think I would be more of a person. I'd have a richer social life, that's for certain. I'd be able to talk to other men in public.'

'Rather than skulking behind the back of buildings.'

'Oh, you don't count.'

'Thank you. I *am* a man, you know.'

'No, of course you are. A whole man too, even without Sarah.'

'No need to go that far. I'm happy to be half a man.'

'*Really?*'

'No, I am, really. I'm half the human being you are and Sarah's twice the human being I am. It's a rare instance of a clichéd phrase saying something particular and profound.'

We had been passing the joint back and forth.

Lizzie closed her eyes to think and giggled. 'If Sarah's twice the person you are, she should call you "my super-fluous half" then.'

I really didn't like that. I tried to giggle back.

'Or do you become her other third?'

She giggled again. I was becoming stoned in a different way to her, feeling the weight of my predicament pressing down on me from overhead, screwing me into the ground. It's incredible that I forget so often that this is what being stoned feels like to me. Contemporary art galleries are usually the exception because they feel like the inside of spaceships, open space and no clutter, my life on earth far away. I passed her the joint back.

'I'm going to need a beer or two to even me out.'

'Don't worry,' she said. 'You've still got two arms, two legs, a whole head of hair. So what do you have half of? A brain? A heart?'

108

'We're still on this? I have both of those, half a brain, half a heart. But let's not carry on in this vein as I'm not about to admit to having half a penis.'

'Good to hear.'

'I'm glad you're pleased.'

'I would feel sorry for Sarah otherwise.'

'Probably don't let that alone stop you.'

'Oh, enough of the self-deprecation. We're not in England now. It's not as charming as you think it is.'

'Fine. Lucky you hanging out with brilliant me. Now please put out that spliff and come and have a beer with me.'

We sat outside on the café terrace and ordered beers. Lizzie pulled out her pack of Marlboro Reds. People don't often smoke full-strength Marlboros in England – the middle class are compromisers and the working class smoke cheaper stronger brands. But the Marlboro Red was the perfect cigarette for Argentines, colour-coded for the Malbec-and-red-meat candour of their desire.

She was telling me more about Arturo's jealousy, the hourly emails while she had been away, the arguments if she proposed to meet a male colleague for a drink without him.

'It's hard working out if it's the culture or if it's him. He of course maintains it's the culture. The *correct* culture, the way things should be.'

But perhaps it is *you*, I thought. I was having a hard time trying not to stare at her too intently. She was a talkative doer of a stoner to my wistful spectator. I was very much enjoying spectating her face, a long face, freckly with her reddish-blonde hair held back in a loose ponytail, strands of which constantly escaped. She was always interfering with it, flicking the strands of hair away, fluttering her fingers around to emphasise points or resting her chin on her hands for the briefest moments of contemplation. She was not elegant or demure but how she was sexy. I wanted to see her eat a steak, I wanted to see the blood run down her chin, I wanted to feel her sink her teeth into my arm.

She grinned at the waiter as he brought drinks and flirted with him, rolling her Rs with relish.

'I can sort of see why you might make men jealous, you know,' I suggested.

'Because I'm friendly?'

'*Exactly*. You're friendly.'

'Aren't you friendly to other women?'

'I certainly am.'

'Well, then, why can't I be friendly to other men?'

'I'm not saying you can't. Of course you can. But not by comparing yourself to me. Who says my friendliness to women is proper?'

'Isn't it?'

'I mean it to be. Or more likely, I want something out of it.'

'Friends.'

'Yeah. But every time? Every time I talk to a woman in a bar I'm only after a friend?'

'Are we talking about you or me here?'

'I'm just saying it's easy to lie to yourself. I've spent my whole life trying to make people like me and I thought I'd got to be quite good at it. I feel at home with women. I love the conversation of women, the thoughts of women, the company of women. And I love the bodies of women, the touch of women. Being with Sarah hasn't stopped me from wanting to make women like me. It's addictive and vain. And sometimes it's friendly. And sometimes . . . I don't know.'

'Liam?'

'Yeah?'

'That's you, that's not me.'

'Well, maybe it's a male thing.'

'Desire and vanity are not male things. I'm not even sure if self-indulgence is either, despite what often seems like overwhelming evidence. You sound like you're just being too hard on yourself.'

'That's not what Sarah thinks.'

'Liam, what have you done?'

I really wanted to tell her. I wondered if I could. 'I . . . I don't know. I used to agree with you. I thought you could do things that aren't you, that are a lie in themselves, an experiment in character. And if you tell someone about them you make them more true than if you didn't.'

'The thing is to not do them in the first place.'

'Of course.'

'But sometimes you do do them.'

'Regrettably.'

'Let's get some more beers,' she said, waving the waiter over. 'I haven't told this story to anyone. Can I trust you?'

'Of course,' I promised.

'You've heard the beginning of the story, when you asked how I met Arturo.'

'At his gig. You grabbed him to have your way with him.'

'I grabbed him but I didn't have my way with him, not that night.'

'Oh?'

'He was, he is, such a sexy kisser. I wanted to. But it's a risk with you idiots, putting out on the first night. Some of you get bored if there's nothing to chase, start assuming that if it was that easy it can't be worth it.'

111

'Not me. I'm always overwhelmingly grateful.'

'Always? Anyway, you're aware of the phenomenon. So I didn't go back with him. I took his number and he had work early so he left. I don't think I mentioned I was on a pill when I first kissed him. I didn't tell Arturo at the time actually. But I *was* on a pill, a really strong one, and regretting not going home with him, feeling really, really horny. I got talking to this guy Hernán and he took me off for a line in the toilets and then I was in such a *wild* mood . . . I mean, it's OK to fuck people you don't really like, isn't it? It's people you do really like who you can't just fuck.'

I kind of admired her logic. A few months earlier I would have found it profound and true. But my rule was simple now: don't fuck anyone, ever.

'Obviously it's important not to make the wrong impression,' I said.

'I knew you'd understand. Except, you've met Hernán – the singer in Arturo's band. *That* Hernán. I was so out of it and wrapped up in Arturo I didn't even notice the guy I was getting off with was his singer until six weeks later when I saw Arturo's band again, sober, and watched Hernán stare right at me from the centre of the stage for the whole performance. I hadn't returned any of his calls, and by this time Arturo and me are properly together, have had this wonderful month exploring the city together. And Hernán has known all along who Arturo's new girlfriend is but doesn't seem to have said anything to him – I don't think he's told him, anyway, at least not directly. I think he likes having this secret over me, to insinuate he knows something about me. If he has said something, it's worse, and it's Arturo and him who like having this hold on me. But I don't think it's that. Arturo's too confrontational to keep something like that to himself. I do my best not to go to the gigs now, to find excuses, but they keep playing more and more.'

I thought of the look on Hernán's face as he had watched Arturo flirt with the girl after his gig last week.

'Lizzie, you didn't do anything that bad – why don't you just tell him?'

'I think I missed my chance. It's so stupid, that embarrassment can grow something so small into such an enormous lie. I feel like I've got a bomb ticking under me. What do you think I should do?'

I didn't know. I was worried she was right, that there is a point beyond which telling the truth can still stand in your favour. I had been miles beyond this point when I had told the whole truth to Sarah about the half-night stand I'd had in Frankfurt, but who was to say Lizzie wasn't slightly beyond it now, with the same consequences? The people out there who never lied, they were so intolerant of we who did. Was it really their courage or just their lack of imagination?

I wanted to believe it was courage. I wanted to believe that this could be me. I decided then that I would tell Lizzie about my split with Sarah. In a minute I decided I would tell her.

Lizzie had stubbed the joint out before it was finished and she lit it again before we went back into the exhibition. This time I enjoyed the high and winked at the girl on the desk as we went past. We slid through the galleries, talking less, caught up in our own impressions. I could almost pretend I had a girlfriend again. I moved up to Lizzie, who was staring at an enormous mural, and I opened my mouth to speak –

'Don't you dare tell me the name of the artist, where

he's from, who his sister was or how he faced the challenge of the military dictatorship between 1976 and 1983. I'm enjoying looking at this.'

'Lizzie,' I said. 'I have a confession to make.'

'Yes,' she giggled, and I felt so happy at that moment I could not spoil it.

'Lizzie. I know nothing about Latin American art.'

'Is this you being charming again?' She pretended to yawn.

'I came here yesterday and memorised all the texts on the placards. That's why I recognise so much of the art and know about the artists. I looked them up on Wikipedia.'

That stopped her yawning. 'Why would you do that?'

'To impress you with my erudition.'

'But that would make you a complete psycho –'

'"Beginning in 1957, coinciding with the space race, Forner's attention turned to imagined scenes of interplanetary travel" –'

'Stop it! You *are* a psycho. So all that pointing and pondering before, that was all an act to impress me?'

'It was.'

She screwed up her fact in disgust and looked me up and down. Then she punched me in the arm and laughed.

'That's brilliant,' she said admiringly.

Chapter 10

Living begins to look possible when you have a friend; the world lightens. I hugged Lizzie goodbye, though it was perhaps more of a don't-go hug. She extricated herself in the end, and we arranged to go for dinner with Arturo later in the week. In the meantime she offered to ask around to see if she could find me an apartment; she thought she knew a colleague at her college who was looking to sublet his place for three months while he went travelling. She talked me through other practical matters too: where to buy a cheap mobile phone, what I would need to get a library card if I wanted somewhere quiet to work.

The mobile was a good idea and I immediately went and bought one. My mum would be happier now I had a number she could call me on. It hadn't escaped me that there was a precedent for my sudden flight: my father's disappearance. I worried I was making the past present again, that time when he left her for the woman who would so briefly become his second wife. His disappearance shortly after that completed the derangement and since I was sixteen I had never slackened the pace of intoxication. I was making sure to call Mum every week from a payphone, to email regularly and keep in touch with my sisters. But it was hard to keep up a conversation because the one thing I needed to talk about was the one thing I was still too ashamed to admit. It wasn't that I minded admitting my faults but that I knew they'd understand and suffer any of my pain alongside me. I remembered looking at Mum the evening after Dad had gone, how the four of us multiplied by four every bit of sadness. I could still hear the echoes.

So I told them I had been suspended from the job, not sacked. I told them I was hoping Sarah would arrive soon. I changed the subject and made jokes. It must have worried them more than ever.

I had stopped trying to call Dad. I refused to chase him. But a couple of days after I had passed my new number on, one of my sisters must have had a rare conversation with him, for I was woken one morning at 5 a.m.

'Hello. Dad? Do you know it's five in the morning?'

'No, it's not, is it? It's midday!'

'You're ahead of me.'

'Definitely? I thought you were ahead of me.'

'Definitely.'

'Oh.' He sounded crestfallen.

'But now you're here, how are you?' I said, trying to cheer him up.

'How am *I*? *You're* in Argentina!'

'I am that.'

'And you've been suspended from your job?'

'You're only just getting started.'

'Wow!'

'You sound exhilarated. It's generally regarded as a bad thing.'

'It's just rather spectacular. What are you going to do?'

'No fucking idea.'

'What about Sarah?'

'I cheated on Sarah, and now she's dumped me. It's a disaster. I didn't even do it properly, I just flirted with doing it and couldn't go through with it and then lied and got caught out. Not that it matters. She says it's the lying that destroyed things, not the cheating. And she doesn't really believe me about the not cheating anyway. I wouldn't if I were her.'

'Ah,' he said. 'Your sisters were concerned. They thought something might have happened. But you haven't told *them* this.'

'No.'

'Why not?'

'Embarrassed? Ashamed? I don't want them to know how miserable I am.'

'Oh, Liam.'

'You're not allowed to tell them how miserable I am, by the way. Let's share that together, us *men*.'

'You make men sound like a horrible word.'

'*We* make men sound like a horrible word.'

It had been years since I'd attacked my dad. At first I hadn't dared to, in case he disappeared again. And after that, it was hard to summon the energy. The anger had retreated somewhere inside me, seeped into cracks and corners. Forgiveness, in its first stages, is more passive than active.

'You don't sound like you like yourself much at the moment,' Dad said, eventually.

'I'm trying to be a better judge of character. Do you like yourself?'

He sighed. The long sigh I recognised from years ago

whenever I asked if he had rung my sisters recently, if he had taken their calls, arranged to see them. The refusal-to-think sigh. The running-away sigh. The sigh that ended the call.

'Don't fucking hang up,' I said.

The sigh again.

'I'm listening, Liam,' he said. 'For what it's worth, I'm sorry too. Tell me what happened.'

'I don't want you to be sympathetic. I don't want you to make me feel better. I don't want to feel bet –'

'Liam,' he said. 'Tell me.'

The morning after the best day of my life – it must have been years, but it felt like a day – I woke up in bed in another country with the wrong woman. I wished I didn't remember how I got there but I did, meeting her that afternoon, staying out with her when the colleague I was sharing a flat with went home before me with the only keys. I had known full well that he would fall asleep drunk and not wake up. We'd ordered a bottle of champagne to her room in the Frankfurter Hof – just, I'd told myself, because I wanted someone to talk to; I had wanted someone to *talk* to. Cockburn, who had introduced me to her earlier, had seen his Frankfurt drug dealer Klaus earlier in the night and now neither Isabela, an Italian editor, nor I was ready to sleep. We lay on her bed and talked for hours and when she leaned over and kissed me I felt a surge in my heart, tasted rust on my lips, and let it go on and on, until I could not forget about her, until the lust for death turned into the perfect recollection of Sarah's face. When I said I had to go – I would sleep on a park bench if I had to – Isabela started to cry. I told her I was in love with someone. She told me it was always the same, we were always in love with someone. She didn't know how we behaved the way we did when we were in love with someone. Nor did I. I put my arms around her and held her against my chest. I reassured myself that I had not gone too far. I tried to reassure myself. That was when she fell asleep. I lay there with the perfect awful weight of her head on my chest and then I was dreaming, falling, dreaming more than I should have.

Chapter 11

The days were quiet then, Spanish in the morning, lunch with Hans, afternoons on the terrace, writing in my notebook. The weather grew cooler. Every morning I scanned the shelves for a new arrival, a book I wanted to read, and went back disappointedly to sip from *Bleak House*. The narrator was unreasonably virtuous and made me feel the opposite. Every time I got excited about the story a new subplot and set of characters arrived to take it further away from me. The novel was brilliant, occasionally enjoyable, the last thing I needed and all I had. It was a cheap edition and its nine hundred pages were set so tightly I would occasionally lose focus and seem to stare at a blank book crawling with ants. But at least not having anything to read was forcing me to write. That was Chandler's two very simple rules for writing a novel: four hours a day when, one, you don't have to write and, two, you're not allowed to do anything else. Eventually you write a novel just to keep from being bored. But Chandler's study wasn't on the top of a hostel roof constantly renewed with multinational young women (in bikinis, when it was sunny). More fool him. Nevertheless, I was getting *some* work done.

On the second night I asked Hans if he'd like to accompany me to the bar in San Telmo, where I was going to try to track down Alejandro Miguel Marques Montenegro.

'Will Lizzie be coming?' he asked.

'I'm seeing Lizzie tomorrow. Her boyfriend is monopolising her tonight.'

'*Boyfriend*. Please tell me some good news about the boyfriend.'

'Although he's better-looking than Johnny Depp, he's substantially poorer.'

'Substantially poorer than me?'

'Mmm.'

'Please. Try again.'

'Although his eyes are hypnotically gorgeous, his job as a motorcycle courier exposes him to considerable personal danger in this city of terrible drivers and bloody accidents.'

'Now tell me how you have interfered with his brake cables and you will put me in a good mood.'

After I had assured Hans of Arturo's imminent demise he agreed to come with me. We walked to an old-fashioned wooden bar with sleepy fans swirling around the ceiling. We avoided the long counter and sat in the corner. It was nine in the evening, early for Buenos Aires, and there were only three or four others in the place.

An elderly bartender was polishing glasses, elegant in his white shirt and black bowtie. Hans went to demonstrate his Spanish-class proficiency and came back with two small glasses of greenish-brown liquid which he placed nonchalantly on the table.

'What the fuck is this?'

121

'Fernet. The national drink.'

'I believe I asked for a beer.'

'Look around you. This is the real Argentina. It's not a place for a beer.'

'They have beers. I can see them in the fridge. What are you talking about? Everyone I can see is drinking a beer.'

'That's not the point.'

'I've drunk this before,' I said.

'So have I,' he said sorrowfully.

'Don't they normally have it with coke?'

'This is the real Argentina,' he repeated.

We sat there, sipping, wincing, looking around us. It was quiet. I couldn't see anyone who looked like my idea of an Alejandro.

Halfway through our Fernets I stood up and ordered us a bottle of wine. We finished it slowly. I liked being with Hans. Conversation was like playing tennis, with little breaks between rallies when we found out about each other. We always had the good grace to resume the game at the saddest moments of the conversation.

His sadness, like mine, like so many men's, was over a woman, a woman he had lost through carelessness and becoming caught up in a job (the difference being that his had earned him lots of money and that I had liked mine). He had been an analyst for a stockbroker's in Frankfurt, working sixteen hours a day six days a week before he quit. I turned off when he began to talk passionately of the beauty of pure algebra. Other people had tried that on me, including one or two Hollywood movies. Hans was travelling for another four months before he would go home for his sister's wedding, to the village near Hamburg where he had grown up. After that, he didn't know what he would do. His travels around South America had not led to the epiphany he'd hoped for. I wasn't surprised by that: I thought then that epiphanies were a narrative convention encouraged by teachers of creative writing degrees.

'You're shocked that changing location every couple of weeks, constantly getting drunk with strangers and doing no work at all isn't focusing your mind?' I asked.

'When you put it like that, fuck you.'

I was beginning to get quite drunk and armed with this courage I approached the barman and asked him if he knew Alejandro Montenegro. '*No lo conozco, conozco a muchos Alejandros. ¿Como es?*'

I was stuck here. I had no idea what he looked like.

I thanked him and excused myself and returned to our table with another bottle of wine. An hour or so later I noticed a new man had entered and sat at the bar. He was the right age, in his mid-forties. I had imagined him as a Latin version of Bennett but in translation, if this was him, he became tall, broad-shouldered and handsome. I watched him drain a whisky.

As I walked to the bar, resolved to ask him if he knew Alejandro, another man walked through the door of the bar, younger than me, slim with gelled dark hair and earrings.

'Alejandro!' he called to the man at the bar. This was exciting. The man called Alejandro stood up and they kissed each other. This was the usual way men greeted each other here. The casual way the man rested his hand against the other's waist and stroked it lightly was something else. It was a discreet gesture and I would have missed it if I had not been staring. They stood there, talking in a low voice for about a minute, and then they began to argue. The small man pushed Alejandro in the chest and Alejandro pushed him back. Next thing, the small man had taken a swing at Alejandro, which he blocked with one arm before pushing the small man back with his other arm. He spat something dismissively at the smaller man before pointedly turning and sitting at the bar with his back to him. The small man stood there, staring, and threw at Alejandro a volley of *cornudos, gils, hijos de puta.* Alejandro knocked back his drink and turned round slowly to watch him with immaculate disdain. With that, the smaller man turned on his heels and left.

The old man behind the bar had watched them sleepily. He reached out with a bottle and poured another measure into Alejandro's glass.

'*Gracias. Perdon.*'

The barman just raised his hand. '*De nada.*' He turned to me and I ordered another bottle of wine.

While he was opening it, I studied Alejandro's profile. He was an attractive man, well-dressed in a fitted white shirt, his silvering hair cut stylishly and complemented by a close-trimmed beard. He turned and trained sad mahogany eyes on me. '*¿Que?*'

'*¿Vos sos Alejandro Miguel Marques Montenegro?*' I began tentatively.

He looked at me bluntly, uninterested and turned away.

'*¿Amigo de* Craig Bennett? *Soy amigo de* Craig Bennett.'

'I wouldn't be surprised if I spoke better English than you,' he said, looking back at me. 'But I'm not friends with Craig Bennett and not only because he's dead.' He turned back to his reflection in the mirrors behind the bottles and in the awkward seconds of silence that followed I decided I should leave him alone. But then he spoke. 'You're too young to be his friend anyway.'

'I'm no younger than your friend.'

'I think you may have witnessed the end of that particular "friendship". Are you one of those people who like to use the word "friend" euphemistically?'

'Er –'

'People do, you see. "Why don't you bring your *friend* for dinner, Alejandro?" Well, because he's an uncivilised drama queen and he's my lover, not my friend. Because I'm embarrassed I dredge such depths. But Craig Bennett, he was your *friend*, was he?'

'Nearly. We only knew each other for one night.'

'You *are* using the word euphemistically.' He raised an eyebrow at me now, more interested, flirtatious.

'Not like that,' I said. 'But I did sort of fall in love with him. Whatever that means. And then he died.'

The bartender served me my wine. Alejandro had finished his drink and I pointed to it and asked for '*uno mas*'.

Alejandro made a flat, humourless chuckle. 'Your Spanish is cute.'

I paid the bartender and slid Alejandro's whisky across.

'You were his friend, though?' I asked.

'A long time ago.'

'I was supposed to be looking after him. I work in publishing. I mean, I did work in publishing. My girlfriend left me on the day I met him. He took care of me.'

Alejandro exhaled and stared into his drink. He looked very sad.

'And you didn't take care of him?'

'No. I didn't do a good job of that.'

Alejandro pushed the whisky back to me and stood up sharply. 'I am afraid I cannot drink with you. I do not want

125

to discuss Craig Bennett. I do not know why you came looking for me but I do not have what you're after.'

With that, he slapped two notes on the counter, turned his back and walked out.

Chapter 12

I had arranged to meet Lizzie and Arturo the following evening for dinner in Arturo's favourite restaurant, a place owned by his cousin. I'd spent the morning in my Spanish class, before writing an email to Amy Casares to describe my meeting with Alejandro. In my letter I conceded defeat. I had met Bennett's friend and he hadn't wanted to know. Why should he care? I was still struggling to answer that question for myself. I was curious why Amy hadn't told me Alejandro was gay – from her emails I had constructed the impression of them as a talented heterosexual pulling partnership – but I didn't mention his encounter with the younger man, or his weary flirtatious camp. We should be sensitive not to send messages other people may have gone to lengths to avoid sending themselves. I have, I admit, a vested interest in recommending this scrupulousness.

Every day I looked for an email from Sarah. I had not sent her one for weeks now and wondered if curiosity would eventually make her write to me. That afternoon, as usual, there was nothing from her, and, as usual, before

I logged off I navigated to her Facebook page to try to deduce what she was up to. She wasn't the type to post confessional statements, so I had been marking her progress by the increasing number of friends she was making, most of whom had Latin American names. Every time I saw her name followed by the information 'Is in a relationship with Liam Wilson' it brought home the reality of what I had lost.

Today I was 'no longer in a relationship with', news illustrated by a small broken-heart icon. I deleted it, felt sickened. My sisters might have seen that, my friends. A child's cartoon scrawled to announce a tragedy. Why not print T-shirts? What was 'in a relationship', anyway? Why did they make the wording so coy, so passive? Be brave if you're going to tell the world, operatic. Sing it like a tango. Liam loves Sarah. Sarah does not love Liam any more. Liam's heart broke. Liam is trying to mend it with alcohol, cocaine and indiscriminate lust. Liam is in trouble.

I deleted my broken heart and returned to the hostel, feverishly composing lines for my love letter. The letter, perhaps about fifty pages long now, was written in various styles. Chief among them was the lyrical nostalgic, manipulatively dredging my memory for our loveliest times together, a form I hoped was more Proustian than sentimental. (I did not re-read the love letter, only added to it.) The other mode competing for prominence was the angry jeremiad to lash the societal hypocrisy I claimed had destroyed us. But when I sat down in a quiet corner of the roof terrace and began to add again to the letter I felt its overwhelming futility. I had my third cigarette and first and only very small cry of the day (I was beginning to feel like Clint Eastwood) and then I felt able to put the love letter away and pull out my other notebook. Four hours later, I felt more optimistic. Things were beginning to fall into place. I had three great characters – Craig, Amy and Alejandro – and I knew just little enough about them to simplify them into life without having to worry about accuracy. Amy blurred into Sarah. Craig blurred into me. A love triangle took shape.

When I had exhausted myself writing and settled down to relax, the thing I had been dreading all month happened. I finished *Bleak House*. Disconsolately, I trudged back down to the communal bookshelves and began to reassess what I might consider reading. There were the eight copies of *The Alchemist*. There were the five copies of *The Beach*. There were the four copies of *Tricks of the Mind* by Derren Brown; three of an instruction manual on how to exploit women with low self-confidence. *On the Road. Zen and the Art of Motorcycle Maintenance. The Dice Man.* I was thirty years old. And that's when I saw it: an English translation of *El Diego* by Diego Maradona. I flicked through and read a bit: it was the flipside of the native literary tradition with its formalist restraint, puzzles and experiments: this was operatic melodrama, the real Argentine sublime, with headings progressing from The Passion to The Resurrection to The Glory, The Struggle, The Vendetta, The Pain. I understood *this*. I was delighted and returned to the roof to read my new guide to Argentine life.

I arrived at the restaurant at half nine. I was more confident at the basic stuff now and asked for a table at the window for three, and a gin and tonic. Twenty minutes later, I was still on my own. I hadn't taken *El Diego* with me so I spent my time staring through the window, imagining what Craig might have thought twelve years ago waiting for Amy to arrive and meet him.

A man in a suit with an enormous bunch of flowers hurried by, looking at his watch. Across the street the door to a block of flats opened and a uniformed maid stepped out, buttoning her coat.

The restaurant's tables were almost all occupied by couples, a lot of them young: the men in tight T-shirts, showing off their trim torsos and biceps; the women small and fragile with shampoo-advert shiny hair and mini-dresses, taking constant trips to the pavement for a Marlboro. I was feeling lonely.

At half past a moped pulled up, a long, limber woman gripping onto the driver, the nylon gloss of her legs slicked against his white jeans. Arturo pulled off his helmet and shook his hair loose. He grinned at no one and showed the white of his teeth. His face was full of the delight of driving his English girlfriend around, attracting glances, the star of his own movie. He hadn't looked over to the restaurant yet but I sensed he knew he was being watched. It is a common feeling (and failing): to suspect you are the only person in the world and that everyone else is performing for your benefit. I never felt it anywhere else as profoundly as I did in Buenos Aires. Everybody moved as if they knew I was watching them.

Now Lizzie took off her helmet and waved at me. Arturo, pretending he hadn't known all along I'd been there, turned and directed his smile at me.

I stood to greet them as they came in, hugging Lizzie hello and giving Arturo the handshake, kiss and stubble-rub that now felt so natural. Arturo, who made jeans and T-shirts look expensive, was smarter than I'd seen him, in a black shirt with three buttons undone. That's a hard look to pull off without coming across as a salsa-class Casanova. He managed it. I looked at the hollow where

130

the low slope of his neck dipped into his shirt and wanted to press my fingers into it.

From over his shoulder, Lizzie winked at me. She was more dressed up than I'd seen her too, blending in with the rest of the *porteños* in a royal blue dress made of a sleek material that ruched around her waist. But below the dress and the dazzle of her legs she wore a pair of cheap-looking leather flats, one of the straps frayed and hanging on by a thin thread. They were the sort of shoes Sarah wore when I first met her and seeing them made me want to curl up and lay my head on them.

'Arturo!' a voice cried from the kitchen. A man in a chef's apron bounded over to embrace him, the cousin. I pursed my lips and winced at Lizzie: the theatre of pain a man might show his friend when a woman walked past who hurt him with desire. It was a popular look in Buenos Aires. She mimed her own look of shock and then we both started laughing.

'He does scrub up well, doesn't he?' she said.

When we had all sat down and Arturo had ordered a bottle of red, Lizzie attempted to explain to me what the different steak options on the menu referred to. Arturo quickly cut her off: 'This one is the best.' Lizzie began to explain the difference between that and another but he repeated it again sternly: 'This one, *bife de chorizo, al punto*,' to a wilful child demonstrating the correct solution to a maths problem. Lizzie shook her head at him affectionately; giving him the benefit of the doubt in his cousin's restaurant. And Arturo was in a good mood, calling over to other tables where he knew people, putting his arm round Lizzie and resting his head on her neck, offering waiters good-natured insults whose tone I could understand if not the substance.

'What's made you so happy?' I asked.

'My beautiful girlfriend, this wine, the company of good people . . .'

I looked around me. 'Good people?'

'You are not so bad,' he told me, looking directly into my eyes as if he had been reading Derren Brown's *Tricks of the Mind*. (I had taken a furtive browse of this to see if there was a section on how to brainwash women into forgiving you.)

'Talking of good people, I got an email from Sarah this morning,' announced Lizzie.

Dread blotted through me. Oh, it wasn't *worth* it. I gripped the table and tried to say something.

'I wrote to her to tell her what a fun day out we had together, how nice I thought you were.'

'Did she correct you?' I managed to say.

'She just said she was glad I was looking after you. You didn't tell me she's in Brazil.'

'*She's in Brazil?*'

They both looked up.

'She's in Brazil, of course she's in Brazil,' I continued calmly. 'I must have got the dates confused, you lose track of time out here.'

'It's a shame it's so soon after I'd just been or I might have gone to see her. Aren't you tempted?' she asked.

'I'm really tempted,' I admitted. 'How far again is it from here to . . .'

'Sao Paulo's what?' she asked Arturo.

'Four-, five-hour flight,' he said. 'Bus, maybe two days.'

'I guess she's very busy with the conference.'

'That's it,' I said. 'She will be. We have a sort of pact. I stay out of art events, she stays out of book events. That way we don't distract each other, feel responsible for the other's boredom.'

'But she could not arrange to come here afterwards?'
Arturo asked.

'Oh, the conference had already booked her flights,
they're not changeable I think.'

I must have looked very glum then. 'You'll see her soon,'
said Lizzie, reaching out and putting her hand on my arm.
She changed the subject before Arturo could ask another
bewildered question about my and Sarah's lack of desire
to see each other.

'How are you finding the hostel?' she asked. 'You know
I lived there for the first month when I arrived?'

'Didn't you find the company terrible?' I asked.

'No,' she said, surprised. 'I liked the people there.
Obviously, you have to hope they're different people to
the ones still there now. But what's the problem with
them?'

'Well, I have a nice friend, Hans. But the young ones,
they're all so uncynical. It's like nothing bad has ever
happened to them. It's impossible to talk to them.'

'You'd like bad things to happen to them?'

'Only for their own good.'

'Oh, yes, *their* own good. You're a terrible traveller, you
know that, Liam?'

'Yes.'

'You're not really a traveller at all, are you? You just
sit around, reading.'

'That's the nicest thing you've ever said to me.'

The food was delicious. I did my best to keep my mind
on it and not on the growing fear that I was about to
miss a chance to surprise Sarah and redeem myself. I
wanted to leave the restaurant immediately and importune
Google for her whereabouts.

But I didn't. I suggested we should order another bottle

of wine. Arturo was still on his first glass but put his hand up and made a gesture at the bottle I'd finished five minutes ago. A new one arrived in its place.

I had wondered if there would be some awkwardness between Arturo and me, the complicity with each other's misbehaviour (if he had misbehaved) making us wary of each other. Our conversation often fell into an unnatural earnestness because of Arturo's good but not perfect English and my concern to be understood. I spoke slowly, reduced my vocabulary and held my gaze to see if my meaning had been made clear. It was the way you might speak to a woman you were convincing of your love. Look into my eyes and believe me. Waiting to see if the lie would take. I'd lost the ability to give this look to Sarah. Her face had twisted up in revulsion when I'd tried.

Once we'd finished the steaks Lizzie went to the toilets and we were left on our own for the first time.

'Thanks again for last week. That was a really good time,' I said.

He smirked. 'You should enjoy your holiday. You liked Ana-Maria?'

'Oh, *no*.'

He frowned.

'Sorry, I didn't mean *no*. Of course I liked Ana-Maria, she's great. I mean earlier, I wasn't saying it was a great night *because* of Ana-Maria, that's what I mean. It was just fun.'

He looked amused. 'Relax, *ché*. I saw her yesterday. Lizzie and I have dinner at hers.' He smiled. 'The look on your face. You really are frightened? Don't be. *Tranquilo*. I'm not stupid. I don't tell anything next to Lizzie. Or Ana-Maria. We have, what do you say . . .'

'Discretion?'

'Manners, I think you say.'

'In that case, you have wonderful manners. Thank you. But I don't like you having to lie for me. It was a mistake.'

'Not saying is not a lie. You are too English about this. Make it what you want it. It don't matter. And, Liam, I see you. Lizzie says Sarah is in Brazil, there is something you don't tell us. *Vale*. You say what you have to say. I think you like to lie.'

'That's not true. I hate to lie. It makes me feel sick.'

'Then don't. Try, anyway. I don't think is possible. Life is lies. *Viveza Criolla*. Is like your footballers. They do not go down, even when is foul in the area. The truth is a penalty but because your player is truthful he gets the lie. Is why you lose. You have to make the truth. Now: tell me the truth about what you did with my girlfriend on Tuesday. When you spend the whole day with my girlfriend. What do you tell her about me?'

It was interesting to watch the thought occurring in him that he might have reason to be annoyed with me, to see it develop from a whim to inflame his face as if I had just bragged of cuckolding him.

'I didn't tell her anything about you. What was there to tell? I saw you talking to a girl.'

He smiled at this and relaxed. 'That's right. That's all I did. Talk to a girl.'

'Lizzie and I didn't talk about you at all,' I said; he looked less pleased at this. 'Not much, I mean – I told her how much I liked your band.'

He looked even less pleased. 'She never comes to see my band. Perhaps you should say something then about Lucila, a hint, something to make her know there is danger if she is not with me?'

'I don't think it ever helps to make a woman think she

135

can't trust you,' I said. 'Not the women it's nice to go out with. It's best just to be honest.'

He waved his hand dismissively. 'Do not lie if you are not good at it, if you are an Englishman, yes. Tell me, do you like Buenos Aires?'

I thought about the question. I supposed I did like it, despite the strangeness and crippling homesickness and heartbreak. I had me to blame for that, not Buenos Aires.

'I do, yes, I do like it here.'

He looked pleased. 'I'm glad you like it. It is home. But there are many terrible problems.' He told me about them. Lizzie was taking a long time in the toilet. 'We are different to you English and the same too, but it is hard to know which bits are the same,' he was saying. 'I don't understand Lizzie. I feel like you do, and I don't like that you do.'

'She's just free-spirited. There's nothing to understand. Just let her do what she wants, trust her, you'll be fine, she's great.'

'And you trust Sarah?'

'Are you still talking about Sarah?' Lizzie said, suddenly sitting back down. 'Arturo, give poor Liam a break. You see he misses her.'

'Oh, yes, I see that,' he said.

'What are you doing on Sunday?' Lizzie said brightly. 'Arturo's going to the football so I'm free.'

Arturo frowned. 'Would you like to come with me, Liam? I find out today I have one more ticket.'

'Liam doesn't like football,' she said.

'I do like football,' I said.

'Really?' she said. 'But you read books. You don't look like you like football.'

'I'm currently reading the autobiography of Diego Maradona.'

136

'I meant you read real books.'

'*Lizzie*,' said Arturo, shocked. '*El Diego* is *obra maestro*, a tragic story of glory and betrayal. Of course,' he said, turning to me, 'it is a shame he played for Boca.'

'So it's not Boca you're going to see?'

It wasn't. He was a *millionario*. I avoided making the obvious joke and asking why then did he deliver parcels on a moped every day? He was a sensitive man, I could see, behind the beauty and swagger. He perhaps wasn't best suited to the machismo he felt the city required of him. And I knew, because I clung to football in this country like a life-raft, that by *millionario* he was identifying himself as a River Plate fan, the bitter enemies of Maradona's old club. It hadn't escaped me that he had only offered me a ticket when he heard Lizzie and I were planning to spend another day together without him. It wouldn't have escaped Lizzie either.

'You should go,' she said to me. 'If you do like football.' The scepticism in her voice was not directed at me alone.

And at that moment, with Arturo staring malevolently at me, I hated football, but I said the opposite and Arturo and I made arrangements to meet at Aleman's bar in walking distance of the stadium Monumental.

There was a scene when it came to paying the bill. I'd assumed we'd split it three ways but it was incredible to Arturo that he would not pay for Lizzie and as I was on the table that meant he would pay for me too.

'But I drank most of the wine,' I said. 'You had one glass. At least let me pay for that.'

He wouldn't. 'You are my guest here. When I am in England, you will look after me.'

We'd spoken about the peso and the economic crash at the start of the century, the rising inflation today. The currency, while fine to live well in Buenos Aires, was never enough on his wages to afford international flights or the cost of living in England. It was a sad offer, full of bravado and a proud hospitality. But Lizzie seemed bored with the display and I wondered then how much it was for my benefit.

That was Thursday. As soon as I got back to the hostel I went online to book a ticket and the next morning I caught a flight to Sao Paulo to find Sarah.

PART TWO: MY LIE

Chapter 13

An extract from *My Biggest Lie* by Craig Bennett, published October 2009 (Eliot, Quinn)

Amy was still filming. Craig chose a seat with his back to the bar's door; he didn't want to spend hours watching for Amy to appear in it.

After an hour, he had a sore neck and moved to the other side of the table to stare more easily at the door. He attempted and failed to read, to write, to drink slowly. All he had managed was to rehearse speeches.

He had tried a 'remember the good times?' speech. Sad, manipulative and true. They had been the best times.

He had tried an 'I will overwhelm you with the strength and eloquence of my emotions and convictions' speech.

He had tried an 'I have wronged you but less than you think' speech.

A 'let's go back in time' speech.

An 'I forgive you for wronging me' speech.

He had tried an 'if you had suffered what I have suffered' speech. A mitigating circumstances defence. A mendacious plot device in literary novels: the warping past.

An 'open your eyes and see' speech.

A 'he's a fat old bastard' speech.

A 'you need to respect yourself more' speech.

The 'I will make it easy for you to forget why you loved me' speech.

There was nothing he could say and then she came in.

By then, he had abandoned his attempts to look busy. When she stepped through the door she bumped straight into his gaze, his yearning, his hope. She hadn't had time to prepare her face for seeing him and, before she made herself calm, he watched her flinch and show the panic she was feeling. Her curls were falling out of the band she'd used to tie her hair back. That's what they did, what I expect they still do. He recognised the black dress she was wearing. Looking at her in it was feeling her against his skin. Her sandals, they were new. They were nice sandals. It had only been a month since she'd waved goodbye to him at Ezeiza airport but already he could spot the small things that had changed. She smiled at him the brilliance of her smile. She changed her mind and made herself look serious. And that made him smile and made her struggle not to.

When he stood up to embrace her the beers he had drunk surprised him and tipped him into her arms.

'Craig,' she said, holding him there. 'What the fuck are you doing here in Madrid, really?'

'I've come to tell you I love you.'

'That's not the issue. I know you love me. This isn't fucking Hollywood.'

'I know, it's independent Spanish cinema. But love, you are Hollywood.'

She tipped him back upright and set him on his feet. 'That's very sweet of you to say so, Craig. I presume you're complimenting my looks rather than my vacuousness.'

'It was a glib metaphor. You're actually too beautiful for Hollywood.'

'And you're too cheesy, even for Spain. I need a drink. I need three drinks. How many have you had?'

'Fewer than necessary. But give me a second and I'll fix that.'

He brought her back two drinks: a brimming rum and coke and a bottle of beer. They had fallen in love being drunk and impulsive. They had remained in love when they were sober. He didn't want to believe that events had changed this, that any decisions were necessary or unalterable.

She looked at the drinks he placed in front of her and narrowed her eyes at him to let him know she knew what he was up to.

'How's the filming going?' he asked.

Her face lit up. 'It's the most fun I've ever had, I think.'

He tried to look as if he was as happy at hearing this news as he would have been if they were still together. But it was a stupid thing to feign, this ambivalence to what was most important to him. Love had never been about altruism. He wanted her triumphs for his own and he wanted his own for her.

'I'm really happy, I really am,' he said, reaching out and putting his hand on hers.

'Thank you.' She smiled a sad smile and pulled her hand away.

'Nothing that's changed is necessary,' he said.

'I'm sorry I haven't said this earlier,' he said.

'We can go back to the way things were,' he said.

He had said much more than this. She smiled sadly throughout all of it and by the end she had taken his hand back and was holding it.

'We can't go back,' she said. 'I prefer it like this.'

Chapter 14

I flew back into Jorge Newbery on Saturday afternoon. The horror I had experienced in Sao Paulo had not happened to me yet; it was a cinema dream, a flicker in a dark place. As I stepped out of the airport, the sun was up, a cold breeze coming in from La Plata. I was an implausible character in this landscape but I blinked my eyes and didn't wake up. Too drained to defend myself from a taxi driver, I waited for a bus. My first trip to Brazil had lasted less than twenty-four hours. I was in no hurry to go back.

I found one comfort that day: when I stepped off the bus in Palermo I recognised it for what it was: *home*. So this was it, this was where I lived now.

It would be worth narrating if I *hadn't* made a mess of myself that Saturday night. As it was, when I headed to meet Arturo in Aleman's bar – Achtung! – on Sunday afternoon, I was shaking, the sun was glaring and I was thinking what a relief it would be to sit down at the side of the road and weep. I didn't do that; I trudged on, tripped over a cracked paving stone and scraped my hands on the pavement as I broke my fall. I was consumed by *bronca*. I kicked a brick wall and hurt my foot. A man passing shouted something too fast for me to understand but it sounded comradely. I'm with you, brother! Capitalist dogs! Kick down the walls!

I was in this furious mood when I arrived at the bar, forty-five minutes late, unreasonably so even here; but Arturo was unfazed, sipping a coke at the bar, chatting to Aleman. I suspected he'd just walked in. 'How are you?' he asked, glancing at his watch when I sat down next to him.

'Fucking awful. This fucking place,' I said, showing him my skinned hands. 'Fucking pavements.'

Arturo looked at Aleman and they laughed.

'I'm glad you both think it's fucking funny,' I said. '*Una cerveza muy grande por favor.*'

They laughed again. '*La bronca*,' said Aleman, nodding at me.

'Liam, *felicidades*,' said Arturo. 'You are now a *porteño*.'

'Fuck off,' I said.

He reached over and put his arm round me. 'Would you like for me to recommend to you the psychoanalyst of my aunt?' I shrugged him off. Aleman and he were delighted by my bad mood. I had become real to them.

I drank half of my beer down in a couple of gulps and felt a bit better. It was a proper bar, just a small wooden counter with glasses hanging upside down above it. There was an old-fashioned TV on a high shelf in the corner of the room, a pool table on the other side, Arturo, Aleman and me and an old guy reading the paper underneath the TV.

'How long before we leave for the game?' I asked.

Arturo looked away for a second. 'A change of plan. We watch it here.'

'Sorry?'

'We watch it here. But you tell Lizzie we went to the game.'

He explained that he had never had another ticket, just his own. He had tried to get another for me but it had been trickier than he expected, and in the end he decided it would be easiest to watch the game in Aleman's bar. We could not let Lizzie know that because it would confirm to her that he had lied to prevent us spending the day together on our own. 'It is not that I don't trust you, *ché*,' he said, 'or I don't trust her, but this is the right thing. You and me, watching the football on a Sunday afternoon, no? This is what we men do. *I* take my girlfriend out, not you.'

Arturo spoke so casually I could not take what he said as a threat. But I was annoyed. I would have much preferred to spend time with Lizzie than with the machos who were beginning to fill the bar. It was a day when I wanted to admit my weakness instead of laughing about it to show how strong I was. I like to think I would have told Lizzie the truth about Sarah that day, and then we would not have fallen out so badly.

River Plate were playing Banfield, a Buenos Aires derby, but this was strictly a pub for the *millionarios*, the red and white flag of River now pinned across the window. The bar filled up as we got close to kick-off. Arturo was talking to everyone, introducing me, and I was *Lo siento, hablo solo un poquito Castellano*-ing away, smiling broadly and occasionally managing to understand and make myself understood. The more beer I drank, the less language mattered.

The game kicked off. Hernán arrived and sat next to us at the bar after kissing and embracing Arturo. All I got was a nod. Arturo and Hernán began to talk to each other intensely in rapid tongue-rolling Spargie I could not hope to follow. Nevertheless, I strained to catch words, trying to work out if Lizzie had anything to worry about.

Whatever they were talking about stopped as River Plate went one–nil down and the bar erupted into a mixture of outrage and delight; a crowd delighted at being outraged. The goal was incredible. A Banfield player had rounded five players and the goalkeeper in an astonishing run. When he side-footed it towards the open goal a defender dived at full length and tipped it around the post with his fingers. I had never seen such an audacious foul, such a sublime affirmation of cheating. The defender was immediately sent off.

I remembered Arturo's theory about why the English don't win football matches and asked him, 'Was that a good foul? Do you approve?'

He thought for a moment. 'Only if he misses the penalty. No, is not a good foul so early in the game. Last minute, *viveza Criolla*; first half, fucking stupid.'

Banfield scored the penalty.

The bar swore loudly, beautifully.

Hernán and Arturo were disappearing to the toilet at regular intervals and soon we were all chatting away at full speed in a mixture of broken English and Spanish, each of us trying to provide the definitive analysis of the game we were barely watching. River Plate came back in the second half with a goal from a corner and it ended one–all. The *millionario* crowd complained bitterly and half of the bar left. We carried on drinking.

At one point, I returned to the bar from my own visit to the toilet to find Hernán leaning in to Arturo, his hand on his arm, speaking close to his ear. Both looked at me suspiciously as I sat back down.

'What are you talking about?' I asked.

'Lizzie,' said Arturo, and they both stared at me. 'Why she is angry at me.'

'*Olvidate!*' said Hernán.

'You will tell her we went to the game?' Arturo asked me.

'Yes,' I said wearily.

'You said on Thursday you will not lie any more,' he pressed.

'I was lying,' I said.

He seemed happier with that. Hernán continued to glare at me before he left to talk to a friend on the other side of the bar.

'What's he saying about Lizzie?' I asked Arturo.

'Nothing.'

'Really?'

'I should not say. You are her friend. He is saying that he thinks he sees her in clubs talking to other men, you know, more than talking.'

I laughed. 'She's not like that.'

'It is not funny,' scowled Arturo.

'No, it's not. She's a friendly woman who talks to other human beings. So what? Don't fuck it up, Arturo.'

'Fuck you. How do I fuck it up?'

'By listening to rubbish like this.'

'You people. "Friendly." You do not care about each other.'

'Us people?'

'Look at you: you leave your girlfriend on the other side of the world. Why? Why are you here when she is not?'

'*Us people?* Do you want to know where I woke up yesterday morning?'

He shrugged.

'I'm getting out of here. See you later, Arturo.'

'Where, then?'

'Fuck you, Arturo. Really, fuck *you*.'

He looked up at me and saw the expression on my face. His anger softened and he put his arm on my shoulder. 'Liam, where?'

So I told him.

I saw her first. I found the lecture theatre and there was no one stopping to ask for my name so I walked straight through. I arrived just as she was giving her paper, watching her through a glass porthole in the door. She stood, shuffling her papers, bookish in her reading glasses, sexy in a black curator's dress that I had bought her last Christmas. It was the most money I'd ever spent on an item of clothing. I'd imagined her wearing it in interviews or at the openings where she'd meet the people who would make her career and our life what it would become. The room held about fifty students, all looking intently at her. She had once come home to me. The dress had been a bit too tight when I bought it for her. Not too tight, but it couldn't have got any tighter without it being too tight. Now there was give to it. She looked different. She looked the same. The straight drops of the black dress skimmed her hips and I could feel the fabric and the curve of her between my fingers, in my throat, in my lungs. She pressed

149

a button on the laptop; a line drawing covered in stamps was projected behind her, and she began with the words 'In presenting my paper here I was interested why that . . .' And I, the idiot who had driven her away, not only by lying to her, wondered if I should improve her grammar later.

I watched her speak for the next half hour. I watched the way her lips moved, the way her nervous pauses disappeared quickly, the way she looked up to the back row as she made the room laugh with a joke, looking down at her feet shyly then back up, the way her eyes kept returning to one spot where her smile grew bigger. I didn't want to follow her eyes to that spot. I found his name out later, from her Facebook page. He was the first to ask a question when she had finished. It was in English but I didn't understand it; the speaker was Latin but there was nothing wrong with his English. I hadn't listened properly to her words either, too enraptured by the fact that Sarah had spoken them, too terrified of the way she was looking at the asker of the question, an older man, perhaps forty-five, with tightly-cropped silver hair and a serious expression. He was not the Don Juan I had feared, a macho cocksman, a stereotype, a holiday Casanova. He looked intelligent, serious, slightly overweight, a man, and I feared him more because of it. He was real. He was different to me.

She didn't see me until the questions had finished and she had left the front to sit back down. When she glanced up and saw my face in the window she staggered. The whole room was still watching her and the woman nearest to her called to ask if she was all right. Sarah composed herself, took a cold look to reassure herself that I was not a ghost, or perhaps to reassure herself that I *was* a ghost, then she shook her head and sat back down, next to the man I would learn later was named Fernando Salvatierra, the man who put his hand around her shoulder and pulled her into him. A supportive hug of congratulation, that's what I told myself it looked like. I watched her whisper something in his ear before quickly writing something down and passing it to him. He looked up sharply and I side-stepped away from the window. I had a chance then, I realised, to turn and walk down the corridor, out of the building and away. But I didn't. I sat down in the corridor instead with my copy of *Hopscotch*, pretending to enjoy it. I was here in the spirit of fun and affection, not desperation. I had to look like I believed this when she came out. I wanted her to think we could still be an adventure.

Fernando was out of the door before her. He strode down the corridor, looking directly at me. What did he see? A threat, I hope, a threat disguised as a pale Englishman, hiding behind a scruffy beard and a paperback.

'Hello,' he said, as he passed.

'Hello,' I said, turning around to watch him walk away, and then back to the throng of people leaving the room. At the back, catching my eyes and looking purposefully away, was Sarah, walking towards me. I stood up and put my book away. She made as if to walk past me and I thought for a moment she was going to manage it, but she turned back, telling the woman she was talking to that she'd be back in a few minutes. And then she looked at me.

'Liam,' she said.

'Just someone who looks like him.'

'Liam,' she repeated as I stepped towards her. We hugged each other.

'You were brilliant,' I said.

'Thank God I didn't see you before I was brilliant. What are you doing here?'

'Making a grand gesture. Do you remember? This is what I used to do.'

We were still hugging.

'Your grand gestures are getting grander. And less effective. You're going to have to let go of me soon, you know.'

'Is it me holding onto you?'

'Not only.'

She let go. I held on. Then I let go.

'I'm really cross with you,' she said. 'You shouldn't be here. I've got stuff to do here all weekend.'

'You're not pleased to see me at all.'

'I'm dismayed to see you. I'm dismayed that part of me is pleased.' Her smile went serious. 'This is just a ten-minute coffee break. There's stuff happening all night too. I've got no time to see you.'

'That's all right,' I said.

She looked at my face and relented. 'There's a bar across the road. Wait there for me. I'll be out about six, we can get an hour or two. This is fucking awful timing, Liam.'

'I heard you were here.'

'You stupid fool.'

We hugged again and then walked together down the corridor and some stairs to where she was taking her coffee break. Once the weekend was over, she was travelling to another city, Recife, for a month, to catalogue an eccentric artist's private archive. In just two months our lives resembled nothing like our lives.

When we went downstairs, Fernando was leaning against a wall, waiting for her. I knew for certain then. 'Er, this is Fernando,' she told me when he stepped towards me. 'This is Liam.' We nodded at each other, no handshake, no fucking kiss. 'I'll see you later,' she said, and I walked away from her as she walked into the canteen with him. As I opened the door to leave I turned around at the same time as she turned and looked at me. Our eyes met and an awful punch of hope hit me in the stomach.

Arturo had gone pale as I told him this story. He had his head in his hands. Hernán had come back and lost interest; now he was talking to Aleman.

'Liam?' Arturo asked, eventually. 'How are you alive?' He stood up and embraced me. I felt the strength of his arms, smelt the fruitiness of his shampoo, hugged back and held.

'Thanks, Arturo.'

'Will you break up now?'

'I . . . it's my fault. I don't want to break up with her.'

'Did you not hit him?'

'I did not hit him.'

'Strange.'

'It was only a suspicion at this time.'

'Still. A suspicion. Strange.'

'So, you don't actually suspect me of desiring Lizzie.'

'Why?'

'Or you would have hit me.'

'Ah. *Naturalmente*.'

'Why not me?'

'You're too . . . *nervous*, English. I am not jealous of you.'

'Thank you.'

'You sound upset.'

'You should be jealous of me.'

'That's funny.'

'That's not funny.'

'No, it *is* funny.'

'What about Ana-Maria, then?'

'You get lucky.'

'Fuck you.'

Hernán turned round. 'What are you laughing about?' he asked Arturo.

'He thinks I am jealous of him.'

Hernán fixed Arturo with a *telenovela* star's pregnant stare.

'Oh, for fuck's sake,' I said, and went out for a cigarette. When I came back they had begun to argue and I quickly lost track of what they were saying. I tapped Arturo on the shoulder, pointed at Hernán and said, 'Ignore him.' Hernán spat an insult in my face. I got off my stool and went outside for another cigarette. The sky was dark now; we'd been drinking for hours. My heart was jumping and I breathed deeply, slowly, trying to put myself back into real time. I hadn't eaten all day, too sick with jealousy in the morning, too full now. If I kept this up, perhaps, like Bennett, my heart would just give up the fight. Was that what happened when you forgot what it was fighting for? When I collapsed, would anyone rescue me? Sarah had rescued me once already after Bennett had died. I couldn't keep expecting her to.

Back in the bar Hernán was at one side of the counter, talking to Aleman; Arturo was at the other, brooding.

'Can I ask you something?' I said to Arturo.

'What?'

I looked up at Hernán. 'In keeping with your philosophy, why haven't you hit *him* yet?'

'You think I should be jealous of him?'

'He isn't as good-looking as you, I admit. Or me. But

doesn't he always want you to think bad of Lizzie? How much is it him? I saw him after your concert, watching you talk to Lucila. He looked at you like he hated you.'

'No. Hernán is my friend.'

'OK. Well, Lizzie is your girlfriend.'

'You don't understand.'

'Don't start that again.'

He screwed up his face. 'I need something.'

I rummaged in my pocket.

'This is not what I meant,' he said, and he walked away in the direction of Hernán.

I ordered another beer and listened to the sounds of the bar swarm into white noise. I shut my eyes and dropped my head and . . .

An outraged shout snapped me out of my trance. I looked up to see Arturo push Hernán. Hernán pushed him back and shouted something else, and in response Arturo swung and punched him in the face. Before Hernán could reply, Aleman had rushed from behind the bar, grabbed Artruo and bundled him out of the door. Hernán addressed the room, his hands outspread. There were only a few of us left and soon his eyes rested again on me, on my own at the bar.

I got up, unsteadily, looked around to see if I was leaving anything behind. Hernán strode up to me and pushed me. He said something nasty about my mother that I could understand by now. He was ridiculous. I had an urge to lean over and kiss him on the cheek. I stood up and pushed past him to the door but he grabbed my shoulder and spun me around. I blocked his punch but it knocked me back and I tripped over my feet. I was scrambling back up when he kicked me in the side. *Ooh*, I heard. He backed off then, unsure if he'd gone too far.

I stood up again and looked at him. He was smaller than me but tougher-looking. He came forward again and I blocked another of his punches with my arms. Next thing, we were rolling around on the floor together, grasping each other's wrists. Aleman arrived and pulled Hernán off me. My glasses had fallen off somewhere and a kind old man handed them back to me, shaking his head. It is very hard to be a hard man who wears glasses. That was my excuse. Hernán was struggling to break free from Aleman. '*Vamos*,' commanded Aleman, and even I understood that.

Outside, Arturo was preparing to do what was dramatically demanded: return to the bar to announce passionate threats to Hernán. I played my part and physically restrained him from this, while Hernán struggled with Aleman. Each struggling pair could see each other through the door and Hernán and Arturo shouted back and forth at each other. We were all performing well. Arturo wasn't struggling very hard. A few metres down the road, a phone box, or what I had thought was a phone box, opened, and a policeman stepped out, looked towards the commotion and strode towards us.

'*La policia*,' Arturo shouted through the door, and led me calmly round the corner before breaking into a sprint. I ran after him. This was becoming fun.

Now we were in Mundo Bizarro, my favourite bar, just round the corner from the hostel. We'd slowed to a walk after running around a couple of corners and then hailed a cab. I'd thought the running was a bit excessive, but Arturo knew his police better than me. We were in the extremely good mood that comes from having had a fight and successfully fled from a policeman. He was very pleased I had hit Hernán: 'We are brothers now.'

We sat at the bar, drinking Fernet-colas and taking trips to the bathroom. I waved at a couple of women I recognised from the youth hostel. They came over and we flirted with them, we were charming and funny and deranged and stupid. We were some of these things. I bought us all drinks, and when the women gave us chaste kisses on the cheeks and went home it was disappointing but OK, like something awful had been avoided. The relief quickly vanished as I realised I was going to have to go home with myself again soon.

Half an hour ago it had been nine, but now it was two in the morning. I was out on the street with my arm round Arturo. He was slurring something about brothers in my ear. He stumbled and we fell against a shop front, laughing. He grabbed onto my belt and pulled himself upright. Careful, I said, as we walked past one of the phone boxes the policemen sat in. I wasn't sure where we were walking; I was just walking, with Arturo. When he disappeared into an alleyway and started pissing against the wall, I copied him. We finished and zipped up and then I came towards him.

He was surprised when I put my hands on his waist but not shocked. He smiled at me, a cocky smile. He didn't pull away when I kissed him. He let me kiss him. I put my hand in his hair and kissed him more firmly. He put his hand in mine and kissed back. We kept going. He took my hand and placed it on his stomach, pushed it down into his jeans. And just as I felt his cock and wondered how I was going to get out of this, and whether I wanted to, he spun away, laughing, spinning through two more circles back into the street. His hand shot up suddenly and for a second I thought he was requesting permission to ask a question, that or making a Hitler salute – and then a taxi pulled up behind him. '*Adios, Inglés*,' he called, opening the door and getting in.

But before the car drove away he wound down the window and stuck his head out. 'Remember,' he shouted. 'Tell Lizzie we were at the game.'

Chapter 15

Despite the unalterable pain of every breath in this foul Sarah-less world, I still went to Spanish class and was beginning to improve. I ordered my morning cortado and lunchtime ravioli with a disciplinary flourish and could comment, idiotically, on the weather to incredulous waitresses. I would normally run into Lizzie in the corridors of the language school, but after three days I still hadn't seen her. On the fourth, I saw her appear at the end of a corridor. She glanced in my direction, held my stare for a second without expression and walked back into a classroom. It wasn't a look that encouraged me to wait for her to come out again.

Later that afternoon, she sent me an email. The hostel's communal living room was quiet that day and I read it on the computer there. Lizzie knew what had happened in Sao Paulo; Sarah had written to her the next day while I was out with Arturo.

She hadn't wanted to tell me that you had split up because she realised you hadn't told us, but after you surprised her like that she felt she had to. I don't want to have a go at you, Liam. It's weird you didn't tell me you and Sarah had split up, but I can see you hoped you hadn't. You cheated on my oldest friend and she dumped you: it's not the best basis on which to begin a friendship. I think you came close to telling me back at the gallery that day, and it sounds like you half-told Arturo at the weekend. I can see you're a mess. But you being a mess doesn't entitle you to mess up my life. Arturo came back ranting about what you said about Hernán, about how he'd worked out what was going on, how you'd helped him see what was happening. I can't understand why you'd break my confidence like that. I trusted you. Why would you do that? Sarah's obviously better off without you and so are we. You've left me with a pile of shit to deal with, but I will deal with it, and Arturo and I will be fine. There's nothing for me to hide any more. Thanks for that. I suspect that's not the case with you. So long, Liam. I hear Mexico City's nice this time of year. Lizzie.

Tangled together with the shame of being caught out in a lie was the usual relief. The slow doomy wait to be revealed as the person I like to think I'm not was now over. And just as I had feared, so too was my friendship with the person I liked more than anyone else I had met here.

I wrote back a quick reply, accepting her judgement of me. There was a moral certainty to the email I couldn't help thinking was sometimes dubious. Any moral certainty from our untested generation appeared that way to me, but that was probably my flaw and it wasn't the time to argue about that. I promised her I had never told Arturo her story about Hernán. I was sure I hadn't; I'm not one of those drunks who loses track of what they've said to people. I'm too well-practised at being drunk to do that. I regret what I say with awful clarity. So I told her that I had seen Hernán bad-mouthing her and tried to protect her. I apologised that this had gone wrong, thanked her for looking after me, and then I retreated to my room to absorb myself in my sentimentally noble sign-off and feeling sorry for myself.

Lizzie didn't reply and the next day I skipped Spanish. Hans came to find me afterwards. It was his last week in the hostel; he was flying back to Germany on Saturday.

'What have you done to that attractive teacher?' he asked me. 'I said hello to her in the corridor today and she looked like she wanted to spit at me.'

I took him to a bar and told him the story. When I'd finished I waited eagerly for his put-down, for the insensitivity that might transmute the situation into comedy. It didn't come. Instead he reached over to give me a hug and I struggled to resist the urge to push him away. When he left two days later I was glad. We'd taken our friendship into the emotional territory it had been designed as a holiday from, and as we 'celebrated' his last night, in Mundo Bizarro, we talked to everyone except each other.

The next week I started Spanish classes again. I needed something to concentrate on. Lizzie avoided me successfully and each time she did I grew more melancholy. I began to spend my afternoons in Alejandro's bar. I'd sit right up at the counter, drinking coffees for the first half of the afternoon and beer into the evening – adding new pages to Sarah's epic love letter but devoting more and more of my time to the other notebook, to piecing my novel together. I had to do something. I couldn't eat food any more. Sleep was a pornographic dream, starring Sarah, Sarah, Sarah. I don't think I had ever been more miserable, more furious. Writing the novel was a distraction from that, a discipline in self-awareness, in forgiveness and contrition.

Alejandro arrived most evenings at six and sat at the other end of the bar. He would give me a curious glance and then pretend to ignore me while he bantered with the barman in his impregnable Spargie. For the first two evenings, we said nothing to each other at all. The young man I had seen him argue with before never appeared again and by the third evening Alejandro and I were smiling at each other. Our game had become quite amusing to ourselves. '*Uno mas cerveza para mi amigo aqui*,' he ordered and the bartender placed a small beer in front of me. '*Por favor*,' I asked the waiter, '*dices "gracias" de mi al Señor*.' '*El pibe dice gracias*,' the old bartender said solemnly to Alejandro after wincing at my Spanish. Alejandro turned to me and smiled and held his glass aloft. I mimicked him. '*Salud!*' we said simultaneously, and I went back to writing about him in my book.

That evening, with a polite nod towards me, he had left the bar before I had chance to buy him a beer back. I was ready the next day when he walked in and nonchalantly ordered him one, barely glancing at him. He grassy-assed and carried on his daily chat with the bartender. He was wearing a good suit, dark blue with a very faint, almost imperceptible grey stripe woven within, matched with a paler blue shirt and a dark tie loosened to undo the neck by one button. I noticed it because I was writing it down in my book. Alejandro wore a full beard that might have looked scruffy without the balance of his impeccable tailoring. There was something in his smartness that was trying to rebel. That was one way to look good in a suit. I struggled to imagine him as a lawyer.

'So, someone is writing the world another novel,' he announced suddenly.

'How do you know I'm writing a novel?' I asked.

'How do you know you are someone?' he said. 'But look at you. I struggle to imagine you're doing something *useful*.'

I raised my beer to him. 'Salud.'

'What are you writing about?' he asked.

'I'm trying to distract myself from writing the longest love letter in the world to my ex-girlfriend by writing instead about Amy Casares and Craig Bennett.'

He went quiet then. 'How is Amy?' he said eventually. 'You know her?'

'She's a friend. She writes me nice emails telling me I'm not worthless.'

'Do you write emails to her telling her you *are* worthless?'

'Oh, God, yes, I suppose I do,' I admitted. 'Poor Amy.'

'Poor Amy . . .' he repeated absently. 'Which makes me think, is this going to be a good novel?' he said, gesturing at my notebook.

'It's going to be better than the love letter. Perhaps you could help me?'

'And how could I do that?'

'You could tell me about your friendship with Craig, with Amy, about the good times you had.'

'You want the good times?'

'The good times.'

'I could tell you about the good times, I suppose. On the condition you promise not to ask about the bad times.'

163

I promised. But Craig and Alejandro's good times became samey after a while. Drugs, women, rebellion; the insulting of bores, the besting of the authorities; the stoical receipt of punishment, the avenging of slights . . . a chemical Don Quixote and Sancho Panza whose antics I could see stretching out for the same thousand pages.

'So why would you stop being friends?' I asked.

He looked at me and seemed more relieved than angry I had broken my promise, but he said, 'I really don't want to talk about this. If I give you a quick summary now, will you truly promise not to ask me any more questions?'

Again, I promised.

He sighed and signalled to the barman that he needed another drink.

'This was Craig's place. He had never been as happy as he was here. It wasn't just that he felt free of his father. The atmosphere suited him, the chaos, the confusion, the bureaucracy. It was a stage for him to be exasperated on. Behaving nobly in the face of a culture that provoked all-consuming *bronca*, yes? It was the trick of his charm, his persona. And it suited him, because of that crazy upbringing alone on a vineyard with his father, it suited him to be a man apart from the culture, to always meet people from across a distance. So he didn't follow Amy when she left for Europe and, in order to make this seem logical, he continued to take his pleasure in Buenos Aires. But she had gone, and the pleasures he took now made it likely she was gone for good. But if he had followed her . . . he'd have left me behind for one, and I was so much part of his pleasure back then. Some states of mind can only occur in a certain space, in certain company. When she went, I was pleased. She'd been in the way. We worked better one to one. But when she was there I was

164

all the good things for Craig that she wasn't; as soon as she was gone I was all the worst things, a mirror reflecting what he had lost. It took such a short time for him to realise this, for me to realise what I had become for him. If he had gone with Amy, I think the reverse would have happened. He didn't want to have to choose and so when he did, he wanted what he hadn't chosen. And I do not want to think about what finally happened.'

He turned his face away in embarrassment.

'What? I asked.

He looked hard at me now. 'You are ruining our friendship,' he said quietly, but then he continued.

'We were fighting in my kitchen and I waved a knife at him. I can't remember what we were fighting about – maybe money or drugs, or a lie one had told the other, a deflection most probably from what we were really arguing about. We were close to being drug addicts. As close as you get. And I was waving this knife, getting into the whole performance of it. I would never have used it on him, on anyone, and of course Craig knew this. And, what, to teach me a lesson he did what he did? This is why I stopped talking to him. I held the knife out and waved it, and I think we both then realised how ridiculous this was. He grinned, and then he jumped straight into the knife, as if to teach me a lesson. I don't know, as if to prove the knife did not exist, that I was not holding it up towards him, that his imagination was greater than mine. I pulled it away but it hit an artery in his arm. We were both covered in his blood. After the hospital patched him up he flew to Spain to try to make up with Amy and I never saw him again. I nearly killed him.'

'I did kill him.'

'Oh, yes, so you claim.' He chuckled bitterly. 'He was

the kind of man to leap onto a knife. If I had been there I would have warned you. I would have tried to warn you.'

They were the people I thought I loved, the bad role models, the fearless, the futureless, the ones who jumped onto knives. Emulating them was bad faith, pure style, and dishonestly against my basic inclination to hard work and kindness – though that was easy to forget in bursts of delighted excess. It was harder to forget in my year of disasters, when my actions energised the persona I had tried on for size and began to efface the person who had been there before.

When I went back to the café the next day Alejandro didn't turn up, or the next. I felt guilty that I had deprived him of his routine and changed mine so he might think it safe to return.

I had been avoiding looking at my money after my expensive trip to Brazil and a few transactions with Aleman and El Coronel, which, while not particularly expensive in themselves, led to ruinous generosity in bars and impetuous dealings with taxi drivers. I was shocked to find out at the start of July that I had only enough money left to stay for another month. While I yearned for England, it was an England that no longer belonged to me – and I dreaded moving back to my mum's house in Blackpool. I imagined it as the beginning of the end of my life.

Thankfully a few days later I received notice that my application for a writing grant from the Arts Council had been successful. They were giving me nearly five thousand quid, enough to support six months more in Buenos Aires. It was the happiest thing that had happened to me since

I had arrived, and despite everything I tried to call Sarah to tell her. It felt like a sign that I could be something else, someone she would like more than the bad memory of me. After the fourth call rang out without answer I rang my mum instead and told her the good news. It wasn't such good news to her. I had finally come clean about my circumstances and she thought, quite sensibly, that I should come home and get another job. I did my best to reassure her I was OK and promised I would be back for Christmas.

Mexico City's nice this time of year. I never saw Lizzie any more in the corridors of the language school. I thought of her all the time and wished I could share my good news with her, my good money with her, on a splendid night out to celebrate. She never replied to a second email when I tried again to present myself more positively; and so I had no choice but to leave her alone.

My Spanish course finished and without it my days lengthened and I grew more lonely. I began to work in the library, a short walk away. Being lonely, bad for myself, was good for the novel. I sat back and made Amy, Craig and Alejandro talk to each other. Craig said to Amy what I wanted to say to Sarah and Amy said to Craig what I wished she wouldn't. I was learning. I was hurting. I was writing, and I began to feel the thrill of approaching the end of a first draft.

As strong as the buzz of composition was, I craved company in the nights. I tried the bars but my confidence was shaken; I couldn't find it in me to talk to anyone.

The hostel contained more teenagers than ever before and I worried I would only be able to talk to gap-year students for so long before I was reduced to begging them to take me to bed and have mercy on me. I'm not sure I would have survived a refusal. Or an acceptance. After days of this, I logged on to the internet, intending to book my return flight. I never got that far, though, because of a surprising email waiting for me. It was from James Cockburn, and he was arriving in Buenos Aires in two days' time.

Chapter 16

It was an extraordinary act to take two flights and eighteen hours to pitch to an author, so it was the kind of thing James Cockburn did regularly to justify his mythic reputation. That's why people thought he did it. I knew these excursions were not always so rationally calculated and explainable.

The last time I had been out of England with Cockburn was nine months ago at the Frankfurt Book Fair. There, in a toilet cubicle, I had held him in one arm as he sobbed into my shoulder about the suicide of David Foster Wallace, while, with my free hand, a *zwanzig* and a credit card, I tried to break into prelapsarian form the rocks of crack we had erroneously bought as coke from a street prostitute. I had wondered if we shouldn't give up on the crack, but James was adamant: 'We're turning it back, we're making it harmless!' We were in Gleis 25, a twenty-four-hour dive bar by the Hauptbahnhof on the edge of Frankfurt's red-light district. It was a popular hang-out for a certain type of publisher at 5 a.m. and beyond. It had more than a hundred Prince songs on the jukebox. What did the regulars think when we showed up each year? Perhaps in the week preceding there is always a group of insurance salesmen who would drink us under the table. I find that hard to believe and even if there were, they would lack our élan. There is a celebratory myth we tell to each other: that during the Fair all Frankfurt's prostitutes go on holiday (so incestuously adulterous are we, the visiting bon vivants). I was glad it was a myth: we needed the prostitutes to score drugs off.

I remember the moment that night that James disappeared with his friend Veronique, a French publishing director who would pop into the office every few months when she was in town, to show James her new shoes. I was chatting to a Swiss rights executive, Anneliese, when I saw him look over at me. I had met Anneliese and her wonderful fringe earlier that day in a meeting. She was intelligent and funny and spoke many languages: they are always intelligent and funny and speak many languages. She was explaining to me about the texture of Thomas Bernhard's prose in the original German. It's the kind of thing I ask women about when I've accidentally taken crack. There were more women in the room than men: there are always more women in the room than men. I was thinking it would be nice if Anneliese would make regular visits to *my* office to show me *her* shoes. They were turquoise, patent-leather, with three-and-a-half-inch heels. They were the type of shoes I had thought profound beautiful women did not need to wear. I was not letting her ankles distract me from her remarks about the texture of Thomas Bernhard's prose in the original German. Or her calves, with their shop-front-dummy sheen of tan nylon. Matt-laminate.

Sand meeting sea in the Caribbean. A perfect holiday read. Guilty pleasure. James smiled at me as he pulled his satchel over his shoulder. Just *buy* it. Take it off the table.

My mentor. My shadow. Myself.

It was an expensive cab ride to the airport but, a dutiful disciple, I went to meet Cockburn at the gate. His email announced he was arriving at eleven in the morning to ensure 'the new Bolaño' signed a contract with him. Who this new Bolaño was remained unclear.

It was not hard to pick Cockburn out from the crowd of arrivals. He was in a typical publisher's outfit: dark jeans, white shirt, three buttons undone, a skinny-fitting grey blazer and rapier-toed cowboy boots with Cuban heels, making his 6'3" into a frightening 6'5". His dark hair reached his shoulders and divided in a parting over his high forehead, sharp nose and moist lips. Cockburn was forty-three and looked like a *Top Gear* presenter: like a midlife crisis. I was relieved to see he was still wearing his wedding ring.

Despite the way James dressed, I looked up to him (literally, unless I wore his cowboy boots). It's easy to believe that the whole world has heard of James Cockburn, but of course he's a niche celebrity. Cockburn is 'the coolest figure in British publishing' (*Guardian*), adored by the geeks who write the literary pages and hated by at least half of those who publish books for a living in a more modest, profitable way.

It was a joy to see him. I ran over and we hugged.

'Liam, we weren't sure you were still alive – it sounded too *outlandish* that you'd just fly away to Buenos Aires, look at you, you've got a *tan*, summer, no *spring*'s barely started back home. Though it's ending here, right? Still, this isn't so bad,' he said, looking towards the door, where it was a sunny late autumn day. 'How long's it been?'

'Three months.'

I noticed he was struggling slightly with his wheelie case, limping alongside it, and I leaned over and took it from him. 'Give me that. How are you recovering? I thought you might be in –'

'A wheelchair?'

'I didn't know. Plaster, crutches?'

'Ah, yeah, for a bit, then they whisk them off you and force you to walk around, even though each step hurts like a kick in the bollocks. But you know me, Liam, I have a powerful constitution. I rather think it is the curse of us both. So this is really the morning, hey? I don't know what time it feels like. Fancy a beer? A beer in the morning, God, this could be a book fair.'

When he mentioned book fairs, I bitterly wondered whether I had been to my last one, but I stopped myself from saying this out loud. I never let myself sound a negative note in Cockburn's company; we spoke only of the successes we were having. Consequently, after jumping in a cab and accelerating away in the direction of his hotel, we took unequal shares of the conversation.

'Now, Liam, *buddy*, you may be able to help me out with a small favour – but that's for later, wow, *look* at this place, man – it's been ten years since I was last here, the Buenos Aires book fair it must have been, I met this wonderful girl there, was it . . . Charlena? No, that sounds more like an Aussie – Charlotta? Yes, Charlotta. *Wow* . . . How are *you* finding the women here?'

'Well, I –'

'You don't want to talk about that, of course you don't want to talk about that. The favour I mentioned being – fuck me! – did you see that? – we nearly died! Anyway,' continued James, fully recovered, 'we're going out for dinner tonight, the author, his name is Daniel Requena, the guy can't speak any English, my Spanish is *muy rustico*, he's fallen out with the Argies who were going to publish him; those handballers are being no fucking use at all. I did my best to persuade Javi to come out with me but he claims he has to *work*, so – how *is* your Spanish? I noticed the nifty way you directed our taxi driver.'

'It's basic. I can direct taxis, order steak sandwiches and score cocaine.'

'Not a bad skill-set,' he mused. 'You may also be able to help me out with the second favour I was going to ask you . . . but first things first, are you good enough to translate for me over dinner?'

'I'm afraid not.'

'Ah.'

'If you showed up with me as an interpreter, I think he would find it hard to take you seriously. Of course, he may have a very rich sense of humour.'

'Well . . . naturally, we expect he will. But let's not risk it. You must know someone out here who'd help. Someone Daniel Requena will be impressed that I know. Someone fascinating.'

Of course, I thought immediately of Alejandro. There was symmetry in the betrayed friend meeting the wounded editor, Bennett's ghost (and Bolaño's?) floating above the filled ashtrays, envying the young hotshot, wishing we'd cool it with the cocaine and adjectives.

'I know someone,' I told Cockburn. 'The only thing is, I think he's hiding from me.'

Cockburn kept quiet for once while I told him the story of Craig Bennett's early twenties in Buenos Aires with his best friend Alejandro.

'Jesus, that's wonderful,' he said, when I'd finished. 'Heartbreaking!' he declared with a broad smile. 'What a story!' And then, like a politician, his face set and he reached for the sombre notes. 'I'm sorry we haven't spoken about Craig's death,' he said, reaching over and putting his hand on my shoulder. 'We will, mate, we will. I fucking miss him. No one blames you. Except Belinda. And the estate. But no one *really* blames you. I wonder if we could work on the estate; you might be in a brilliant position to write the biography . . .'

'The estate *hates* me? Who *is* the estate anyway?'

'Oh, some sister in Australia. From what Craig had told me they didn't see much of each other. They were separated when they were kids, Craig went with the dad, she went with the mum. He didn't have a girlfriend. His parents are dead. I guess there wasn't anyone else.'

'That's sad. And his sister hates me?'

'She's expressed certain sisterly anger towards the man who was supposed to be looking after him on the night he died.'

'And I suppose Belinda supplied her with her impression of me.'

'Well, Belinda wouldn't have mentioned the drugs and nor have I. But you admitted to the police that you were taking drugs with Craig, so she knows from them you were in it together. Like I say, it's understandable, and probably not irredeemable. You're a charming lad. Don't lose heart. We'll see what we can do.' He reached over and gave me a hug I didn't want. 'Come on, let's find this Alejandro!'

So I let things drop. James was excited. He could scent another book to hunt besides the one he was here to capture. And I wanted to be excited too. My old boss was back and we had some work to do.

I gave the driver new instructions and we drove through to Alejandro's bar. It was empty when we arrived. The polished wood, clean glasses and neatly aligned chairs shone with the optimism of an early-morning Eden. There was only a memory of beer beneath the pine air-freshener.

'Remind me what I drink here,' said Cockburn, squaring up to the bar and startling as the bartender rose from behind it like a lift reaching our floor. He scowled when he saw me.

'*Buen dia*,' I smiled. '*¿Vos ves Alejandro?*'

'*Lo vi hace dos semanas!*' he accused me. '*A causa de vos!*'

Cockburn liked this bit of aggression. 'What's he saying?' he said, raising his eyebrows.

'He thinks it's my fault Alejandro stopped coming here. I think he's basically right. I wouldn't be surprised if Alejandro was his best customer.'

The bartender was still talking.

'Tell him you think you're going back to England next week,' Cockburn suggested. 'Tell him you need to find Alejandro before you return. Tell him you'll let him know you won't bother him any more.'

I tried. The barman spoke fast Spargie in reply. I looked at James and shrugged.

'Tell him if he sees him to call this number,' said Cockburn, scribbling something down on a napkin before handing it to the bartender with a fifty-peso note.

Cockburn had never forgotten how to tell me to do

things and, haltingly, I asked the bartender to call us if he saw Alejandro. '*Por favor, dos cervezas,*' added Cockburn to my speech.

The bartender was more friendly now, though he needed another fifty before he parted with a list of other bars Alejandro was known to frequent. Unfortunately, he didn't know the name of the company where Alejandro worked so we were limited to this list. Cockburn wanted to try it straight away but I explained that Alejandro would still be at work.

'Did you see that?' he asked me as we took our beers outside to have them with a cigarette. 'That was like Philip Marlowe.'

'Felipe Marlowe. You know that's actual money you've just given him.'

He pulled out a note from his wallet and looked at it curiously. 'Doesn't look like actual money to me.'

It was now past midday and Cockburn had several hours until his dinner with the new Bolaño. I'd presumed we'd meet, have a quick catch-up over lunch and then he'd go to bed for the afternoon – but he didn't seem at all jetlagged. His energy was frightening. You looked at him and could almost see someone else beneath his skin, trying to get out.

After I told James about Aleman and his bar, he wanted to go there immediately and score – it was essential for his 'body-rhythms' that he did not sleep until late in the night. I flat-out refused to go so early. After coke there would be no real talk; just speechifying and mutual incomprehension. It would be easier to raise the harder topics and more futile when we did. Anything could go; anything would; and all would be forgotten, excused, as long as it wasn't permanent. I knew now that sometimes it was.

Even so, cocaine might have been useful for bringing the conversation back round to Craig. He deflected all my attempts to bring Craig up: Cockburn was the editor of this trip, this chapter-in-progress, keen to begin with a bang, in *media res*, straight to adventure before the boring bits, the backstory, my downfall. It was how he had encouraged me to approach my life, the old adage, 'show don't tell'. I understood it instinctively. It was easy, too easy. Action over reflection and the reflection takes care of itself. Not in my experience it didn't, not in time. The problem wasn't that I wasn't Hemingway but that now I knew I wasn't. The innocent days were finished. Craig died.

James continued to dominate the conversation, telling me plot after plot of the novels he'd recently acquired, laying down adjective after interchangeable adjective to describe their unique prose and saleability. I lost my cool and begged him to slow down, to tell me about the last three months, what he knew of the funeral, what people had said, what people were saying, about me, me, me, what had become of me.

James was embarrassed at my outburst. We were still sitting outside and he looked away from me to an office block as he lit another cigarette, a man and a woman in suits emerging for lunch, the moped courier who'd just parked dashing in through the open door. I had broken the rules. He had not wanted to think about my unhappiness.

'The funeral, well, I couldn't make it, I was still lying up in hospital,' he said formally. 'I was surprised to hear you weren't there.'

'Really? But I wasn't allowed to be. No one would tell me where it was!'

He looked even more uncomfortable. 'Don't be like that, Liam.'

'I don't want to be protected from what people think about me. Belinda told me not to go. I know what she thinks about me. What about everyone else?'

'Who is everyone else? The people who like you, like me, they still like you. The people who don't know you, they still don't know you.'

'I just want to know what I have to do to be forgiven.'

James pursed his lips like he was disappointed with me. 'You want acquittal, not forgiveness. You want your job back, you want your girlfriend back. Of course you do. You won't feel forgiven till you get a new job, a new girlfriend.'

'I want the old ones, not new ones.'

'Well, I certainly can't help you with Sarah.'

'What about with . . . ?'

He turned his profile to me and gazed into the distance. When he turned back to look at me I noticed new lines in his face. 'Liam, *you* resigned. If I could help, you know I would. My stock is not at its highest this year. A couple of big bets didn't pay off. My biggest-selling author is now dead and you are perceived as having had the power to prevent this. I am also perceived as responsible for this, as though you were my ambassador, my embodied bad practice. Well, yes. Nothing unusual, it all evens out. We'll have another Booker winner next year. But there was the thing about my office too, which pushed things with Belinda a bit too far.'

James had reacted badly when we had moved into the new open-plan office system that had been finished a month after I had started. I had been to his office to see him before I was his colleague, in the days when I was

178

'punching above my weight' as an editor at a small press. We'd met at a prize ceremony and he'd invited me for breakfast the next day. His office was like a spoiled teenager's bedroom: a battered leather sofa, ripped music posters, an expensive stereo, a small fridge for beers and champagne and a locked desk-drawer containing two wraps of cocaine and some excellent ecstasy tablets. It was Friday. At 10 a.m. we had had a beer and a line each while the industrious women outside (one of whom I would become) began their working day. Then we had headed out for a fried breakfast that lasted twenty-four hours.

When Belinda decreed James was to lose his office, he had passionately argued that the authors he brought to the firm needed his space to hang out in. 'Bring a different type of author to the firm, then,' she had finally warned him, 'or find a different type of firm. It's like this now.'

He had made a go of it. It was weird to see him sitting at a desk in the corner of a long room, sending emails, and then it was less weird because he was rarely there. He began to take all his author meetings in the pub round the corner, rather than just half of them.

It was in one of these meetings that he joked about sneaking in one weekend to rebuild his office. Jeremy Deller loved the idea and offered do it with a team of technicians, provided he could film it. That night, they waited till ten and went back to the office with a tape-measure. Two weeks later the logistics were entirely plausible, and all that was needed then was for James, in a fit of hysterical realism, to give in and see what the consequences were.

I had only been at work there for a couple of months when I arrived that Monday to find a gang of around thirty people staring at a perfect white hut enclosing the space where James' desk used to be. One of the walls was flush with the side of his nearest colleague's desk. People had been trying the lock but it wouldn't open and there was no sign of a key. The walls were smoothed off and painted the same white colour as the walls of the office. There was no sign of Cockburn. Belinda angrily sent everyone away but stayed herself, running her hands over the walls of the new structure and looking nonplussed. At eleven o'clock James walked briskly into work, turned a key in the lock of his office and shut the door behind him. When Belinda made him leave and accompany her to a meeting room, he left the door open. Inside was a meticulous reconstruction of his old office, the sofa, the posters, the old bookcases.

The story reached the trade press and then the nationals. James' aura increased and, as much as Belinda wanted to sack him, he was such a popular figure, such an extravagant self-publicist, it was easier just to discipline him. The marooned office remained for the rest of the week. James was not allowed to use it, but he had left the door unlocked, and for the rest of the week we took turns sneaking into it, lying on the sofa, reading manuscripts after-hours and taking beers out of the mini-fridge. The following Monday, it had disappeared again, and we didn't see Cockburn for the rest of that week either. Later, a film of the office being reconstructed appeared in a retrospective at the Hayward Gallery.

'It was probably the right thing for you to stay away from the funeral,' Cockburn concluded. 'There are some people, a publicist, a CEO, maybe one or two others, who think you really fucked up with Bennett. Well, you did, he's dead. You and I admit that. We know there was little you could do to stop Craig doing whatever he wanted, but you drew the short straw when he did his stupidest thing yet.'

I didn't believe it. 'I could have stopped him. We chose to believe he was as incorrigible as he pretended he was. Someone should have broken the chain. I was the one there, *I* should have.'

'You're too hard on yourself. People will respect your courage in admitting you had a part – if you have to admit it. There'll be other jobs. Everyone loves a resurrection story. You know what I think? You want your crime to be greater than it is so you can excuse yourself from redeeming yourself. Excuse yourself from the hard work of getting on with your life.'

I kept quiet. It was possible he was right about Bennett. And my mind leapt with delight to the possibility that perhaps I was being too hard on myself about Sarah too. That I deserved her back. How easy it would be to succumb to my old good opinion of myself. Why was I resisting?

With Cockburn sat beside me I had begun to feel the thrill and satisfaction of what I had used to do, what I had really done in the office from half-nine to eight o'clock every day, the hard work and not the cartoon hedonism. I knew Cockburn, if he took Fridays off, was putting in at least four long days Monday to Thursday, working through the weekend and reading every hour he wasn't drinking. The drinking was the work too, it was with the agents and celebrities who gave him access to the books we maintained that only he could make happen. I remembered the less dramatic way I had worked, the buzz of reading a manuscript late at night that was worth telling

181

people about. It didn't happen all the time but it still happened. There are writers left who understand Bolaño's words, that literature is a dangerous calling, and Cockburn was here with me hoping to find one of them. It was time to find out more about that.

Cockburn smiled when I asked him to tell me more, relieved to be back on safe ground. 'Liam, this is fascinating. Javi hasn't even spoken to him yet. Only his Argentine agent has met him, and I haven't even had direct contact with her. All I've got is a forwarded email from the sub-agent suggesting a restaurant to meet at this evening. And the manuscript. Javi says it's the best thing he's read for years. I haven't heard him this excited. The work-experience girl's done a rough translation of the first five pages for me . . . It's a bloody shame Craig's not around – he'd have read it for me. I've got the same feeling about it I had about *Talking to Pedro* before it won the Booker.'

'Does Belinda know you're out here on the strength of this feeling?'

'No.'

'Translated Argentine fiction doesn't sound very commercial.'

'There are more important things in life than that.'

'I hope Belinda hasn't heard you talking this way.'

I looked at James and tried not to interpret his idealism as crisis. Belinda wouldn't tolerate another outright rebellion. Why was he really here? What had driven him onto that plane? If this was another breaking point, I hoped his survivor's instinct would see him through it – he'd go home to his wife and baby and might last a year or two before he felt compelled to do something stupid. He might be lucky all his life. Someone had to be.

'And Ella, how is she really? How's the baby?'

He breathed out a sigh. 'Ella's great. Mandy's great. I nearly made such a mistake there.'

'Craig told me before he died.'

'God, I miss Craig. He talked me out of it, you know. I didn't want to listen at the time so I made that stupid climb round the wall. "He who makes a beast . . ." It makes me feel so guilty sometimes. If I hadn't been such a prick, if I hadn't fallen . . . Ella's perfect, you know. She lets me stay out late in the week when I have to, knows it's part of the job. That's the problem, I get in the mood when I think I don't want perfection. She lets me fly off to Argentina on a whim. You know this is a whim, don't you? Of course you do. Sometimes I get this feeling in me, like I'm going to do something awful just so I can observe myself doing it. Do you know?'

I did.

'So this came up and I knew you were here, and I thought this might be the lesser of two evils.'

'Is the other woman Craig mentioned the greater of the two?'

'No. That's over.'

'Good. Look at me. This is how you'll end up.'

'You don't look so bad.'

'I'm thirteen years younger than you. But I'm unemployed, perhaps unemployable. I've lost the woman whom I loved unrequitedly for five years before somehow, incredibly, I managed to make her love me. Now I'm terrified to leave this country that I hate living in because of how little is waiting for me at home.'

James fidgeted impatiently. He sighed. 'That sounds quite bad,' he admitted.

'Exactly. So control yourself. We're not invincible. We're just untested.'

It was approaching one o'clock now. The beers we'd drunk made the sun hazy and rhythmic, a psychedelic pulse in a Seventies film. James' idea of scoring cocaine was more and more tempting. It is always tempting to feel invincible.

'Let's go and try these places for Alejandro,' I suggested, to take my mind off the hunger. 'He's probably having lunch somewhere.'

We drained our beers and set off. James leaned over and put an arm round me briefly.

Chapter 17

We walked along the waterfront in Puerto Madero, searching for Alejandro. The waiters knew who he was in two of the restaurants we tried. We left our phone numbers with messages to say that we wanted him to have dinner with us and translate the conversation of a 'talented young author'. Cockburn tipped the waiters. (I had seen Cockburn tip a bus driver in the past.) All of this killed an hour, but soon we were having another drink. Cockburn was beginning to worry. If Alejandro didn't come through, the conversation with the new Bolaño might never take place. If Cockburn came back to the office without a book, he was going to have a lot of explaining to do. I had been thinking of Lizzie as we made the trawl round the cafés and bars, of how flawlessly she would have performed the role of vivacious translator. I knew Cockburn would adore her. *This is my great friend Lizzie; I've asked her to interpret tonight. Afterwards, perhaps we can go out dancing.* She would fit perfectly into the club of excellent people he used to sell membership to his own excellent club. And the more I thought of her the more I was not prepared to have her dislike me, not without doing all I could to make her my friend again.

I described Lizzie to Cockburn as we made our way to the language school, how funny and intelligent she was and how – well, she *was* – beautiful.

'Liam?' he asked, after a while. 'Despite what you said earlier, are you sure you're not beginning to get over Sarah?'

Of course I was in love with Lizzie – but it didn't help.

'I think I'm getting over Sarah every time a woman smiles at me,' I explained to him. 'And it lasts for perhaps thirty seconds before I shut my eyes and see Sarah looking at me, the way she used to look at me.'

'You fucking romantic.'

'Well, don't you fall in love with Lizzie too,' I warned him as we walked up the steps to the school.

We strode purposefully down the corridor to the classroom I'd seen Lizzie coming out of most frequently. She was there, behind the closed door. I could hear her slowly conjugating English verbs before they echoed in Latin accents. James and I sat down on the floor against the corridor walls. It made me think of waiting for Sarah to come out of her lecture, of her new lover and what they would be doing if they were together now . . .

'You know,' said Cockburn, 'there's nothing like a quest.'

I gave him a weary headshake, but I had been enjoying myself before too, so much it had left me uneasy. I couldn't carry on as I had been doing, pretending that writing an unreadable love letter and a penitential novel was a purpose in life. Something had to change.

We sat there waiting for fifteen minutes. Cockburn filled me in on the activities of my old colleagues and the new boyfriends and girlfriends they had commissioned. Six months ago I would have been very interested, but now . . . well, I wasn't naive enough to think it made me a deeper person that I'd lost interest in my fellow human beings. I should try harder. 'So, you didn't really answer me before,' I said. 'What's it like being a dad?'

He opened his mouth as if he was about to pitch, and I waited for a torrent of delightfuls and wonderfuls, but he shut it again and looked sad. 'I'd be able to give you a much better idea if I wasn't here in Argentina, wouldn't I?'

At that moment, the door opened and a series of office-smart young men and women began to file out. My stomach lurched. I stood up and almost collided with Lizzie in the doorway.

'You see,' said James, refilling Lizzie's glass, 'there hasn't been an internationally popular Argentine novelist for, well, for ever.'

We were in a café over the road from the language school. I was only half listening as he carried on but it sounded plausible. You had living literary superstars from Peru, Colombia, Mexico, Chile (with Bolaño, dead for years, still managing to publish a book a month), and the backpackers' favourite from Brazil, but no Argentines had really made a sales impact in English since Borges, and he wasn't a novelist. Cortázar had been lauded, Sabato too, but how many English-speaking readers really knew who they were? What was it these people withheld from English?

Lizzie's initial anger at being ambushed outside her room had turned to confusion as she made out James swaying behind me in his Cuban-heeled boots, 36-inch-long skinny denims, half-undone shirt and greying hair. I had pleaded passionately then for her to come and sit down and talk to us, to understand I had not meant to deceive her or cause problems with Arturo. My English sounded melodramatic, Argentine. She brushed aside my apology as if it was bad form. She was looking at James curiously, and so I introduced him and let him make his own speech, something about how highly I had praised her, how much he trusted my judgement, how little he now needed to due to the evidence of his own eyes and ears. (Cockburn's English, I realised, had always sounded Argentine.) He elaborated on the tremendous opportunity available that evening, the chance to speak to a prose-stylist of profound originality, to contribute to a mission which, if successful, would in some small way correct the philistine reading habits of the British reading public. Lizzie looked to me after hearing this, as if I would confirm whether or not it was a joke, and when I simply nodded, neither confirming nor denying, she agreed to have lunch with us and hear James out.

The waiter brought us our food and asked if we would like a second bottle of the Malbec. Of course we would.

'So what's this guy's name?' she asked.

'Daniel Requena.'

'Never heard of him.'

'He's not even published here yet. My friend Javi from Barcelona's just bought Spanish-language rights. The buzz about him is enormous, though.'

'What's he like?'

'As a person, no one knows. Even Javi hasn't spoken to him on the phone. I'll be the first European publisher to meet him face to face.'

This seemed to have less effect on Lizzie than James intended: 'Look, this is all very appealing and interesting, and I'd be happy to do my best. But I've made a promise to have dinner with my boyfriend this evening, and he gets upset enough when I do things without including him.'

'Oh, well, look,' said James, sounding slightly deflated. 'A boyfriend. I guess you can bring him too – why *don't* you? I mean, if you *want* him to come.'

Lizzie pulled out her phone and sent a text. And then my phone rang. This was still a rare enough occurrence for me to spend ten seconds returning other diners' smug disapproval before I realised the noise came from my own bag. My mum was the only person who rang regularly and, having been used to checking my phone every five minutes in England, where I had friends and purpose, I had accustomed myself to its new silence. But we had left this number alongside James in the places we had searched for Alejandro, and now an Argentine number was calling.

'*Hola, esta* Liam,' I said.

Alejandro's voice said something long and rolling, and when I could only um and er in response, he switched to English. 'I see your Spanish has not improved. So, Liam, what is the meaning of this elaborate trail you have left for me? You have realised by now that I do not enjoy remembering my old friend Craig Bennett. I will be very angry if this is a pretence for asking me more of your indelicate questions.'

'It is not a pre –'

'Who is this James Cockburn? Is he real? Is that a name, cock-burn? In my society it is the symptom of too pleasurable an evening.'

'He pretends it's pronounced Co-burn. He is real. He's sitting next to me, frowning. He was the-man-whom-we're-not-talking-about's editor. Would you like to talk to him?

189

'In a minute. And have you seen this beautiful young author?'

'I –'

'And by the way, I am not such a *tart* to accept an unusual assignment for the mere sight of a boy with talent, particularly when summoned by a crassly scribbled note on the back of a business card.'

'I –'

'I will come anyway. Will you present me with James Burningcock, please?'

I handed him over and James started up. 'Hel-*lo*, I'm so glad you *called*. Liam's told me all *about* you.' He stood and strode outside. He couldn't conduct a phone conversation except at a brisk walk. I was alone with Lizzie for the first time in weeks.

'Is he always like this?' she asked.

'Only in the company of people.'

She made a wan smile and looked at her plate. There was a sudden shyness to her I hadn't noticed before.

'Liam.' 'Lizzie.' We said each other's names simultaneously.

'You first,' I said first.

'Sarah wrote to me. She said you'd written to apologise to her. She said you wouldn't be the type to be indiscreet. She said your problem is the opposite, that you think too much about the effects of what you say. She stressed the word *say* as a direct opposite of *do*.'

She trailed her finger in a circle in the crumbs of her tostada and looked down into the swirl she'd made.

'I can't argue with that but can I tell you –'

'Shut up,' she said, looking up. 'I guess I should accept that if you let Arturo know about the business with Hernán it wasn't through carelessness.'

'I didn't let Arturo know anything. I tried to defend you from Hernán's attempts to make Arturo jealous. I just pointed out Hernán seemed very keen on you himself.'

'Which, if Sarah's right about how deliberately you think things through . . .'

'You think I wanted to cause trouble deliberately?'

'I don't know.'

'Sarah said that?'

'I wouldn't say that exactly. She said you're not malicious. Not on purpose.'

'I don't think I'm malicious even by accident, even if you can be malicious by accident. I'm straightforward, really. An idiot, yes, but straightforward.'

'You're not an idiot. You hide behind that. That's exactly the sort of self-deprecating non-straightforward statement I expected you would make. So why did you lie to us from the start about you and Sarah still being together?'

'It wasn't simple. I hoped it wasn't over. I didn't want to help make it over by announcing it to everyone. If I hadn't skipped over that, we might never have had a chance to be friends, never had a conversation, let alone an honest conversation. But we did talk honestly, didn't we? I love talking to you. You're the best person I've met here.'

Despite herself, she made a weak smile. 'You're not like me. I would have just told you. I would still have been your friend if you'd told me what had happened with Sarah.'

'No, I'm not like you. But I didn't know that then.'

She looked at me suspiciously. I was so weary of wearing the wrong costume.

'Please don't think I tried to screw you over,' I said. 'Why would I try to cause trouble for you and Arturo? What would be my reason? I love Sarah. Can't you tell?

I flew all the way to Brazil for a day just to see her. Please, Lizzie, let's be friends. We make *good* friends.'

'You know traditionally it's women who cry to manipulate men?'

I rubbed my eyes and looked directly at her. 'Forgive me,' I argentined with a hand on my heart, 'like a man forgiving a manipulative woman.'

People had begun to look over both curiously and approvingly at us. This was a good lunchtime scene. It might not be long before people started to offer us advice.

'Okay, okay,' Lizzie sighed, embarrassed, 'for God's sake, you're forgiven.'

I reached out and squeezed her hand. A woman at the next table beamed at me. James came striding back towards us. He sat down and took a swig of wine.

'Go all right?' I asked.

He finished his glass. 'Er, yeah. Friendly enough guy. I tried to tell him we didn't need him any more now we have the talented Lizzie at our disposal but he wouldn't listen and kept asking what time, what restaurant. Apparently, the food's magnificent, extremely expensive, and he will see us there at nine-thirty.'

'Great, my boyfriend's looking forward to it too,' said Lizzie, looking at her phone.

'I intend to bring no one but myself,' I declared.

'Good,' said James, looking ruffled.

Lizzie had classes after lunch so, at four o'clock, I was left on my own with James.

'You probably need a sleep?' I ventured.

'Very kind of you to concern yourself, Liam, but I'm

not going to desert you so soon after our reunion. How about we try your mate's bar?'

So it was that, after five hours in Achtung!, we made our way to one of the finest restaurants in Latin America without the slightest hope of eating there. We had recently done another large line of cocaine to 'sober us up' and when that had not made us sober we had smoked some luminous skunk with Aleman to 'tone down our chat'. These cures had pasted us to the back seat of a speeding taxi.

We looked at each other warily. 'We shouldn't really have done that to ourselves,' said James. 'Are we really in Argentina?'

'Probably not,' I replied.

The streets pulsed past like the beginning of a cinematic car chase. By the time the film had finished I hoped I might be able to speak properly again. The ride proceeded for a few moments in silence.

'Are you ready to offer your theories to the table about the lack of internationally famous Argentine novelists?' I asked James. It was a sentence that had taken me no more than six minutes to prepare.

'Oh, God.'

'And what you propose to do to change this?'

'Oh, God,' he said and scrambled to wind down the window and poke his head out. He held it there for five seconds while the driver addressed me with a stream of animated Spanish, then pulled it back in. 'That helped a bit,' he said.

'Really?' I asked.

'Optimism, Liam, optimism.'

When we pulled up, the taxi driver asked for a fare three or four times the going rate. James surprised him by doubling it and politely asking for a *recibo*. There was not a language in the world in which he did not know the word for a receipt.

We were standing outside a restaurant with windows that glowed with intense white light and made me think unpleasantly of an operating theatre. Lizzie and Arturo were standing in its doorway, lit up like angels taking a fag break. They looked at us and laughed.

'There are two of you!' Arturo called, coming forward to hug and kiss me. 'This will be fun!'

Over the last few weeks I had not thought much about our kiss in the alleyway. It belonged to a me I didn't really believe in. But seeing him there, black jeans, shirt and jacket, brown skin and dark hair, smarter than I'd ever seen him, autumn-eyed, clean-shaven, smirking with our shared secret – I had to turn away quickly to Lizzie.

Which did not reduce my desire. I wanted them both.

Chapter 18

D aniel Requena was (still is) a woman.

As I entered the restaurant, I staggered at the sight of the severed heads of mythical beasts that lined the walls. Recovering, I concentrated on walking in a straight line and maintaining the calm facial expression of a reformed criminal. James, always more ambitious, accelerated towards a corner table where Allen Ginsberg circa 1947 was sitting with a woman friend beneath a unicorn's head.

'*Hola, soy* James Cockburn!' James bellowed: the words we had practised earlier. The young man in horn-rimmed spectacles flinched. Some peas, or substance made wittily into the shape of peas, fled from his plate. I watched the peas-or-not-to-peas roll to the floor in slow motion. James shouted even louder: '*Encantado! ¿Eres Daniel Requena, no?*'

'No!' said wide-eyed Ginsberg and his startled girlfriend. The maître d' strode towards James as if he was about to rugby tackle him. Two tables along, a young woman began to laugh and stood up.

'James Cockburn! *Encantada! Soy* Dani Requena.'

As if his mistake had never happened, James strode towards her and bent to kiss her on each cheek. It was quite a bend because she was tiny, nearly two feet smaller than him, and he narrowly avoided headbutting her. She was maybe my age, with straight brown hair falling around her narrow shoulders and a slim face with neat features that made me think of girls from the home counties. She looked like a writer, or rather, she looked like a writing instrument, like a freshly sharpened pencil.

James gamely introduced Lizzie with the words she'd taught him earlier, '*Mi amiga y la intérprete*', before Lizzie took over in fluid Spanish and made her laugh immediately. I presumed they were laughing at James and me. After they'd embraced, Lizzie introduced Arturo, who had been waiting behind her, looking sideways at Dani through his fringe. Dani spent a couple of seconds taking him in before giving him the standard kiss hello. I was left to introduce myself. I gave her my name and when she continued to look at me expectantly I reached for words to describe my role that I didn't even possess in English. I settled on, '*Soy un editor muerto.*'

She raised her eyebrows, looked round at all of us, amused, and spoke to Lizzie.

Arturo translated before Lizzie had the chance. 'She says we need a bigger table.' The maître d' had been hovering, trying to size up which of these strange characters to deal with first. Arturo spoke to him immediately, and it seconds he was arguing and laughing with him. His personality was quicker and brighter in his own language, inaccessible to me. I could tell Lizzie was annoyed at being usurped in her role by Arturo. She made an attempt to join in the conversation with the maître d' but he continued to talk to Arturo and ignore her until we were led to a larger table at the back of the restaurant.

James took one head of the table and invited Dani and Lizzie to sit either side of him. Arturo chose to sit on the other side of Dani rather than next to Lizzie, leaving me to sit next to her, facing Arturo.

I began to think we might pull this off. The sudden change of company had shocked me from my introspection, and James' incredible self-belief was bulldozing its way through any of his own residual paranoia.

'*Supones soy el hombre*,' Dani said to James and he caught the meaning before Lizzie could translate.

'*Si*, I admit it,' he said. 'Everyone kept calling you the *new* Bolaño, not the *female* Bolaño. And the pages I've read seemed so . . . precise and cold and spare.'

Lizzie, looking grumpy, finally got to do some interpreting, though when I looked at Dani tilting her tiny chin up at James I had the feeling she had understood each of his words.

'Do you think only men are precise and cold and spare?' Lizzie asked James.

James and I looked at each other. We were the precise opposites: scattershot, febrile and superfluous.

'No, of course,' apologised James. 'There's probably no such thing as male or female style. But there is such a thing as male or female *nombres* and Daniel Requena is to me a *male nombre*.'

'Like George Eliot,' I suggested, glad to have something to contribute.

'No, not like that,' said Dani in English and then she spoke some rapid Spanish we could tell was politely refuting our suggestions. Already it seemed the Englishmen abroad were destined to play the idiots in this exchange.

'One,' translated Lizzie, 'it is not like that really, because Dani or even Daniel Requena is my real name, short for Daniela Requena, so I have not misled you; rather, you have misled yourselves. Two,' she paused dramatically, 'flattery will get you everywhere.'

We all laughed and Dani smiled at us tolerantly. She seemed to have some sympathy for comic characters, if that's what we were. It was a change from the role of the villain I had been getting used to. So I sat quietly and did my best to sober up. Sin, guilt and repentance: it was some sort of structure for a life. Instead of disappearing to the toilet, I watched James, Lizzie and Arturo fight for Dani's attention. Alejandro had not arrived and I felt like an interloper at a double-date. Whenever Arturo succeeded in distracting Dani from James, Lizzie and James took their revenge by flirting heartily with each other until Arturo was forced to bring them back into the conversation and revert to English. The spotlights shining on the mounted unicorn heads above us made them glow white as bone. I stared at them until eventually, exhausted, I slipped out for a cigarette on my own.

Dani arrived, just as I was stubbing mine out. 'Hello,' she said, pulling a cigarette out of her bag.

'*Señorita*,' I said. My anxiousness at speaking Spanish often led to this type of Tourette's.

She giggled.

'I mean, hello,' I said, smiling back. '*Hablo solo un poquito Castellano*.'

'*Tengo una confesion*.'

'*¿Una? Tengo muchas confesiones*.'

'Your accent is cute,' she said. 'I appreciate the effort.'

'Well, it certainly is effortful. Thank you.' For a moment

I felt very proud of how my Spanish was progressing until I realised we had switched to English.

'Well, of course, I speak English,' she said.

'Yes, I can see that now. Is that your *confesion*?'

'I do not realise how good I can speak English until I hear your Spanish.'

'*Gracias*. I'm glad I came in useful for something. So, why go through all that interpreting?'

'Oh, I thought it might be interesting. To have distance. I was not sure I wanted to meet James. Being private is working well for me. I didn't want to ruin things.'

She'd understood perfectly how to intrigue a publisher like Cockburn. Agents are so keen to tell you about their authors' physical blessings, their advantageous networks and starring roles in incredible personal melodramas, that to be refused any information at all is suspense of the highest order. James was not such a sophisticated reader as to refuse the pleasure of seeking the great revelation, and I could see how he was now delighted with the current twist. The story of his meeting with her in itself was valuable for him even if he failed to buy the rights to her book.

Dani went on: 'But in the end I became too curious. I wanted to meet this character James Cockburn my agent makes sound like Jim Morrison. My agent exaggerates. It is more easy to have a mystery through a translator, to have a distance. That is also why I wanted to meet the English first, because you *always* need a translator with the English. And perhaps I worried that *distinguished English publishers* would speak English so well I would be confused.'

'*¿A que hora llegan los distinguido Ingléses publishers?*'

She looked at an imaginary watch. 'They're supposed to be here now.'

'I'm surprised you've managed to get away from one of them.'

'Yes, I had to pretend I go to the toilet.'

I finished my second cigarette and stubbed it out. 'You're interesting,' I said.

'You're interesting too,' she said. '"*Editor muerto*".'

'That's only half of it. What's Castellano for "murderer"?'

'*El asesino o la asesina.*'

'*Soy el editor asesino.*'

'You guys have read too much Bolaño. You need to lighten up.'

I laughed or I would have liked to. She picked a bad night to offer me this advice. The wind was beginning to pick up, there was a chill in the air, the coldest I'd felt since being in Buenos Aires. I shivered.

'Don't you want to tell me who you murdered?' she asked.

'If I have to. Do you know Craig Bennett?'

She nodded. 'Of course.'

'I was with him when he died, it was partly my fault. I murdered my career that night, whatever happened. I murdered myself. Now I'm stuck here in purgatory.'

'I don't believe you're a murderer. And please, as if Bolaño wasn't enough, now you're going to do Dante?'

I felt suddenly as if I was choking on the dust of all the unread books I had left in boxes in my aunt's basement. 'Oh, God, books, let's not talk about books, I'm so sick of books.'

'What should we talk about?'

'We could always try . . . not talking at *all*.'

My reflex attempt at flirtation surprised me, as much as it was in keeping with my normal behaviour, my mid-binge leaps for transcendence. I slowed my voice and held eye-contact with her. She was about my age but her green eyes examined me from years away, and her laugh, when it arrived soon afterwards, was kind but not entirely unhurtful.

It was then that the taxi pulled up and Alejandro leapt out with a shout and came towards us. 'My young friend, hello!'

He looked suave in a black suit and white shirt. He kissed my cheek and turned to Dani. He had never greeted me with such affection before. '*Buenos noches*,' he said, offering her his hand and looking to me for an introduction.

'This is my new friend *Daniel* Requena, the novelist I mentioned who is about to set fire to the Argentine literary world. Dani, this is my friend Alejandro, friend of writers, muse, entertainer, bon vivant. We had asked him to join us to interpret for you before Lizzie accepted – and before you revealed to me just now that you can speak English very well.'

'You are *not* the gorgeous young man?' Alejandro asked Dani.

'I suspect I am. I understand why you thought I was a man,' she said, turning to me. 'But how did you know I was gorgeous?'

'A lucky guess,' I said, and then she began to talk too quickly to Alejandro for me to understand.

Back inside the restaurant it was time to order. I had gone without cocaine for two hours now but any preference for food was still purely abstract. What type of food *would* a food-eating human prefer? James seemed back to his perkiest but was mainly engaged with the wine list. It appeared Dionysius had already drunk the greatest share of two bottles. There was talk around me of suckling pig, of octopus, rabbit in white wine, unicorn fillet served with figs and soaked in cognac, the thigh of a centaur, slow-roasted with lemon and thyme, salt and pepper gorgon hair, dragon tail and fennel risotto. In the end, with help from Alejandro – 'What is the best small meal for a man recovering from a daytime cocaine binge?' 'You look pale, my friend, you need some red meat in you.' – I ordered the only steak on the menu, bloody, expensive.

Alejandro was making a useful impact on the table, helping to diffuse the resentment brewing between Cockburn and Arturo, between Arturo and Lizzie. He poured water on Arturo's jealously by showing him a fascinated attention while simultaneously shunning Cockburn. Cockburn was trying to court Alejandro, perhaps thinking of the important role he could play to Bennett's biographer. His tactic to win Alejandro over was to talk without interruption about his, James Cockburn's, lead role in Craig Bennett's history, in long, excitable sentences which confirmed my suspicion that he would not be eating his dinner.

'Liam,' Alejandro asked me, pretending not to hear another of Cockburn's questions, 'why did you not bring Arturo to the bar when you came to annoy me? Then I would have been much happier to be annoyed by you.'

Arturo was not the sort to refuse flattery from man or woman. He sat back, amused, enjoying James' rejection and talking to Alejandro in quick bursts of Spanish which he would, with his instinctual good manners, alternate occasionally with slower English to keep me in the conversation.

I was grateful for that. As I receded from the conversation, I was happy just to watch his face. I could see no sign that he was the man who had kissed me in the alleyway, and I found this an enormous relief. There was at least one other man at this table who played the roles he chose to, and he had done me the kindness of letting me, and perhaps me alone, see this. I smiled at him and watched him almost imperceptibly purse his lips at me before he resumed speaking to Dani, having spotted Lizzie laughing at one of Cockburn's jokes.

At the other side of the table Dani was contributing more and more in English but still seemed to enjoy having Lizzie translate to James for her. From the way they smirked at each other I suspected they were conducting a private conversation about James.

As the evening wore on, all of the flirting in which I was hardly involved made me feel alone. If I would only take my medicine I could happily impose myself on others and not notice I was unwelcome. But I was determined to eat some of my dinner and to look the waiter in the face when he came to collect my plate, determined for once to behave with some manners. Cockburn too had begun to flag and fall out of the conversation, and as he took time to breathe the conversation switched to Spanish between the rest of the table. Cockburn's eyes met mine and travelled to the other two men at the table. Alejandro had his hand on Arturo's arm and was leaning in to tell him a story close to his ear that was making Arturo laugh steadily, economically, as though to preserve his energy for what was to come. It wasn't just Arturo who was attractive: some girls would certainly have preferred Alejandro, who, though fifteen years older, with his well trimmed and silver flecked beard, presented a more classically masculine picture of beauty.

James and I, pasty-faced, red-eyed, with droopy hair and dishevelled faces, were not obviously well-matched opponents with the Argentines. But, as usual, if they had the skill, beauty, underhand tricks, we Brits would hope to win the day through sheer doggedness. James raised a non-existent cigarette to his lips and we left the table for a team-talk outside the restaurant.

'Not very friendly this Alejandro, is he?' said James.

'I don't think he likes *you*,' I said.

James spread his arms with the mystified innocence of an Argentine defender receiving a yellow card.

'You're going on about Bennett too much. I told you he's touchy about him. Every question you think you're asking him is prefaced by such a long anecdote about one of the classic adventures of Cockburn and Bennett that it's a direct challenge for Alejandro to prove his stories are as good as yours. He's not interested in competing.'

'Oh, well, thank you for reassuring me.'

'I worry about you in that office without having me around to offer advice.'

'I really wouldn't worry on that count, Liam: there's no shortage of people left who are happy to point out my shortcomings.'

'How many more lines have you had?'

'None! Well, one. And to be frank, I need another.'

'No one *likes* Frank. At least wait until after dinner.'

'Dinner. How unedifying.'

We went back in and James tried once again. 'So, Alejandro, Liam tells me you and Craig used to get up to all sorts of trouble.'

'Well, we were friends and we were young and brave and stupid,' he said and turned back to Arturo.

'Well, go on, please tell us a story,' James persisted.

'I am afraid,' said Alejandro, 'that it was always Craig who told the best stories, certainly in public. I am shy, you see.' He turned again to Arturo and said. 'I need more intimacy to tell mine.'

'Oh, *please*,' said James, and Lizzie and Dani joined in to ask Alejandro to tell us more.

'Yes, tell us a story,' said Arturo.

Alejandro swatted an invisible fly. 'Must I? It really was the usual shit. Heroin, cocaine, fraud, extortion. Young boys' games.'

'Oh, come *on*.'

'I do not know how to tell it without cliché. Liam? Perhaps you have found a way?'

Everyone looked at me.

'Has he not told you, Cockblock, that he is researching the life of Craig Bennett in Buenos Aires and writing a novel about him? I have watched him writing it next to me at the bar. You write quickly, Liam. I have read it over your shoulder. There are some sentences I quite enjoyed.'

Cockburn had sobered up suddenly and was looking at me. Dani had become more alert too.

'How do you do it, Liam?' Alejandro continued. 'How should I tell our story? Any tips?'

I mumbled something glib about avoiding sex scenes and lyrical descriptions of taking ecstasy.

'That doesn't leave us with much,' said Alejandro.

Dani spoke and Lizzie translated: 'You never tell a story about someone else, only yourself.'

'What about biographies?' asked Cockburn. 'Don't you believe in them?'

'I believe in their *existence*,' said Dani through Lizzie. 'I have seen them in the biography sections.' She looked up at the unicorns on the wall. 'They are not mythical creatures.'

'Homosexuals,' said Alejandro.

'Pardon?' James asked.

'It's something we started at school. No women around then. It's what wrecked the friendship in the end. I didn't have as much trouble believing in it as a category of existence as he did.'

'He never did settle down for long,' mused James. 'But it was always Amy he talked about.'

'Amy's a friend of mine,' I said. 'He was talking about Amy on the night he died.'

'You never write about someone else, only yourself,' said Dani, this time in English.

'Oh, I know *Amy*,' said Alejandro. 'I am sure you will want to tell it like he did,' he said, looking at me sadly.

The starters arrived – not for James or me – and I appreciated their quality as abstractly as I would that of a well-made violin bow.

Alejandro and Arturo went out and came back giggly and red-eyed from a cigarette break. Dani was increasingly having to interrupt James in English as she realised interrupting was the only tactic available to take part in a dialogue with him. Lizzie, however, was still contributing clarifications and explanations in English and Spanish, and I began to feel jealous. As James got into his flow, selling the imprint, his ambitions for the book, for her, for the future of modern letters, Lizzie, with her pithy summaries and asides, came across as his new, improved, more-talented lieutenant. While I knew this was only for tonight, I knew too that there was someone in London just like her, my real usurper.

Even surrounded by friends, I experienced the usual Buenos Aires loneliness, the unbelonging, the fear of waiters. As I watched Alejandro and Arturo giggle like children under the skulls of legendary beasts, I felt as if it was me who had just smoked a spliff.

I could have done some coke, one can always do some coke, and that's exactly why I didn't.

Instead, I slipped out of my seat, out of the restaurant and round the corner onto the busy main road. Here I found a quiet neighbourhood bar, bought a beer, found the darkest corner and called my father.

I woke him up. I heard murmurs from a woman in the background before he promised to ring me back in five minutes. He had mentioned a new girlfriend before. In the minutes while I waited for him to ring me back, the bar's darkness began to oppress me and I walked outside to the street again. I leant back against a wall and looked out at the traffic flying past, so far from the woman I loved, and I tried to imagine the insensible vastness of so many other roads, so many versions of myself in every country staring at cars rushing past and seeking something other than fragments of their reflection in electric windows. I wanted home and I did not know where it was. Then Dad rang back.

'Liam, how are you?' he asked. 'It's nice to hear from you, even if it is so late.' He sighed the type of bone-weary sigh he had sighed on the phone shortly before and after he had disappeared for three years.

It was easier to forgive a sigh like that now. I hoped it wasn't how I had sounded to Sarah in the weeks before I left England.

'Are you all right, Dad?' I asked.

As usual, he began to tell me about his work. After he had crashed out of teaching, he had become a freelance copy-editor, and now we were in the same industry he was always keen to talk shop. As I listened about his deadlines for Sandra and Jonathan and the problems with Indian typesetters I found myself patting my pockets for a cigarette despite already having a lit one in my hand. Dad had become old without the support system, without the almost-paid-off mortgage, the wife, the salary. What could be passed off as light comedy for a younger man was dark and threatening to him. I see now he was looking to me for reassurance, for tips I could never give. But all his talk of money reminded me of my own dwindling resources and I couldn't help interrupting him.

'Can we talk about something else, Dad?'

'I'm sorry, Liam,' he said, sounding hurt. 'What?'

'It's not that I'm not interested,' I lied. 'It's just I rang because I really needed someone to talk to and I haven't done any talking yet.'

'Well, talk.'

'Um . . .'

'Where are you right now, for instance?'

'I'm walking up and down a street outside a bar. It's about half-ten. Round the corner is a fancy restaurant I ran away from twenty minutes ago. I was having dinner with my old colleague James Co –'

'I saw him on the telly last night discussing the future of the book.'

'Really?' I was disappointed but not surprised. He loved being on TV. 'How boring of him. Anyway, I was having dinner with him and the new Bolaño –'

'The new Bolaño! What's he like?'

'*She*. You sexist. *She*'s all right.'

Dad chuckled. He had a good chuckle, stronger, more plausible than his sigh. He should have sounded like this a lot more. It was easy to make him laugh. He liked my stories, about my friends, about women I met, and especially about publishing. He envied me for getting to meet novelists while he got to email academics. He would have liked me to spend more time telling him stories about them so he could relay them to his friends from the pub. We had a good time together in the pub. He wanted to be proud of me. We put on a show for each other. His friends would keep congratulating us on how close we were to each other.

'You sound like you're having fun out there.'

'I'm losing my mind, Dad, that's what I'm trying to say. I'm not joking. I'm losing it this very minute. I've got no one to talk to. Everyone's young and annoying or incomprehensibly Argentine. I miss Sarah. God, I miss Sarah.'

'I'm sorry, Liam.'

'Oh, I'm all right really.'

'I bet you tell yourself that a lot.'

'All the time. Always with a manly swig of a drink or pull on a cigarette.'

'Ah, *cigarettes*. I've had to give up smoking.'

He'd been giving up for years, it was almost his hobby.

'I just can't seem to get my blood pressure down,' he continued. 'The doctor says I need to do more exercise, but when I do . . .' Dad's voice was tired out. He hadn't meant to cause all the pain he had. He just hadn't thought hard enough. My heart went out to him. I didn't mean it to, but it did. I wanted to tell him I understood. Subtract at least that from your sadness. You are forgiven.

'I don't do much exercise here, either,' I said.

'I've been getting DVDs, magazines, *Men's Health*, I've even started running. I can't do it. It's shown me how knackered I am. Really, Liam, I am.'

'Perhaps you just need to try to accept you're slowing down. Tell me, is there any point after thirty when you stop comparing how knackered you are with how much less knackered you used to be?'

'Is there? Let me think. Certainly not after thirty-five. No. No, there isn't. It gets worse and worse.'

'I thought it might.'

He laughed again. 'Don't tell me *you're* worried about how old you are.'

'Sometimes. But no, not really. I'm more worried about how young I am and what I'm going to do for the rest of my life now I've fucked up everything that mattered to me.'

I had tried to say that lightly. The line went quiet for a few seconds and then Dad spoke. 'I don't think that hurts less when you get older.'

I shivered. It was getting colder. I took a deep breath, threw down my cigarette and asked the question I had given up asking him years ago.

'Dad? When you went missing, where were you, what did you do? All those years, what were you thinking about?'

There was a long pause, a sigh I could draw by now. 'I'm sorry, Liam,' he said eventually. 'I will. We need to talk. I'd like to talk actually. It might be good for us both. Not like this, though. Face to face. When are you coming home?'

I had not been greatly missed in my absence. Most people had finished their food, except for Cockburn. Lizzie and Dani were giggling as they bullied him into taking mouthfuls of octopus or perhaps kraken that he was doing his best to avoid. Arturo and Alejandro were watching them and laughing. A severed human heart lay on my plate, leaking blood. My stomach amazed me with a carnivorous lurch. I cut a piece off and chewed it, reached for a bottle of red and filled my glass rim-full.

I remember heading next to Mundo Bizarro . . . an argument, a drink being thrown . . . by a girl? At Arturo? Or was it Lizzie? A pill placed in my palm. El Coronel shouting. A punch aimed at James. *Las Malvinas son Argentinas!* We left. Lizzie and James in a taxi. Where was Arturo?

I was lying in a corner of a nightclub. *Porteños* were pointing at me and laughing. I staggered to my feet and checked my pockets. There were two packets of crushed cigarettes but I no longer seemed to own a wallet. I found my phone and saw someone else's smashing against a wall, shiny innards glinting against the streetlamp. It was 3.45 a.m. now and I had seventeen missed calls.

In the bathroom mirror I checked my face. My lips were covered in black filth, but when I washed this off I was semi-presentable. With enough cigarettes and gin-and-tonics and hardboiled irony I hoped I could lose the permanent seen-a-ghost expression of the ecstasy overdosee. Incredibly, as I dug my fingers in the ticket pocket of my jeans, I found a small plastic bag that probably contained coke. There was a wedge of notes I had folded up and squashed in there too. They'd both help. I splashed more water on my face, smiled at the guy next to me and left.

I was at least two drinks below normal. Once I had headed to the bar to make a start on the gin-and-tonics, I began to look around me. I didn't recognise the club, but in other, less disorientating circumstances I would have loved it. Heavy, Freudian house music played and blurred into the dry-ice and hot bodies dancing. The room I was in was dark, narrow and low-ceilinged, and seemed to stretch forever into the distance. Mirrors on each side of the wall drew all the dancers who had ever lived in a procession towards the centre of the earth. It was a club as Borges would have described it in one of his interminable stories. It was likely I would be here for all eternity.

Such thoughts, at first a relief, began to oppress me, and I headed through the endless dance floor in search of my friends. I hoped I still had them. I had a feeling bad things had happened. The E – yes, it was certainly an E I could feel, and there was an awful suspicion that I had had two – made me forget my predicament in short flashes, and I found myself grinning at the boys and girls I passed.

And, eventually, above me, unmistakably, was James Cockburn, shirt undone to the navel, dancing on giant speakers in the middle of the antechamber I had reached after several miles of dance floor. I watched him turn to hug the gleaming man in a pink musclevest beside him, and then he caught sight of me and held his arms aloft before stepping down from the speakers and mingling me in his damp embrace.

'Where've you been?' he shouted. 'This place is incredible!'

'I'm not dead, am I?' I shouted back. 'This isn't actually the afterlife?'

'No, mate,' he shouted. 'Afterlife's in Rio, I think. We're in Library of Babel!'

This didn't seem strange then. 'Where's everyone else?'

'There's only you and me and Lizzie! We thought you'd left. Where've you been?'

'Unconscious, on the floor.'

'Nice one!'

'Not really, no.'

212

The crossfader switched and a piano riff of simple, yearning optimism dropped into the room like the news in the midst of a natural disaster that your loved ones had survived. It took my breath away. We stopped talking and hugged and danced and the happiness I felt brought tears to my eyes. I wished Sarah was there so I could communicate my soul to her in the same joyful chords I would not remember tomorrow. It was at this point Lizzie arrived with a new girlfriend, a small brunette with a mod fringe and panda-eye make-up. I watched them dancing closer and closer, slowing down, gazing into each other's eyes, and then . . . and then . . . and then they were kissing, and James and I didn't dare move, and then we were all kissing, back and forward, the softness of Panda-eyes' lips and open mouth a surrender, the muscularity of Lizzie's tongue a carefully-controlled tour, the soaked sharp stubble of James an unpleasant joke we quickly laughed off. This was what I loved about ecstasy and as close as you could get to the emotion artificially. We had a kiss to remember when we were coming down. It was how the past could redeem the future. Or doom it.

We were still there at six. I'd given everyone another half E by then (I had found three in a back pocket). Lizzie had tried to tell me about the big argument she'd had with Arturo that I couldn't remember – apparently he'd punched me after I stuck up for her in the middle of an argument they were having. I had struggled to hear her over the music. Arturo had taken Dani and Alejandro to another bar. It was just after he'd left that she'd thrown her phone against a wall in anger. 'If he wants me to cheat on him, he's made me feel completely up for it,' she shouted. Cockburn moved in and put his arms round her waist. She pushed him away and kissed Panda-eyes again. Cockburn put his arms around both of them.

Later, when I was in a cubicle with Cockburn, my phone rang again and I realised it was Arturo, that he must have been trying to reach Lizzie on my phone for the last couple of hours. That, or apologise to me. That, or threaten me. 'Shall I answer it?' I asked.

'What do you think he's going to say to her if he finds out she's in a club doing ecstasy with both of us?' asked Cockburn, digging around in the wrap with his key.

I didn't answer that. We silently watched the phone until it stopped ringing.

'Quick, turn it off,' said Cockburn.

I did. We each inhaled a quick keyload of coke and unlocked the door.

'I can't believe I'm in Buenos Aires, in Library of Babel, having just kissed two beautiful bisexual women,' said Cockburn, looking in the mirror.

'They're no more bisexual than we are. It's not real, it's a dream. That's just how people on ecstasy shake hands. We understand; others won't. So don't do anything else. Ella's at home.'

'Thank you, Liam,' he said, suddenly thoughtful. 'You're right. Always looking after me.' Then his face broke into a broad, excited grin. 'Shall we go and find the girls again?'

It was dawn when we returned to James' hotel, seeking his mini-bar. Our friend Panda-eyes was gone, frightened away by what in re-telling this story I will describe as Cockburn's wandering hands; we hugged her goodbye and lamented her loss and would remember her for ever as perfect. James' jetlag had finally caught up with him: the drugs weren't working on him at all as we left the taxi. He was slurring something about having left his coat in the garden of forking

214

paths as Lizzie and I propped him up and marched him across an enormous shiny foyer to the lift. The receptionists brightly called out to us in English, 'Good morning!' Perhaps the speakers in the foyer were broken; there was no electronic tango music playing. Once in his room, James collapsed on his bed immediately, and Lizzie helped him out of his jacket and shoes and tucked him up. It was important to keep moving at a time like this: we had had a wonderful time and perhaps it was worth it but there were many frightening consequences to face if we allowed ourselves to, not least this crisply cold dawning morning. 'Have you got anything left?' asked Lizzie. There was a tiny bit of coke left and a whole pill we didn't dare wait to digest. We crushed it down and did the business. It was a big, spacious white room. That helped. Our noses stung horribly. We took a beer out onto the balcony and lay on the deck, watching the sun bleed through the night. The drug kicked in and made us feel incredibly nice again. We talked and talked. The air was chilly. I brought a duvet out and we lay under it, smoking fags, passing the beer back and forth between us, explaining to each other everything we had ever done or dreamed. The ecstasy magnetised our bodies, her legs across mine, my arm around her waist, her head on my shoulder. At one point I couldn't resist kissing her again. It only lasted a few seconds and didn't mean anything, but it felt wonderful. 'That wasn't romantic,' she warned me, and I lay back with the new sun shining in my face and laughed. I was so happy.

I was alone when I woke up. For a few moments I didn't know what I was, let alone who I was or where I was. The distant noise of traffic said this was a world where cars existed. The concept of what a car was – *just*. Turning onto my side, I found a note under an unopened can of Quilmes, scribbled in biro on what looked like a page torn out of my notebook. My satchel was open nearby, but when I looked inside it my notebook wasn't there. This was a worry too awful to contemplate and so I pulled the note from beneath the beer, hoping for some instructions. *Your name is Don Martinez. You do not remember anything. Not even about your wife, who is in grave danger. You must find her. Now, go to the bathroom.*

No, it was not as useful as this.

Dear Liam (and James)
You fell asleep. Now I've started worrying and won't be able to rest. I'm going back to face the music with Arturo. It will be easier now than later. Thank you for a very lovely evening.
Lizzie xxx

After I had read the note, in a gesture that was all to do with the coping mechanisms of style and little with desire, I opened the can of beer and took a swig. It was wet, I can say that for it.

'Bravo!' called James from the bedroom. He appeared out on the balcony in a clean shirt, wet hair and sunglasses.

'What on earth do you look so pleased about?' I asked.

'You may well ask,' he said, raising his clenched fists to his shoulders and gyrating his hips in a sickening motion as if he were hula-hooping.

'Stop that,' I croaked.

He complied but pulled out his BlackBerry and brandished it at me. 'Email from Daniel's agent, expressing her client's desire to sign a contract with us. Job *done*.'

He put his phone back in his pocket and began to stretch his right arm behind his neck and over his left shoulder, repeating again the other way.

'She probably wants to write you *into* a novel,' I said.

'And so she should.'

'As a sort of grotesque Dickensian caricature.'

'Now, Liam,' he said, stopping stretching and returning inside the room, 'that's hurtful. I'm going to order us breakfast from room service, and then we can start.'

'Thanks,' I said. 'Start what?'

He didn't answer and I heard him back up the phone and order two *desayunos Inglés*, coffee and orange juice.

When he came back onto the balcony he was holding the notebook I had recently finished my novel in. He flourished it at me like a red card.

'You know, I think this could make everyone a *lot* of money,' he said. 'And what's best, in a way Craig would have just *loved*. A fitting tribute, if you will.'

'You read it?'

'I loved it. Well done, Liam: it's really very fucking good.'

'You mean it?'

'Yes, I mean it.'

I felt my hangover lifting.

'Do you think you might want to, er . . .'

'Of course I want to publish it. There's just one big stumbling block,' James went on, 'but I know just how to get over it.'

And then he told me his plan.

Chapter 19

Editor's introduction to *My Biggest Lie* by Craig Bennett (October 2009, Eliot, Quinn)

The night when Craig Bennett won the Man Booker Prize in 2000 exceeded my wildest dreams. Not only was it the first time that a novel I commissioned won the prize; but it was won by a writer who had become my best friend. It was an achievement beyond any expectations for a debut writer whose talents nevertheless truly deserved it.

Bennett's life was something of a boomerang (cultural stereotyping intended): flung from the UK to Australia as a young boy; continuing to spin onwards in his twenties to Latin America (a place that would be enormously important to his writing); before returning back to the UK and the success of first publication, at which point his profile, and the myth of his 'bad behaviour', spiralled out of control.

Bennett was born in Sydney after his parents emigrated from Yorkshire. He was the son of Ralph and Maureen. He lived with them and his sister until his mother left his father for another man. Craig alone continued to live with his father, who gave up his engineering job and moved them to the country, having bought a partnership in a vineyard in New South Wales.

Ralph Bennett is portrayed in Bennett's memoir *Juice* (2008) as a domineering, unpredictable character, capable of great charm and compassion, but also of bleak depression, violence and mania. Ralph never forgave his wife for the affair that ended their marriage and so Craig saw very little of her and his sister. Instead, he was 'home-schooled' on the grounds of the vineyard his father was (only at times successfully) preoccupied with. Craig taught himself to drive at twelve, the same young age at which he describes beginning to drink wine regularly. The rhapsodic freedom he felt at that age – so different to most young people's – is I think the key to understanding his work.

At thirteen the authorities caught up with him and he was sent to boarding school, where he was expelled in his second month, but the next attempt to educate him met with more success and he remained at Victoria Boys School for the next four years, alternating his holidays with his father at the vineyard and his mother in Sydney. It was here he met Alejandro Montenegro, who would be a close friend of Craig's for many years. It is Montenegro who has unearthed this previously unseen 'first novel' of Bennett's.

Montenegro's family was from Buenos Aires, and after finishing school Alejandro and Craig moved together there. Bennett was to spend many years in Argentina and briefly worked in the film industry. After the success of his debut novel, his circle completed as he moved back permanently to the UK, settling on the Welsh coast. It is of great sadness to everyone that at this calmest period of his life he should die of a heart attack during the London Book Fair.

This novel, *My Biggest Lie*, was written in the mid-1990s, shortly before *Talking to Pedro*. The typewritten manuscript was long believed lost and Bennett was trying to reconstruct the novel from memory when he died. Ostensibly an autobiographical novel based on Bennett's first years in Buenos Aires, *My Biggest Lie* explores prevailing themes in his work: the relationship between autobiography and fiction, between person and persona, between truth and lies. The hunt for other 'new' manuscripts continues.

Chapter 20

I wanted to go home but now I was trapped in Buenos Aires. I had work to do.

Seen from the outside, I may not have appeared to be a man in captivity. I had left my monk's cell to move into a pleasant one-bedroom apartment in Belgrano sublet by the colleague of Lizzie's who'd gone travelling for three months. After all the moaning I had subjected her to about the hostel, I should have bounced out the door. But I felt sad saying farewell to another familiar place, handing my key back to the same miserable man who had checked me in on the first day.

'You've been with us a while, ché,' he said mournfully. 'Where are you going?'

In the background melancholic accordion filtered like a melodica through a dub beat. It was a suicide-inducing sound.

'I'm renting an apartment in Belgrano,' I said. 'Listen, do you like this music?'

He looked up. 'Me, I like rock and roll. The Stones. Springsteen.' I hadn't seen him this enthusiastic before.

'The boss – not Bruce, my boss – he makes us play this. For the atmosphere. The guests, *you* like it.' He was slowing down again now. 'Argentine, but contemporary. We have some CDs for sale if you like,' he said, reaching for drawer beneath him.

'No, no, please, *gracias*.'

He handed me my deposit and before I left I put *El Diego* back in the shelves. No one had taken up my old copy of *Labyrinths*, and so I returned this to my suitcase. Outside the taxi beeped its horn.

Cockburn had arranged for Eliot, Quinn to pick up the bill for my new apartment: expenses for my short-term contract as 'on-site project editor'. To the strangers I met in bars now I could tell a story of why I was in Buenos Aires that implied no shame, no crisis, no breakdown. In searching to reverse loss I had found not love but profit. Lying had got me into this and now lying would get me out.

James' arrival back in the UK made national headlines. Not only had he signed Dani Requena, the 'new Borges' (our night dancing in the Library of Babel had strongly affected Cockburn), but – sensationally – he had tracked down a never-been-seen lost novel from recently deceased Booker Prize-winner Craig Bennett.

I read out loud to Alejandro from the *Guardian*'s website:

'It was an unbelievable find,' said James Cockburn. 'I'd heard a rumour from a colleague about an old friend of Craig's living in Buenos Aires. Sadly, they had fallen out. There's a love triangle described in the book which seems to be quite autobiographical. After a day running all over Buenos Aires and chasing leads, I managed to track down Alejandro Montenegro: we immediately became great friends.'

Bennett and Montenegro met in a private high school in Australia and had been inseparable until late in their twenties. They worked together on film scripts in Buenos Aires.

During Cockburn's meeting with Montenegro he was given part of a photocopy of an early manuscript from Bennett. Fifteen years earlier, Bennett had given it over to Montenegro for his opinion. It was marked with crossings out and minor corrections in pen from Bennett.

'Alejandro had always assumed this was a novel that had already been published,' said Cockburn. 'He had always postponed reading Craig's novels, not wanting to be reminded of their painful falling out. He confessed to me that he always hoped he would get a chance to read them once they were friends again. He knew it was worth money but it meant more to him than that.'

But this manuscript was actually the unpublished first-written novel by Craig Bennett, completed when he was thirty years old, a manuscript long believed lost. Cockburn was transfixed as he realised what he was reading.

'This is a brand new Craig Bennett novel, every bit as surprising and brave an expedition into the human heart as his four others. A young man's novel, it's less guarded and more romantic than the later works, and it sizzles with the eroticism of the Buenos Aires nightlife.'

Cockburn and Alejandro are reconstructing a manuscript with the aid of an editor in Buenos Aires, and Eliot, Quinn will rush-release the novel in October this year. 'This is without doubt the literary event of 2009,' said James Cockburn, 'and I will go as far as saying this century.'

This *century*. Not even this century *so far*. This century and the ninety years left of it.

223

Alejandro had not said anything while I read the story and when I finished I turned around to see him staring at me, holding a cafetiere and slowly shaking his head.

'Your boss. He is an enormous arsehole, you know?' he said eventually.

Alejandro had to be in on the plot.

It can be easy to forget how competent and single-minded Cockburn is when it comes to a publishing opportunity. His senses are super-tuned: he had made sure during our night to get a card from Alejandro with the name of the legal practice where he worked, and it was there we headed in the afternoon after our calls to his mobile went unanswered. After a brief argument, Alejandro agreed to let us buy him a drink after work. Here I kept quiet and felt nauseous while Cockburn explained his proposal. Alejandro stared at me throughout.

'And how do you feel about this, Liam?' he asked.

I was tired of feeling. I wanted nothing more than to surrender to instruction.

'I'm in,' I said.

Alejandro was all I could have hoped for in my first editor. We met every other night in the week and on Saturday afternoons at his apartment. He read my pages and corrected my imaginings of what life had been like in Buenos Aires in the early 1990s. Sometimes he would chuckle: 'I wish it had been like that; leave that in.' Other times he would be angry: 'What species of charmless bore do you think we were?' He added magnificent *lunfardo* swear-words and expressions and suggested ways to render them against English style. He told me long anecdotes over our coffee breaks and a few days later I presented them back to him in some reworked pages. My novel became better and less of my own. Alejandro breathed the ghost of Craig Bennett over it and I felt his laughter vibrate though its bones.

By the end of a month in which I worked longer than twelve hours a day, seven days a week, I had typed every chapter from my notebook onto my laptop and reworked each several times with Alejandro. We sent this to James. Now it was time for the next stage. On an old manual typewriter Alejandro owned, I copied the finished manuscript, including extra mistakes and sentences for Alejandro to scribble out and add notes to in a separate colour. This was the typewriter Craig used to borrow to write stories and film scripts. Alejandro had moved it and a sealed spare ribbon between the six different apartments he had lived in since Craig had left Buenos Aires fifteen years ago. As I pressed down on the old levers, I felt Craig's fingers rattling, clashing against the ancient ribbon, tattooing the words onto the pale page. The machine gleamed in black metal and made a racket like a factory. I had hardly drunk while I had been writing on the laptop but now I started on whisky early after lunch, drinking most of a bottle and smoking two packs a day in my lonely apartment. The old hunger for cocaine spread through my body and I lay out on my bed, feeling the flames lick along my arteries and roar in my skull. I was not myself. I was being consumed.

But when the fires died down, there would still be something left of me. I would bring myself back, sit down again and type.

A week later, I brought the manuscript to Alejandro.

We removed pages at random and crumpled them into balls, we set fire to their edges, we spat on them and covered them in cigarette ash, we splashed coffee and beer on them and ground them beneath our feet.

I photocopied them all and we gave this new copy the same treatment, scraping and scribbling, gouging and ripping.

I photocopied them again and FedExed these pages to James.

I had just finished my first publishing assignment since losing my job in April.

Despite my mixed feelings, as I posted the manuscript to England, I was proud of my work.

I was able now to go back home to England, as I'd resolved, but I had my apartment paid for another month and I decided to stay on. I had invoiced Eliot, Quinn for my work/unofficial advance, and James had promised to keep me topped up if I ran low. My money would go a lot further in Buenos Aires, and despite my homesickness it was hard to imagine living with my mum in Blackpool for more than a week or two.

More than anything, what stopped me from running to catch a flight was the feeling of having finished a job in Buenos Aires, of having had a colleague, a purpose, a desk. I was getting used to the place. I hassled James and he gave me a copy-editing job with the promise of some more; I began to toy with the idea of getting my own flat when this one ran out, making a living from doing free-lance work for English publishers. The old fiction began to try and reassert itself over the reality I knew: I would write my second 'debut' novel from exile, live the life of a Beckett, a Joyce, a Gombrowicz . . . as drawn by a child with bright crayons. I was too much of a tart to even attempt to write like them; I cared too much about people liking me.

It was weeks later now, the end of August, and I had not seen Lizzie or Arturo since our night out with James and Dani. I was not very surprised and had anticipated a cooling-off period while Lizzie and Arturo tried to resolve or ignore their differences. I'd sent one email to Lizzie just after James had left, saying how much I'd enjoyed my night out with her and how sorry I was for any difficulties it had caused. She had replied briefly, telling me not to worry about it, but that it would be difficult to see me for a while. She'd get in touch. After a week passed I accepted the implications of this calmly. No one was going to save me from myself but me.

Channelling Craig had emptied me out and now I began to put myself back in. I made regular phone calls to my mother and sisters and reassured them that I was working, had a roof over my head, was seeing how things might go here but would be back in England soon. Their relief brought home to me for the first time how much I had worried them, how much they must have feared me repeating my dad's disappearance. I kept meaning to phone my dad too, but I felt guilty that I was still here, that I'd gone back on my decision to go and see him. I resolved to go to see him as soon as I arrived back in England.

Dani Requena contacted me and I met her for lunch. We talked about – what else? – books, and she probed me about the new Craig Bennett novel James had discovered. When had he discovered it? Why hadn't they mentioned it at the dinner? She knew there was something amiss, something entertaining, and I was very close to confessing to her. So close, I decided I could not be trusted to see her again and put her off when she next suggested meeting up.

This is not a story of a remarkable reform. There were times when the allure of cheap stimulation and easy sociability was too much and I ended up on sofas in strange apartments arguing with people whose names I could not remember in the morning.

On one occasion a man wanted me to fuck his girlfriend while he watched. It was so much the wrong thing to do I decided I really should do it, except: I really didn't want to. I tried to sleep on their sofa, listening to them in the other room, appalled and compelled and crazy, before I ran out into the night, far lonelier than I had been before I met them.

Perhaps I needed those minor, controlled breakdowns that I could attribute the next day to a temporary chemical imbalance. I bled my madness in small doses.

In the hope that it would help me to avoid getting into such situations, I had started writing something else, a novel about a publisher who accidentally killed one of his novelists. And I had resumed my grand undertaking, the best love letter the world had ever seen. I was only beginning now to realise how much I had underestimated the task, just how many hours and drafts would be required. The codes of love had been exhausted, had exhausted her, and I had to break through them now, to the moments of loss and truth that I believed must lie beneath them, the feeling I had within me that it must somehow be possible to make her feel too.

The novel was my morning book. I lay on my bed, remembering and inventing conversations, writing a paragraph an hour, crossing it out an hour later. In the afternoon I copy-edited the biography of an indie-superstar Cockburn was publishing. It was not until the evenings that my work really began. I had my notebook, valentine-card red and leatherbound, the type favoured by pretend Hemingways and Picassos and myself – and I took it with me on walks around Buenos Aires, to cafés and bars, to cheap *parrillas* and pizza joints. The end of the night would often come with me sitting on a bar stool at Mundo Bizarro, straining to read my last sentence in blue sodium lighting while the disco ball spun brighter petals across the pages, autumn falling in the garden of forking paths. I wrote for hours each evening, and after two weeks I had barely ten pages left to fill, a madman's diary. I knew that the greatest love letter in the world would not be this long, would be, at best, the average length of a short story in the *New Yorker*. Still, I continued to work. I would write out all the clichés of love and cross them out and with what was left form a concentrate of pure communicated love. I bought another notebook, and it was on one night when I was filling this in that I felt a pat on my back and turned around to see Arturo.

Alejandro had given me his version of our falling out: 'It was most entertaining and then it wasn't. The two English editors who could already not stand up somehow got hold of some ecstasy in Mundo Bizarro and didn't offer any to Arturo. So when Cockshop had his hands all over the nice English girl, Arturo got angry. It was James he had meant to hit, not you, but you walked in the way and started delivering a lecture about old-fashioned attitudes towards women, and then, when your friend mentioned the Malvinas – he used, of course, a different word – it became, unsurprisingly, an issue of national pride. The house drug dealer took issue. If you hadn't had such a dramatic bleeding lip I suspect Lizzie would have

229

been on Arturo's side, but as it was . . . it ruined a perfectly nice evening.'

I couldn't remember being punched by Arturo, and there had been no pain anywhere on my face the next day, so I had put Alejandro's story easily to one side. Now, as I faced Arturo's dark-stubbled chin and implacable expression, I had no idea if he was planning to hit me, for the first or the second time. Perhaps he was also wondering. I decided to make it more difficult for him by smiling and standing up to embrace him, leaning over to kiss his cheek.

'I am sorry I hit you,' he said.

'I had to have two teeth replaced,' I said.

'No!' he said, trying only to look shocked and not slightly proud.

'No, not really,' I said. 'Sorry. I didn't even know you'd hit me.'

'You knew I'd hit you.'

'No, honestly.'

'I think you know.'

'OK, I know.'

'I'm sorry I hit you.'

'It was very painful.'

'*Vale.*'

'But I deserved it.'

'OK.'

And then we were friends again. I asked how Lizzie was and he sighed.

'It's not good. She's on holiday from the language school, travelling with her friend. I don't want her to go. She says she has to, I have to learn to trust her. We are maybe broken up. We see when she gets back. Tell me, what happened at the end of that night when she got back to her flat so late?'

I told him the truth, omitting one small kiss, just as I had not mentioned one other small kiss to Lizzie.

'That's what she said,' he said, shaking his head, as if disappointed to find out he had not caught his girlfriend, or whatever she was now, in a lie. I think he believed me. I was too poor a liar in his eyes to really represent a threat.

I offered him no more advice about Lizzie. I owed that at least to her. And to him. When Arturo invited me over to join him and his friends, I was tempted, but something made me stop.

'I'm sorry,' I said, 'I need an early night, I've got work to do tomorrow.'

'How long are you staying here?' he asked.

'I'm not sure,' I said, beginning to realise that wasn't true.

'I'll see you again before you go?' he asked. 'You have my number?'

'Just in case I don't, come here,' I said, and we kissed and embraced again. Perhaps I held on too long – it was him who pulled away first. 'If not here, I will see you again in England,' he said. 'The drinks will be on me,' I said, and we both smiled like we believed it would happen. 'The drugs too, I hope,' he said. He looked over his shoulder towards his friends. Then he winked and squeezed my arse and walked away. I sat at the bar and finished my drink, watching him laughing with his friends, sweeping his hair back and scanning the bar's horizon for interest. He was beautiful and I was glad for him.

An hour later, when I got back to the apartment, I went online and booked a flight to Gatwick, leaving in a week's time.

*   *   *

The next morning, after a Spanish lesson, instead of working on my novel I set off on a walk. I headed out into the Microcentro, through the elegant business women, through the wide shopping streets and out west, through Korean neighbourhoods, past desultory prostitutes looking for trade, cumbia smashing out from shop-front ghetto-blasters, bargain shops selling two-peso Marias, graffiti murals of streetcars, Che Gueveras, Frank Sinatras, a sudden white church in a tree-lined square, a kung-fu palace, life fading out into middle-class suburbs, quiet graveyards, end-of-the-line metro stations. North next day, designer shops into wide boulevards, packs of thirty dogs walking one human in the park, past a bronze Borges staring over a fountain at a manicured hedge, a lonely walk that found me turning sooner than I expected, northwest in a circle and back to the centre.

During my walks I would look at people and try to imagine their lives. I say people, I mean women. It was a kind of prayer I found easier than the ones I had been taught. What did she do with those shoes when she got in? Did she kick them off across the floor, collapse on a sofa and light a cigarette? Did she place them neatly in a shoe rack, have a shower and cook dinner? What book was she reading? What food did she cook? Did she go home at all?

Dreaming of such intimacy convinced me I was destined to live a life of solitude for ever. So I was delighted when I bumped into Ana-Maria, coming out of a clothes shop, her smile towards me turning into a look of delicious mock anger. It was almost impossible to imagine that this was a woman who had made love to me one night, who had taken command of me, in this city, a woman in a sleek dark blue dress with hard pointed feet, in the type of shoes that made me crazy, feet that had sloped and pressed into my back.

'You are still *alive*,' she said, coming forward and kissing me on both cheeks.

'I am now. I had been wondering. You look incredible.'

'I intend that,' she laughed.

'Do you know I once had a dream I went to bed with a woman as beautiful as you?'

'It was a *good* dream!'

'You would have thought so, wouldn't you? I don't always enjoy good dreams the way a normal man would.'

'Practice, is what you need.'

'Practice, that's a good idea. Do you want to, er, meet up one –'

'Ha ha! I am, er, with someone at the moment.'

I looked at her. I remembered her room, the dresses she made. She was talented. There were so many talented people. Perhaps I could become one myself.

She tipped herself even further forward on her toes and kissed me goodbye. 'Go home and practise dreaming,' she said, turning around and blowing me a kiss.

I got back to the flat late in the afternoon and settled down at my desk with the two red notebooks. I wanted to send my letter to Sarah before I left Argentina, announcing I was on my way back to see her. I was under no illusion she'd be delighted to hear this news. It really would need to be the greatest love letter in the world.

I looked at the notebooks, their many thousands of words in my neat handwriting, neat even when I wrote drunk. There was always one part I could hold still while the rest shook.

I shut the notebooks. I took a new sheet of paper and wrote my address at the top of it. Its exotic glamour did not escape me. But after that I tried to be direct and simple. I wrote that I was coming home, that I would like to see her. I wrote about the things I'd seen that day that had made me think of her, the way that she had made me see the things I'd seen that day. I wrote that it was becoming harder to imagine that we had lived together, that certain memories were fading and certain ones growing stronger. I admitted I had a stronger image of the first moment I realised she wanted me to kiss her than anything that happened later. That was probably a bad sign, but how to know?

After an hour and a half it was done. I re-read it, and though I knew I'd regret it in an hour, I put it in an envelope, went to buy a stamp and posted it.

It wasn't that day, it was the next day, that my sister called me. I was relaxed now I knew I was going home, determined to enjoy my last few days in Buenos Aires. I'd been out having coffee and reading Borges, who I was pleased and surprised to find no longer made me want to vomit. No one ever rang my phone so I hardly ever took it out with me. But when I got back to the flat I had several missed calls from my sister and a text telling me to ring her. I remember flinging my book on the sofa and collapsing into it with a sense of great satisfaction. Then I called her up. Her voice was strange.

'Liam,' she said, 'I'm really sorry. I've got some awful news.'

That morning my father had headed to his yoga class, as he did every Wednesday. It was a lovely sunny day, my sister told me. I imagined the bright skies as he left the house, how he had been happy, alive. He felt better, and because he wanted to be better he had gone for a run on the common, determined to lower his blood pressure, determined to be as young as he looked and felt, determined that the mistakes of the past would not destroy the future.

A woman walking her dog found him and called an ambulance. By the time they arrived, it was too late.

Chapter 21

The last page of a long love letter:

remember when we came back that night on your birthday,
late in that first summer, the smell of smoke and grass in
your hair, the splayed trees caught like Christs? We danced
around your room, the evening deeper bluing minute by
minute, the day and the night stretched so thin we seeped
into each other. Every one of the first nights was like that
night when we felt like that. I can't imagine feeling like that
now, but I can remember how it surprised us, how we
surprised ourselves into someone new.

Now we have knackered spines and hangovers hurt more.
We own nothing of any permanence. Which could mean: we
are free. We could do it again, surprise ourselves by what's
possible, into the new life.

I mean it, that dirty word love. When I say I love you it is
selfish, hungry and manipulative. I owe you that, at least:
you're gorgeous. You make a glorious possession. I want.
The way you chew your hair. The way you smudge your
stolen make-up. That dance of yours, which no one in the

world before had ever thought to do. I love. I want to make you happy too. I want to make you laugh. I want to be there for you. I want you to be you and for me to try but always fail to imagine what that's like. I want you to be not me. A mystery. I love you. Don't just hate me for it. Forgive me and have your revenge. Love me back.

I know it's hard to answer a letter like this. All I want to know is one thing for now. I'll be back next Wednesday. Can I come and see you?

Chapter 22

He was buried in a wicker coffin, a basket with a lid, with ivy and flowers threaded through the strands. I stood at the base, at the head, and with my sister's fiancé was the first to take the weight of his body from the hearse. He was heavy, heavier than he had looked the last time I had seen him, too long ago, heavier than I had ever realised. Nearly two hundred people lined the path to the hall, both his parents, my mum and the nice one of the two subsequent wives, my sisters, his sister, all the new friends he had made, and we shuffled through them, my shoulder burning, damage accruing. When I turned to my left I was shocked to find out I could see him through the strands of the coffin, his face covered in transparent white gauze like the packaging a new laptop or TV would come in. He had always looked young anyway and the gauze softened his features further; it was me I saw lying there. I had turned down the chance to see his body in the hospital. I didn't know if I would regret that. It was too late for that. I had to change my life or it could be me soon.

Later, when we lowered his coffin down into the grave, his friends from the bands he had played in began to sing. 'Everyone hold hands and make a circle for Michael,' a woman shouted, too cheerily, too conventionally unconventional, and I pretended I had not heard and stepped forward closer to the lip of the grave. I shook off the hand of someone who tried to pull me back and held my head down, getting angry and relishing it, a lone figure inside an enlarging circle of people, pretending I was not aware of what was going on around me. Eventually his half-brother came and placed his arm around me and stood with me. I remained for a few seconds and let him lead me back into the circle. Someone sang *Lord, won't you buy me a Mercedes Benz*. It was something. It was as good as anything.

Afterwards, at the wake, I stayed by Mum while the many friends I had never met came and told me stories about a different man to the one I had known. There were a hundred fathers in the room: none of them sounded like him. The aunt I rarely saw told me what a mature brother he had been, how he'd tried his best to be the man of each of their houses, learning DIY, putting up shelves, fixing things – only for his own absent father, who paid the bills, to move them every couple of years, nearer to whichever new job he had taken. I hadn't thought about the damage done to my father, only of the damage he'd done to us. I had failed to imagine his life just as we had thought he'd failed to imagine ours.

My sisters and I stayed close, making jokes, laughing, drinking. We had all made our own separate speeches in the humanist service (we inherited our Catholicism only on our mum's side). The night ended somehow in a small-town disco, drunk beyond comprehension.

I caught a train the next day back up North, where I stayed with my mum for two weeks. It was a sunny September, and I walked the beach in the daytime while she was out teaching. How did my parents end up here, at the end of the world? It was a place to go to hide from the cops, a violent boyfriend, a drug deal gone wrong. They arrived here with me aged two, fresh-faced teachers in the full bloom of their optimism. So I simplify: I have no idea how they felt washing up at the end of a peninsula, staring across the wide, bleak, beautiful view to Morecambe Bay, the hills of the Lake District behind, all horizon and nowhere to go. It must have appealed to Dad. He found somewhere to stay put and managed to for fourteen years. It was the longest he would live anywhere in his life. I had been luckier than him, than my sisters. For sixteen years I had had my father with me. That was something. I would never again say that it wasn't.

The weeks went quickly. There was a date pressing on me, a date I never wanted the world to see. But no further apocalypses occurred and on that date I caught the train to London.

Chapter 23

L ondon showed itself in the muted colours of an old
TV set, a bad home video of itself.

But it was home. The damp air. The lack of emphasis
in the grumbles of the pissed-off people on the Tube. The
pushers, the shovers, the pigeons, the dickheads on daft
bikes; their rudeness was a welcome-home hug.

I was just around the corner from my old office when
the skies remembered me and I was washed into the
London Review Bookshop to take shelter.

I'd accustomed myself to the constraints of the hostel's
library, so the number of readable books on the shelves
made me giddy. Then perverse: I bought *We Love Glenda
So Much*, a collection of Cortázar short stories imported
from the States, and settled down in the café to read. It
turned out I could appreciate a high level of Latin originality with a proper English pot of tea beside me. I had
completely disowned the barbarous taste of my man in
Buenos Aires when I looked up and noticed my old
publicity and marketing director Amanda Jones walk in.
She was with a fashionable young man with dark hair

and glasses. He was either the newest young writer from Brooklyn I would soon hear about or a gleeful philistine from an agency about to reinvent 'the book'. (Each week now brought joyful threats of violence to 'the book'.) Amanda hadn't spotted me, and watching her I realised that I hadn't spotted that I knew other people in the room too. The agent Bill Flowers was busy talking in one corner with a dealer in rare books. He caught me looking in his direction and gave me a nod. I nodded back and carried on reading, but it was hard to concentrate. I was back in the world, in the book club. Confrontations were heading my way.

A shadow fell over Julio Cortázar, and I looked up.

'Amanda,' I said. She was looking at me like she'd caught me watching pornography late in the office. Cockburn has a funny story about –

'You're back,' she said.

'I'm back,' I confirmed. 'Amanda, I owe you an apology. Would you like to sit down?'

She harrumphed, but sat down anyway. 'This won't take long,' she said.

'Yes,' I said, 'I agree about the uselessness of most apologies. But I never even attempted to explain to you what happened that night. Did you know my girlfriend left me in the morning? I couldn't think about anything else. If you told me that day that Craig had a heart problem, then it just did not go in. I wouldn't have just ignored that. By the time I knew, there was no stopping him. Or me, by then. It was much more difficult than it would have been earlier. Are you sure you told me about his heart?'

'Both Belinda and I clearly said you were to keep him away from drugs. If this is an apology, it doesn't sound like it.'

'I do remember that. I just assumed that was standard advice for all authors.'

'It is!'

'Well, see? I disobeyed you both, I'm sorry. But I thought I was just abandoning basic good practice, not endangering someone's life.'

'You're welcome to defend yourself in whatever way you like. The man's dead. Do you even understand what that means? To be dead? He's *dead*.'

I flashed with anger and tried to stay calm. She didn't know about Dad. And neither, really, did I. I turned away from her. Was it my weakness that I found it so hard to condemn people, or hers that she found it so easy? Behind her the boy she was with had whipped out a laptop carved out of dull gunmetal. Bill Flowers was looking in our direction and I wondered if he had heard what I had said.

'I'm sorry,' I said. 'That's all. Thanks for listening.'

She shook her head. 'I liked you, you know, when you first arrived. You went out of your way to be friendly, to find out how you could be helpful. That's what teamwork is. You and fucking Cockburn – that is not a team. Do you think he defends you in the office? Do you think it even occurs to him? You really did pick the wrong man to emulate.'

'I really am sorry,' I said, beginning to get annoyed at being told what I already knew.

'Yes, well. I presume it's coincidence you're here and you're not intending to come along tonight?'

'What's on tonight, Amanda?' It came out like a challenge.

She pushed back out of her chair and was up. 'Don't you dare think about it,' she said, and walked back to her table.

I would have left immediately if Bill Flowers had not arrived before I could get up. He peered at my book and raised his eyes.

'Cortázar? Showing off? Bloody good writer, though. Where the fuck have you been?'

'Argentina, actually.'

'So that's why . . . Borges, labyrinths, Maradona . . .'

'You seem to know as much as I do about the place.'

'Right. Any good?'

'No good at all.'

'Thought as much. You know, I think I've just realised something. You're the "on-site editor" they mentioned in the *Bookseller*, aren't you? Was it you who really found this Bennett manuscript?'

'Um . . . well . . .'

'I knew it wasn't that *egregious* cunt. What a wanker, taking the credit like that.'

'Well, it may as well have gone to a publisher. These days I'm just an unemployed aspiring writer.'

'Nothing wrong with that.'

'Apart from everything.'

'Apart from everything. Do you have an agent?'

'Probably not any more.' Suzy Carling had never contacted me again and I had never dared to contact her.

'You know where I am.'

'Thanks.'

'Fucking convenient.'

'What?'

'Fucking convenient, that Bennett manuscript showing up, just when Cockburn needs a book that might sell some copies. Not a fake, is it? I wouldn't put anything past that cunt.'

'Um, I, of course it's –'

'Sounds like a fake to me. I'm joking. Tell Cockburn I'll be giving it a close read.'

'Don't do that. I mean, yes, ha ha. I will.'

'Bye then, Liam. Head up. Look after yourself.'

And then he was gone, back to his seat and his antiquarian bookseller, leaving me with an incipient panic attack. I left a fiver on the table for my tea and got out of there, avoiding eye-contact with Amanda. I didn't want to see anyone else from the literary world. I really didn't. But I was too late. As I opened the door to the shop, in came Olivia Klein and backed me up into the literary magazines. A copy of *N + 1* fell off the top shelf and hit me on the head.

'Liam,' she said, looking shocked. I picked up the magazine and put it back. 'How are you? I was at a party last night and saw James. I heard about your dad. I'm so sorry, are you all right?'

Dad was dead. I had begun to feel like this was a world where it was possible it would never be mentioned again. She came forward to kiss me on one cheek and I pulled back to kiss her on the other, like we did, but she held on and pulled me in for a hug. She was nearly as tall as me. The smell of her perfume, the softness of her cheek, it was too pleasant. I was so angry and this was so unexpected. Suddenly my chest was shaking against her shoulder. The same copy of *N + 1* fell off the shelf and hit me on the head again. It didn't help matters. 'Oh, Liam, come on,' she said, 'come out, come with me.'

She bought me a pint in the Museum Tavern.

'What did James say?' I asked.

'Just it was sudden, a heart attack – yes?'

245

'Yeah, he was out running. He didn't know he was so ill.'

'I'm sorry. My father died a year ago.'

Her father, the doctor, with his well-stocked library of European classics. It hadn't occurred to me that these people died too, or that they lived.

'I'm sorry to hear that. How?'

'Cancer.'

I was very sorry then. Comparatively I must have had it easy. I hadn't expected it so in many ways it was like it hadn't actually happened, I said. 'I didn't speak to him enough. In some ways, things are just the same.'

'I don't think it works like that.'

'Why not? It has to work somehow.'

Up close, in daylight, you could see the pattern of freckles that seemed the only thing stopping her skin from being transparent. Her eyes were palest Alice blue.

She shrugged. 'You'll find that out.'

'I thought we didn't like each other,' I said.

'I'm sure you loved each other.'

'Thank you. But no, I thought *we* didn't like each other.'

'I thought that too,' she said. 'We probably *don't* like each other.'

'You'll be pleased to hear that James and I have found the new Borges,' I told her. 'The one you thought was missing.'

She laughed. 'So where was he?'

I tutted. 'Sexist. *She.*'

Sometimes it's the strangers who save you. It feels so light to shed an enemy, so simple when it's done. All our invented animosity turned into laughter. I made a friend. Two hours later, as arranged, I met up with Alejandro in the same pub. I hugged Olivia goodbye; she had been kind enough not to leave me on my own, and Alejandro took over her shift. Eliot, Quinn had flown him over and put him up in a hotel for a week. It had been Cockburn's idea; Alejandro's presence here would authenticate the novel. No one really thought we could have been audacious enough to forge a Booker-winner's novel. I certainly wouldn't have had the courage to start the project on purpose.

When I had said goodbye to Alejandro before I caught my flight home I had told him about my dad. I don't remember much of the conversation afterwards, except that he was kind. I was drinking. He gave me a tight hug when I left for the flight. His dad was dead too. They all died. No one knew what a short time they lasted until it was too late.

We brushed over the subject now. The book was weighty enough and we spoke of it in whispers. Neither of us had seen it yet, apart from on Amazon. There was a strict embargo which no one had broken to review early. The reviews were all to appear in the weekend's papers. For now, it was still as unreal as it was on the morning when, after three hours' sleep and a morning beer, I had agreed to let James take command.

We had drunk a few drinks by the time Alejandro and I left for the launch, but I am good at drinking, it is my best skill, and so I wasn't too drunk when we arrived at the venue. As launches went, this was as formal as they came, rows of seating, and three different speakers. We had assumed I would get in easily as Alejandro's +1 but Amanda had posted a publicity assistant on the door to look out for me. As we mounted the steps to the entrance a slender Arabella whispered in the security guard's ear and he immediately stepped forward and pushed his palm out into my chest. 'Are you Liam Wilson?' he asked.

'I am a guest of honour and this is my invited friend,' began Alejandro, as the blonde girl raised her mobile phone to her ear.

'Leave it,' I told Alejandro, walking back down the steps and beckoning him back to talk. 'I'll never get in if I make a fuss.'

'I'm going,' I announced to the bouncer, 'you win', and I walked off away from the door.

Chapter 24

Five minutes later, I had circled the building and was approaching the back from an empty alleyway. Alejandro had gone looking for a way to let me in from the inside. The men's toilets faced the wrong way, but he thought the women's looked like they connected with the back of the building. I hung up, called Olivia and explained my predicament. 'Are you serious?' she asked. Yes, I explained, I was.

A few minutes later a small window opened, high off the ground, about six feet from the floor, and Olivia's head appeared through it. 'Quick then, hurry up,' she said, with bossy schoolgirl authority. 'There's no one in here at the moment.'

I had to take a running leap at the window ledge and haul myself up on my elbows. I heard my jacket rip. There was just enough room for my head and shoulders to get in and Olivia had to grip me under my arms and pull me through. I realised I was about to drop directly onto my cranium with my arms pinned by my side, but Olivia squeezed my chest in a tight grip and dumped me sideways in an undignified heap on the floor.

At the very moment I landed, we heard Belinda and Amanda's voices. I dived into a cubicle and locked the door.

'The cheek of it,' said Belinda. 'Well done Katy for spotting him.'

'It's unbelievable, isn't it? Hasn't he done enough? Oh, hello, Olivia. Are you all right? You look flushed.'

'Hello, Amanda. Don't mind me. What's happening? It sounds dramatic.'

'Ah, nothing for you to worry about,' said Belinda. 'Have we been introduced?'

'Belinda, this is Olivia Klein, who reviews for the *Guardian*,' began Amanda, and I listened to Belinda ask if she was reviewing *My Biggest Lie*. 'That's gone to our lead reviewer,' said Olivia. Undaunted, Belinda suggested she could interview James Cockburn about putting the book together.

None of this calmed my mood. I had not thought about James doing interviews, but realised now that he might be all over the weekend papers.

Their voices trailed off. I'd never felt as nervous as this. It was shameful for me to be anywhere near this building – so what if it was my book being launched? I'd let Cockburn take that away from me, knowing that he was right – I'd written a passable novel that would sell in large numbers only if it was written by someone else. I hadn't missed out. Not having my name on the cover of my book wasn't the worst thing at all. The worst thing was having let Cockburn convince me that Craig wouldn't mind, that he'd be very much amused, that what we were doing was creating a perfect tribute to his anarchic personality. But this was not our own special memorial for him. However we put it to ourselves, what we were doing was fucking him. He was dead and we were desecrating his memory, trying to make sure that the way he lived on would be forever false. It wasn't a private funeral but a private execution; we were about to finish killing him once and for all. The very least I owed Craig was to be here to witness it.

It was not my first time in the women's toilets. The sharing of cocaine is a pleasant excuse to challenge unnecessary gender segregation. I don't need to say that this was not one of those enjoyably intimate occasions. I heard the door go. Had Olivia deserted me? I waited another minute and was about to make a run for it when the door went again, Olivia called 'Quick!' and I scuttled out to meet her. 'It won't be long till the speeches,' she said. 'You'll be safe in the middle of a row. I've got nothing to do with this any more.' She turned and walked away without looking back.

I came out at the end of a crowded room laid out with chairs in front of a small super-lit stage. There were TV cameras set up to either side. There might have been eight hundred people in the room. I saw Belinda at one side of the stage talking to Alejandro, and steered myself around to the other side of the crowd where she wouldn't be able to see me. I looked out for Amanda, but couldn't see her. This was ridiculous. What was I doing? Lauren Laverne was talking into a TV camera on one side of the room. I began to spot faces I knew. There was only a second or two for me to freeze and try to imagine what I would say to them and then my former colleagues were saying hello to me, surprising me with their smiles, by asking me how I was doing, by saying how pleased they were to see me. They were indignant about the way I had disappeared. *I sent you text after text!* I apologised (unless I tell you otherwise I am always apologising) and took a couple of numbers again on my new phone, gave away my new number. I took a glass of wine from a passing tray, helped myself to a canapé. That such simple remembered actions were still possible felt incredible to me.

I shouldn't have been so surprised at the warm reception. I knew most people were polite and forgiving. But I had expected to detect the bad flavour of myself in the way they breathed next to me, expected their revulsion to be impossible to bear. Perhaps I could bear it. Once, in a clap clinic, the week after Sarah and I came properly together, I had been made to ring one by one the six women I had slept with in the last six months to tell them I might have chlamydia. It turned out I didn't have chlamydia, or anything else, but encouraged by a male nurse with a shaved head I made my telephone confessions and waited to hear what a bastard I was. They were all so kind, so grateful. I had assumed I had given it to each of them and it was only afterwards I realised they had all assumed they had given it to me.

I sipped my wine and took another canapé. I was beginning to feel like I belonged there, and then I was forced to duck and pretend to tie a shoelace as Amanda walked past. 'Take your seats please, everyone, speeches in five,' she called.

I stood up again and looked around. There she was, my pen pal, Amy Casares, talking to James Cockburn. She turned and saw me; I watched her slow, red carnivorous smile. James was leaning into her, flirtatious, and hadn't seen me. Amy, as you may know, is an astonishingly attractive woman. She has the hair of a Scandinavian, skin that has advertised moisturisers. She wears immaculate dresses casually, gives them the slightest suggestion of a messed-up sheet.

I saw she was about to call out to me and hurried over so she wouldn't draw attention my way. It could only be a matter of minutes now before I was spotted and removed from the premises.

I charged into her, put my head in her blonde curls and squeezed her tightly. When I opened my eyes I could see James over her shoulder. I was pleased to see him looking worried. I hadn't told him I was coming.

'Liam!' she said. 'You're looking so well. Considering, obviously. I'm so sorry about your dad. James was just saying how sad he was you couldn't make it.'

'Oh, really,' I said, smiling at James. 'No, I came here to surprise him.' James looked around warily.

'But how are you?' Amy said. 'It must have been such a shock.'

'I'm fine. We can talk about it later. It's so nice to see you.'

'You too. I'm so surprised at this book,' she said. In the shock of meeting so many old faces, I hadn't even spotted the book table but now I followed her eyes to a pyramid of black-and-gold hardbacks. Even from quite far away I could spot the rubbery S&M supermatt finish on the black, a void rejecting the light of the chandelier above while the foil titles glittered in fool's gold.

'So that's them,' I said and James nodded sombrely.

'I can't wait to read it,' Amy continued. 'He must have written it round about the time I was in Buenos Aires with him. I never really believed he was writing a novel then.'

'You might be in for a big surprise. Hey, James?'

'I was just saying that we can't say for certain exactly when he wrote it,' said James. 'Only when he gave it to Alejandro, and he's only really guessing from memory.'

'Weird he gave it to Alejandro,' said Amy. 'He was always so private about his writing. He wasn't a sharer at all.'

'No, he wasn't,' said James. 'Who knows – we may even find another novel!'

'I'm sure we won't,' I said.

'What makes you say that?' asked Amy.

'Just a feeling,' I said, looking at James.

Take your seats, please came over the microphone. Amanda was standing on stage now. I moved so Cockburn's tall body was between us. It could only be seconds now until my discovery. Other people in the crowd were looking at me as they went past to find a seat, not all of them in a friendly way.

Alejandro arrived and made himself smile. 'Liam! Amy! Cockshop! Let's all sit down.'

'I'll see you later,' said James heavily. He walked away from us. He wouldn't want Belinda to blame him for my presence here. I had been wondering for weeks now how much she knew of the novel's provenance. She might not have wanted to ask many questions, even if she had doubts.

Amy took my arm and guided me into the second row from the front, right in the middle, with Alejandro to one side and Amy to the other. A few heads turned to look at me. 'What on earth are they staring at?' said Amy. 'You're very brave coming here, Liam. Ignore those *fucking idiots*.'

She said this fiercely enough to snap some heads back round to facing the stage.

Belinda was walking up the steps now, the cameramen

swinging around to follow her. She reached the top of the stage, stood in front of the mike and looked out.

In that instant she saw me and drew her head back involuntarily. She looked away. Then she looked back and stared hard into my eyes for the longest time before inclining her head towards the back of the room, to the exit. I stayed still, kept her gaze. She couldn't throw me out without causing at least a disturbance, at worst a scandal. The cameras were on and who knew what I might have shouted if I'd been pulled out.

That was the last time she looked at me during her five-minute speech. It was consummately professional, warm, grave, intimate and always correct. How touched she was to see so many people who loved Craig Bennett's writing gathered together. How sad that this was the last time we could welcome one of his novels into the world (unless we're very lucky!). How wrong it is to have to do this without him here with us.

I wasn't listening hard to her. She stood on the stage in front of a black curtain, the kind of curtain you had in small theatres like this. There had been a similar one in the community hall where we'd held Dad's service. We put the head of the coffin down on the edge of the stage and pushed it along to the centre, squeaking against the boards. Belinda held Craig's book in the air; he came in a smaller container.

Towards the end of Belinda's speech, one of the cameramen came in closer to her. I looked behind me. There were familiar faces, book journalists, publishers, rock stars with author wives: the biggest book crowd I had been part of since Craig's last party. The look on so many of their faces, confident of being in a gathering with a noble end: reading.

Such awful complacency. I hated them. There is nothing noble about reading novels. It is an escape, a throwing-off, an evasion. We are not good people.

Belinda finished and we all clapped. She didn't look once in my direction on her way down. Then James appeared on the right of the stage and made his way up the stairs.

'Here we go,' muttered Alejandro. Amy reached over and squeezed my hand.

Standing in front of the microphone, James stared out at the crowd. He put a hand in his hair and swept it back. A chunk of it stood up dramatically and slowly wilted. He coughed. He stared out again. The cameras trained on him made the silence longer. His hair continued to wilt until he swept his hand back through it again. We waited for him to speak, growing more awkward. To my right, the bouncer who had denied me entrance was standing at the end of the aisle, keeping an eye on me, looking more bored than threatening.

'I didn't speak at Craig's funeral,' James began. 'I'd only just got out of hospital after having fallen out of a window during the London Book Fair.' (Titters from the crowd.) 'I suppose that *is* amusing,' he carried on, sardonically, disdainfully. 'You all heard the gossip, I suspect.' James looked from side to side at the crowd then raised his hand to his mouth and stage-whispered, '*I was pushed*. By Craig, of course. Because he was sleeping with my wife.' James now smiled broadly. 'He wasn't sleeping with my wife.' Now he frowned. 'In fact, he never even tried to. We were most offended. My wife is a beautiful woman.' (More titters from the crowd.) 'The funniest reason I heard to explain why Craig pushed me out of the window was that he was angry about how much we were paying him. How marvellous that journalists think this is how the publishing industry works. Everyone here in the trade knows in which case it would be Craig's *agent* who pushed me out of the window. Hello, Suzy, thanks for coming.' I followed the direction of his gaze and saw Suzy Carling for the first time in six months. She wasn't laughing but the crowd were loving the showman publishing, and the TV cameras would too. James paused to let the laughter die down and continued. 'Craig himself was always amazed at how much money his books brought him. I wasn't – he was brilliant, he made people want to read his books: what you paid for what you *received* was piffling. But I remember him saying, "I will never complain about the money I get paid from publishing books in case they realise how much they're paying me." I liked that *they're*. I'm not sure he realised that I was "one of them". He seemed to think sometimes that we were both getting away with the same great scam. I loved that about him. He was generous enough to think that his writing was a very small gift he could offer. Writers don't normally continue to think like that after they've had a big success. Of course, most are never lucky enough to. It is rare that talent is rewarded with money.

'No, Craig's tastes never became more expensive. We'd still get through quite a lot of money together in the pub when he came to London, don't get me wrong. But the rest of the time he was quiet, at home in Wales, trying to live the simple life, perhaps failing as much as he succeeded. All of you here who knew Craig knew his gentleness, knew it through his concern for you. If he liked you, he was concerned. When we argued it was because he was trying to look after me, because he was trying to stop me from falling over. Many of you may remember times he put himself in the way of your fall. No, he was not a pusher but a catcher.'

'Well, that's true at least,' muttered Alejandro.

'He was not a pusher but a catcher,' repeated James sonorously, then laughed at himself. The tone of his voice was changing. He was trying to be jokey, cheerful, professional, but a revulsion was showing through, attacking his usual persona. He looked over at us and smiled again. 'Make of that what you will.' He straightened up again and paused. He suddenly looked stricken. 'He is not around to catch us any more.'

I wondered to what extent he had planned to look like this at this point of his speech, how staged his presentation was. A month ago I had stood in front of the same sort of curtains, making a speech for Dad. Afterwards so many people came up to me and said how moved they had been. I had regretted it every day since, its fluency, its easy humour, cheap sentiment and professionalism. I had treated the occasion like another book launch. My sisters watching me in the front row. My simplifications. An excuse for a public-speaking contest. A brick wall spray-painted with a stickman.

James looked to be learning about that. His face contorted with disgust.

'The next time I decide to do something stupid – more stupid even than falling out of a window – I will not have Craig to prevent me. Except, because he is not here, and will never be here again, I will have to remember him, what he loved about us and what we loved about him. So perhaps he will still protect me. It is one way to keep him alive, to keep me alive. And when I need a reminder of what he was like, or want to share Craig with someone who never met him, I will turn to the books.

'This is why we are here today. There is one more book to read. In a while we will be hearing from this, an extract chosen by Craig's sister Helen, who sadly can't be here with us today as she's expecting a baby this month. Craig's agent Suzy Carling will read the extract, and a message from Helen. I want to thank Suzy and Helen, who together with myself are Craig's literary executors. I want to thank them for choosing to work again with Craig's long-term publisher Eliot, Quinn – we'll have to hope that in his travels across the world Craig has left many more manuscripts lying around. Who knows what he might have left behind in a carrier bag in one of his eighty-four favourite bars? I will certainly be heading to one of them when I leave here tonight.' James looked up at me and his face fell. 'Sadly,' he went on, 'I think we may have already had more luck than we have deserved in finding this book.

'Before I talk about what this book contains, I – I was going to say something in my speech now about another man who loved Craig. I've decided instead, on the spur of the moment, to talk about two other men who loved Craig and who both played an integral part in bringing us this novel – a novel I know you will want to buy and take home with you today.'

James had looked steadily towards Alejandro and me as he spoke, and the audience were turning as one to follow the direction of his gaze. I say as one, but there was a notable exception, Belinda, who was staring at the side of James' head as if, if she concentrated hard enough, she could burn a hole in it. James was careful never to turn once in her direction.

'The reason why I had only planned to speak of one of these men,' said James, 'is because I didn't think the other one would turn up. Specifically, I didn't think he would turn up because the bouncers on the door were given strict orders not to admit him.' James smiled and the crowd laughed, assuming he was joking. 'You think I'm joking but I'm not. What's more, Belinda told me earlier that the bouncer carried out these orders and turned this man away. This is a man, I can tell you, who loves Craig so much I have learned he climbed through the window of the ladies' toilets to be here. I'm talking about my friend and colleague Liam Wilson, who, having seen Craig Bennett have the heart attack that killed him, blamed himself for this, quit his job and moved to Buenos Aires. It was in this city we assume that Craig had written this novel *My Biggest Lie*, which we're all here for today, perhaps at the same age as Liam, just a few years before he won the Booker Prize with his first published novel *Talking to Pedro*.

'It was Liam himself who tracked down Craig's best friend from those days. He joins us here tonight, Alejandro Montenegro. Without Liam introducing me to him at a memorable dinner in Buenos Aires three months ago, we would not be here tonight.

'That is a story for another time. I've said Liam feels in some way responsible for the way Craig died. I'm not going to tell Liam not to blame himself – I won't insult him that way – if he wants to blame himself, it's for him to decide how long he should do this for and for him to go into why he does. I wish he had done something different that night that would have meant Craig was still alive, but I'm not sure what that something is, or that I would have done it. Everyone makes mistakes, everyone could have done something different. We have to remember that it was Craig who made the biggest mistake, and that is why he is not here. I want to thank Liam for being his friend on the night when my own stupid mistake meant I could not. I want to thank Liam for caring about Craig's life when it was gone, for wanting to preserve it. Thank you, Liam.'

Amy next to me began to clap and slowly the room followed, the whole room, until a wave of noise sweeping over me was like something cracking, tightening, splitting, a sound I heard and feared like it was the sound of my heart bursting. I put my head down and waited for it to finish.

'Similarly,' began Cockburn, 'I want to thank Alejandro Montenegro, all the way from Argentina because of his love for Craig.' At this, Amy reached over me and took Alejandro's hand. It was a nice gesture of solidarity, which had the effect of locking me down in my seat like the bar on a rollercoaster. That's what it felt like too, like being on the Big One on Blackpool Pleasure Beach, slowly cranking your way to a height from which only disaster could be conceived.

'I have heard wonderful tales, from Craig, from Alejandro, from their friend Amy, about the closeness of their bond. They grew up in Australia together before Craig followed Alejandro to his family's home in Argentina. Alejandro was the first reader of this novel, twenty years ago. A manuscript we can only guess whether was ever sent to publishers.'

'I'm sure he would have mentioned that,' whispered Amy across me to Alejandro.

Alejandro looked down at his feet.

'It wouldn't surprise me if it was sent to publishers and turned down,' said James. 'Not because it's not good: it's wonderful. No, I wouldn't be surprised if it was rejected, because publishers make mistakes. It is our job to make

261

mistakes, to have the courage to get it wrong so that sometimes we have the courage to get it right.' James was really beginning to choke up now. 'I have a confession to make,' he said decisively, 'about this book.'

This is the moment when the cart reached the top of the hill and teetered on the summit. Now he would not meet my eye. Now he was looking at Belinda and she would not meet his. I made my conclusion about her complicity. I wondered if she had known from the start or only discovered when it was too late. It had been easy at first for us to pretend we were not doing the appalling thing we were doing. Now James wanted to confess. And now was the end of all our careers, perhaps even our liberty.

The human seatbelt keeping me from fleeing grew tighter. 'Ow!' said Amy to Alejandro. 'You're squeezing me too hard.' He let go, and I picked my escape route, preparing to haul myself past all the knees to the aisle – and run. 'What in God's name is he doing?' asked Alejandro, turning to me, pressing down with his hand on my knees as if predicting my impulse to flight.

'What's wrong with you two?' asked Amy.

I looked up imploringly at James and he continued. 'My confession is this, and it's not a good confession for a publisher to make. The thing is, I haven't, to this day, accepted what losing Craig means. Or that there's no bringing him back.' He held up the book, stark gold capitals on sex-shop black. '*My Biggest Lie* . . . This, after all, is only paper and ink. This, after all, is nothing.'

And with that he walked suddenly down the stairs, still holding the book, and strode with his long quick step to the back of the hall, where he disappeared through the door. A confused and excited murmuring broke out throughout the room. Belinda made her way up the steps and back to the microphone.

'Thank you, James,' she said, letting out her breath more quickly than she'd intended. 'We are now going to welcome Suzy Carling to the stage, to read a short extract from *My Biggest Lie* by Craig Bennett, chosen by his sister Helen Edwards.'

'Are you all right?' Amy asked me. 'You're both acting very strange.'

'I'm going,' I said to her, 'this is too weird.'

'You're staying,' said Alejandro, holding on to my arm. 'This is your launch. Our launch. You need to listen to this.'

'What are you talking about?' asked Amy.

People were looking round at us, shushing. Suzy Carling made her way to the stage in a black dress and heels. She surveyed the room before she spoke, her eyes resting on me. There was no anger in the look, just calculation, the assessment a predator makes of its prey.

'Thank you all for coming. I'm going to read you an email from Helen Edwards, Craig's sister, about why she wanted me to read this particular extract.'

She unfolded a piece of paper and read.

'"I've chosen this extract for its simplicity, for its calm and optimism, for it's compassion for people: the facets of Craig's character everyone liked to ignore. This is Craig at his best, the Craig I know."'

'He was a great man,' said Suzy. 'I miss him.' She opened the book, turned the thick, creamy paper to the right part. Then she started to read.

Falling in love was not what he had thought falling in love was like. The other times had been something else, different in kind and degree . . . After they had kissed goodbye and she had gone through to catch her plane, he walked in circles around the concourse, hungrily spinning new sights before his eyes, filling himself up with the world he was now at home in, its new language, his new palate. He sat down, giddy, and looked up at the atrium. He breathed in the air. Then he stood and went outside to the taxi queue.

On the way back to the centre, he told the taxi driver that he had fallen in love. The taxi driver laughed. You are lucky, he said. Craig asked the taxi driver about his wife, whether he had any children. The taxi driver told him about his son and daughter, 18 and 21, the son working in an office, the daughter at university studying science. He was proud of his children. 'And your wife?' asked Craig. The taxi driver seemed not to hear him and told him instead about the area where he lived, Barracas, a poor, working-class area, but not a slum, a proud working-class area, a place famous for its protests. Craig didn't ask again about the driver's wife, you didn't do that here, but suddenly the driver was telling Craig about the night she disappeared in 1978. I think about her in a room, alone with those animals, and how I was not there to help her. She was from a different world to me, a university lecturer. She was out of my league, I thought. I don't know why she liked me but she did. A miracle. I asked her to dance with me at a *milonga*. She would not accept the way things are in this filthy country. It is where the children get their brains. My son was a baby when she went, my daughter was three years old. She would never have left them. I was terri-fied they would come and take me, but, shamefully, they were not even interested. I say shamefully but I am not ashamed I can be here for my children.

It was the first time since Craig had arrived in Buenos Aires that a stranger had told him a story like this, though he may have met many other people who could have. There were awful stories everywhere. The driver told him about his mother-in-law, her illnesses and her passion, the marches she attended and invited him to attend with her. I have to drive, you know? he said. I have to work for my children. But I go with her when I can.

Craig listened and tried to imagine the taxi driver's sadness, his guilt, the way it had felt to be terrorised like he had been. He felt bad about being happy himself, until he realised he had to be happy, it was the only fair thing, because nothing had happened to the woman he loved.

A kid ran in front of the taxi, stooped to pick up a rolling football, and ran off. The taxi driver beeped his horn, opened his wallet and showed Craig two photos, a young woman smiling with a baby, a gawky teenage boy grinning as a girl put his arm round him. The taxi driver wasn't in either photo – but he had taken them, he had looked, he was the invisible part.

'Thank you,' said Suzy Carling, putting down the book and walking back to her seat. Alejandro had been quietly crying. I felt nothing. Amy turned round and looked at me, her eyes dry, glittering, inquisitive. Was there something in the reading, some detail, that had awoken her to its untruth? I would have to go and see her tomorrow, confess and beg her to keep quiet.

Alejandro let out a big sigh. 'Schmaltz,' he said, but he looked sad, sad the way schmaltz makes us when it reminds us how we've been tenderised to it. Belinda made a final exhortation for us to buy the book and we stood. The middle of the row, having afforded a protection earlier, now penned me in.

'I'm going to go and talk to his agent,' said Amy, 'and pick up a copy of this weird book.'

'Before you go,' I started, but she had found a space and slipped through into the aisle. The way she marched to the book stall made me feverish. The bouncer who had not let me in was still waiting in the aisle for me, but he was suddenly pushed back by a crowd of agents, editors and journalists heading our way. Being thrown out was a delightful idea. I looked over to the drinks table, miles away, the clean white table cloth, the endless rows of golden wine.

'Get ready to do some serious lying,' Alejandro whispered to me. 'I'm going to try to get thrown out,' I told him. But it was too late. They were upon us.

It seemed to go on for ever. The questions, the optimistic insinuations. Journalists suggested the most outrageous turns of events, hoping we would be taken aback and reveal their truth, yet they suggested nothing as outrageous as what was actually happening. Nor was it the journalists who set my teeth most on edge, for whom making our story consistent was most frightening. It was worse with my friends, the colleagues and rivals I'd always liked and admired; they were harder to lie to not just because I didn't want to lie to them but because they knew what they were talking about, how incredible it was for an unheard-of novel by Craig Bennett to appear overnight. In our tribute to Craig, our enormous fuck-you to Craig, James and I had consigned ourselves to either a lifetime of lying or a lifetime of disgrace. The two things I had fled to Buenos Aires to try to cure myself of.

I thought the bouncer would never come for me, but after the fiftieth question I found myself with a strong arm round my shoulder, being marched towards the back of the room. I didn't even notice who he was until I was already well away from the pack. 'I'm afraid you're going to have to leave now,' he said.

'That's OK,' I said, leaning into him like a tired girlfriend. 'Are you going to beat me up?' I asked as he led me into a corridor away from the party.

'Do you want me to?'

'There's a part of me that thinks I probably deserve it.'

'A little guy like you? Mate, you don't deserve nothing.'

And with that he opened a fire door and pushed me outside. I was round the corner from the front entrance, but he pointed me in the other direction. 'You're going to walk that way and I'm going to stand here and make sure you do.'

I nodded and held out my hand. He looked at it and pointed in the direction I was supposed to be going. I smiled. He didn't. It was a satisfying exchange for both of us. 'Bye bye then,' I said. I thanked him and went.

Chapter 25

I found James upstairs in the Academy, sitting at a table in the corner using my novel as a bar mat for a whisky. The bar wasn't very busy. A handsome man who looked like he'd been sleeping in his suit was telling the barmaid about his day at work: 'And so I told the designers, if you want to play around with coke then do it at the Christmas party under controlled conditions and not on my fucking front cover.' The barmaid started to tell him a story in return about a cocktail she'd invented last night which used a cooked sausage as a stirrer.

I'd suspected James was going to be here, but I would have come anyway. Craig had brought me here on the night he died. Here, in the middle of my despair, he had filled me temporarily with the greatest of optimism. I walked over to James and sat down.

'He was sitting, staring gloomily at a glass of whisky, when the boy who had killed his friend walked in.'

James looked up and took a deliberate sip. 'Not a bad first line. Hemingwayesque? Graham Greene? Is the "gloomily" essential? What's the next line?'

'The boy looked at him and tried to contain his anger – seriously, what the fuck was that speech? I've had Lauren Laverne trying to interview me for *The Culture Show*. My phone's been ringing non-stop. You've put me in the news.'

'That seems a little melodramatic and implausible now as a work of fiction.'

'It has become implausible. What are we going to do about that? The whole point is for it to *not* be implausible. And now we have a subplot about a disgraced editor who was with Craig on the day he died and who subsequently discovered his long-lost novel. And who then broke in through the girls' toilets to his book launch! Christ.'

'But what a great *story*.'

'Do you mean that?' And in that instant I realised he did. I put a cigarette in my mouth, put it back in my packet. I tried to say something and couldn't. 'You did it deliberately,' I eventually managed, 'for publicity.'

'I did it for you.'

'It hasn't *helped* me. You've just transferred the responsibility for this monstrosity from you to me. You arsehole. Don't think I won't bring you down when we get caught. Don't think Alejandro won't support my side of the story, how you stole my novel.'

James gulped down the rest of his whisky. 'Liam, listen mate. What's all this? Don't think like that. I don't think like that. What we did was a terrible idea, OK, I know, I realised that on stage. I'm sorry. We should never have done it. I wanted to confess. I came this close.'

'Can you imagine what would have become of our careers, of our lives, if you had done?'

'I did imagine,' he sighed. 'I imagined quickly and accurately and I changed my mind. What you said about me doing it for publicity, it wasn't like that. I did it for *you*,

Liam. I didn't expect to see you, I wasn't allowed to invite you, and then having to do a speech for your novel and not mention you – it was obscene. It was your night. I had to say something. It was an awful thing to take your night away from you.'

'That's the least awful thing. It was never my night. Be consistent. Remember how you convinced me? You don't even believe what you're saying.'

'I do believe what I'm saying. I always believe what I'm saying.'

'That's the fucking problem.'

'Liam, Liam, I just wanted to credit you.'

'Then you shouldn't have persuaded me to forge someone else's book.'

'Shhh,' he said, looking around him.

It was pointless for me to try to make him confess his motives. He didn't know them himself. His promotional reflexes were so instinctual they occurred to him as morals. I could never rely on him as a friend, still less, as I had tried to, as a father figure. But I'm not convinced you can rely on most friends or fathers either, and for better or worse I was bound to him.

'Please let's not argue,' he said. 'Get a drink, won't you? After all, this for us is Craig's wake. Let's raise a glass to him. Go on, my card's behind the bar.'

It was not a very funereal drink. I ordered a bottle of the house champagne, the same type I remember sharing with Craig on his last visit here. It was our launch night, after all.

'Would you like me to pop the cork?' the barmaid asked.

'No, please stay alive,' I said.

She looked at me funnily and left the cork in. What

fragile hearts we have. What pathetic excuses I had allowed mine while I had pretended Sarah's wasn't beating.

I carried over the ice-bucket and our two flutes. James nodded. I banged the bottle down on the table like a call to business, twisted off the cork and we watched the foam rise from the neck before I poured two glasses.

'To Craig, our friend,' said James. We clinked. 'Angie, come over here and drink a glass for Craig,' he called to the barmaid.

It wasn't long before we had finished the bottle and another was popping. Enough was never enough. This is what I'd learned from James, from life, and this is what would kill me, like Craig, like Dad, if I didn't unlearn it. I looked at my phone to check the time, noticing the many missed calls I had accrued from unknown numbers. I had to be somewhere else in an hour.

While I scrolled through these numbers, I heard James answer his phone – 'Clara, how are you? Of course, we're in the Academy, bring the gang. Yes, yes, I'm with Liam. Come down.'

'Was that Clara Pembroke?' I asked, when he had put the phone down. 'The literary editor of the *Sunday Times*?'

'It was. She's coming down with some of the crowd from earlier.' He was excited. He had completely forgotten why I had been angry with him.

'I told you I'm not giving any interviews about this,' I said, putting on my jacket. 'You need to keep these people away from me, they are all *yours* now.'

I wanted to tell him to stick the money too, whatever that was going to be, however he was going to sneak it through the company's books. But I was implicated too far already, and I needed the cash.

'Enjoy yourself, I'm off,' I said, picking up his copy of *My Biggest Lie*. I wanted that for later.

'Liam, don't go away like that,' he pleaded. 'You do understand, don't you? We have to forgive each other.'

'If I ever forgive myself, I'll forgive you too,' I said. 'But I don't think I ever will.'

With that I walked away. But I made the mistake at the door of looking back into the room before I climbed down the stairs. James was standing up, looking at me miserably. Craig was dead. We'd made sure of that. I remembered my friend who had tried to save me when I didn't deserve it and walked back to James and hugged him.

'We've done such an awful stupid thing,' he said.

'You never know, we might get away with it until retirement age. And if we don't it will be a relief to tell the truth. Of course, we'd probably have to go to prison. Where better to write our memoirs?'

He managed a faint smile at that. 'I'll find a way to destroy the company's manuscript accidentally,' he said. 'Perhaps I'll burn down the offices. Except there's a copy with the agent. Perhaps I'll burn down *her* offices.' He looked excited now.

'That's a fine plan,' I said.

'Craig wouldn't mind, would he, what we did?'

'Of course he would. He'd be bloody furious.'

'He would have found it funny, I know that.'

'We can only hope so. Let's stop being so funny, though, let's have less fun. For him. For ourselves.'

James put his hands on my shoulders and looked at me proudly. 'A good idea, Liam.'

I didn't like that look. It didn't belong to him. But he could own that pride if he needed it. I couldn't give it to anyone else. He let go and we looked at each other sadly.

'You sure you won't stay?' he asked.

'I'm sure. I have to be somewhere else.'

'Somewhere good, I hope.'

I hoped so too. Sarah had rented a new place close to our old one. She had answered my letter and agreed to meet me. We'd spoken on the phone just after the funeral but I didn't know any of the important details about how her life had changed. I had not dared to ask if she had a new boyfriend.

'Someone good,' I said.

'Good luck.'

I'd need more than that.

On the bus, getting close to our old stop, I took out my pen and dedicated a dead man's novel to Sarah. I crossed out Craig Bennett on the title page and wrote the very last line of the love letter.

I am sorry, Sarah, and I hope you will forgive me. Love from Liam.

It was something I could offer to her that no one else could. My biggest lie. My only love. For a moment, I toyed with throwing it out of the top window. But it was a heavy book, and I had done enough damage with it already.

Acknowledgements

Thank you to:

Peter Straus, Sam Copeland

Francis Bickmore, Jamie Byng, Andrea Joyce, Lorraine McCann, Jo Dingley, Jaz Lacey-Campbell and everyone at Canongate

Alan Mahar, Catherine O'Flynn, Keiran Goddard

Michael Schmidt, Zoe Strachan, Kei Miller

Jacquie, Naomi, Rachel and all my family

Edward Robinson and Lucila Porthe, for Argentina

Rik Evans and Kevin Pocklington, kind hosts in Scotland

Zanna Gilbert

Charlotte Payne, Johnpaul Villafrati, Ian Edwards, Johnny Nichols

Mark Richards, Lee Brackstone

Matthew McLean

Anna Kelly

CANON▌▌GATE.tv

CHANNELLING GREAT CONTENT

 WATCH — INTERVIEWS, TRAILERS, ANIMATIONS, READINGS, GIGS

 LISTEN — AUDIO BOOKS, PODCASTS, MUSIC, PLAYLISTS

 READ — CHAPTERS, EXCERPTS, SNEAK PEEKS, RECOMMENDATIONS

 DISCOVER — BLOGS, EVENTS, NEWS, CREATIVE PARTNERS

 SHOP — LIMITED EDITIONS, BUNDLES, SECRET SALES